Len

by Ryan J. Dareul

Cover art by Hassan Zafar

Independently published via DiggyPOD
Tecumseh, MI 49286
www.diggypod.com

ISBN 978-0-692-05007-1

I wrote this book for the sober dreamers;

the promising, but inhibited;

the ambitious, but poor;

the souls who walk this world each day in the knowledge that they could change it for the better, if only they had the means. I dedicate *Len* to you, in the hopes of our hope.

Contents

Chapter One

Leonard's most recent promotion represented all the promise he'd been searching for. What was more, this promotion even got him a seat alongside a friend of the family. It was Leonard's first day on the job as an investigative auditor, but when good old Wallace stood up – before Leonard even got the chance to reach the desk – and threw him a coat and keys, Leonard had to wonder what on Earth lay in store for him.

"Go start the car," Wallace said. "I saved something special for your first day."

Wanting only to please on his first day, Leonard did as bid. He tried to stay excited. It became hard once his partner started driving and explained the premise of their little adventure.

"Oh, this is just stupid."

"Be that as it may, it's where we're going."

"But this is impossible! How does anyone live in a tree along a highway?" The passenger threw up his head and propped his head against the window. The trees flashed across the window by the dozen. They were jagged, barren of leaves, disinteresting, and clustered. "It doesn't make any sense. Especially when this is supposed to be a teenager."

Wallace acknowledged him with a tilt of his head but didn't take his eyes off the road. "Well, he made it work somehow. We'll see when we get there. With our luck, he'll have moved in with somebody and the place is abandoned."

Jazz flowed out of the radio, turned far enough down that the two men heard it now for the first time in the abbreviated quiet. "This is just so stupid," Leonard said.

Their shuttle, a black Honda, rolled down US-33. It went beneath an overpass, came to the next set of trees thereafter. Then the car pulled over on the side of the highway, and everyone else went on with their day. A pack of cars went by and sped off into the distance.

"Is this the place?" asked the passenger.

The driver threw the door closed. "How many treehouses do you see along Ohio interstates?"

The passenger, watching him over his shoulder, shrugged and faced forward. The driver joined him and they stood abreast on the shoulder, sizing up the task before them.

"This can't be real."

"Guess we'll see," the driver said, and strode forward.

They came to the base of the trunk. As his passenger kicked a particularly pesky cattail from his leg, the driver knocked on the tree. "Hello!" he shouted. "Mr. Campbell! Mr. Campbell are you up there?"

Trimmed round the top with flares of green, a face-shaped shadow popped out of a glassless window. Whoever it was didn't saying anything.

"Hello! Are you Leonard Campbell?" the driver asked at the top of his lungs.

Len saw the two of them, down there among the weeds. He saw both of them; one tall, skinny as anything, bald, white, and downright wussy-looking; next to him, the one shouting, Len saw the mustached driver, a black family man if ever he knew. Both of them had khaki-colored trench coats, shiny shoes, and leather driving gloves. He half-hoped a snake would sprint out of the cattails for them. The Steve Harvey-looking one kept screaming questions. Was he Leonard Campbell?

"No," the boy called back.

The two men exchanged looks. "Is he home?" the skinny one asked. His wiry voice made Len chuckle. It suited him.

"No," the boy said. "Go away."

"If he's not here," the driver asked, "may I ask who you are?"

The fastest reply yet: "Don't worry about it."

Len ducked back into his treehouse and plopped himself on his bed. "Dumb bastards," he mumbled, picking up a book and heading back to his reading. Just as he was about to re-secure his bearings within the pages, he heard the moan of wood bearing weight. He locked the trapdoor shut as loud as he could.

6

"What was that?" the skinny man asked the driver from the third plank rung.

"He's messing around with something up there. Let me try again. Hello! SIR!" The boy poked his head out again. "Do you know where we can reach Leonard Campbell?"

"I don't know anyone by that name!" Len called back.

"But you fit his description!" the driver said. He had a file with him and made exaggerated gestures to it. "Look, we're from the IRS! We need to find Mr. Campbell for tax purposes!"

Len rolled his eyes.

"You're not coming up here," the boy said.

"Can you come down?" the skinny one asked.

"I could," the boy said, "but not for you poor bastards."

The boy's head retreated. The skinny man dropped his arms and paced. "Hold on now," said his mustached cohort, "Maybe if we promise to leave him alone, he'll play nice." He craned his neck once more upward. "Can I at least get your name so I can correct the records back at my office? All the papers I got said Mr. Campbell lives here! If we can correct that then I can make sure nobody else from our offices comes out and bothers you!"

It took a moment, but the boy replied. "Len!" said the wooden box in the tree.

"Leonard Campbell! I knew it was you!" the driver said.

"That's not my name," Len said without poking his head out the window again. "I gave you my name. Leave. Go correct your records."

"But Mr. Campbell!"

Len sprung halfway out the window. "Listen, you thick bastard! I told you to get out of here! Unless you want to drive back without a windshield I suggest you get a move on!"

"He wouldn't do that," the driver said to his companion, at a normal volume. "Please, Mr. Campbell!"

A small chunk of cement, with what looked like a few inches of a street sign's pole sticking out, flew out of the window. It landed in the cattails between the men and their car, bounced, and rolled to a stop just short of the shoulder.

"GET LOST!" Len shrieked. "NEXT ONE'S COMING FOR YOUR HEAD!"

The driver handed the keys to the skinny man. "Move the car," he whispered, even though he knew Len couldn't hear him over the distance. As his companion moved the car down to the exit to give the illusion of leaving, the mustached IRS man walked as quietly as he could to the other side of the tree. When his cohort came around again, parked, and approached to rejoin him, he gestured to be silent.

"Mr. Campbell, really, may we please have a word with you?"

There was, apparently, another window directly facing the highway. The IRS men knew it now because a second, larger chunk of concrete launched from that side of Len's treehouse and landed in a geyser of windshield shards. The Honda bounced on its shocks. The skinny man, hanging his head, pressed a button on the keys. The alarm ceased.

The two of them simply stood, staring, at their ride back.

"I told you," Len said, without need to quite fully shout.

Mustache sighed. "Leonard, we –"

"That's NOT my NAME! How badly do you want to lose some toes today?"

"Mr. Campbell, you're being unreasonable."

"Shut up, Parkjob. Go take your nervous condition and sit down in the grass somewhere."

"He told you," the mustached one said. The skinny one scowled down at him and his grin, but had no retort.

"That's it," the black IRS man continued. "I'm coming up!"

"Like hell you are," Len said, double-checking that he had the trapdoor locked. The man climbed up the crude ladder anyway, and knocked on it. Len ignored him. Len told him to go away, to leave him alone, and of course the bastard wouldn't let it go. Len started reading a comic instead.

Then the trapdoor started to clank and bang and split. The IRS men were trying to barge their way in.

"What's going on here?" Len heard asked by a faint, new voice.

The comic landed on the bed as he rushed to the window.

The skinny man on the ground saw the newcomer first. "Who are you?" he asked.

The newcomer was an Indian teenager, perhaps a year or two younger than what Len looked like and with a clear complexion that belied her adolescence, making her pretty face glow in the open light. With her, she had a bow and a freshly caught rabbit. Her clothes suggested an apprenticeship under Paul Bunyan. She didn't acknowledge the skinny man, but rather saw the one throwing his shoulder against the trapdoor. "Get down!"

The mustached man saw her then. "Wait, what? Who are you?"

"This is so stupid," the skinny man muttered.

"Don't worry about that," the Indian girl told the other. The mustached man rolled his eyes, but made his way back down. "What can I help you gentlemen with today?" she asked once both men were on the ground.

The mustached man straightened up. "We are from the IRS. Orders came down from our offices and we're here to find Mr. Leonard Campbell. It's for tax purposes."

The girl shouldered her quiver and bow. "Okay," she said. "Why are you *really* here?"

Both men's jaws fell open. They exchanged looks, and the end was upon them. The skinny one went to make sure the car would still start. Left behind for only a moment, the mustached man glanced once more up at Len's treehouse. "Are you two... friends?"

"It's no business of yours," the girl said. "I don't care if you two are here for 'tax purposes' or not – you ought to leave this poor kid alone."

The car started. The mustached man took a moment, and finally looked the intruder in the eye. "His family is very worried about him, you know. That's part of the reason we came."

9

The girl released her bow, quiver, and rabbit to the ground. "His family is not one of his concerns." She made to climb the ladder, and pointed over the man's shoulder, toward the car. The IRS man took the hint, and rode shotgun.

Len watched them go. The girl knocked on a very intact trapdoor, and Len let her up. "Thank you," he said as they began cleaning the rabbit. "When does your dad expect you home for dinner?"

Chapter Two

Yes, it was true that Len lived in a rather boxic treehouse, and that the tree itself was but one of the countless lining an Ohio freeway. He lived by himself, with his voluminous green hair as untamed as his prospective freedom. He was of average height for a boy his age. His eyes were blue, his days of living alone had trimmed him of his baby fat, and his favorite food was sliced pear. He dressed comfortably when he could, and precariously when the job demanded it.

Len scavenged, trapped food in the small swaths of forest left standing in the fields along the road, and in this, his third year away from his family, he was content. With October fast approaching, the leaves had given themselves up for his heat. He'd scrounged them up at the first opportunity, before the wind teed them up for the grills and wheels of passing semis, and he kept them bagged at the foot of his bed. When necessary, they were to be fed to the heater on the opposite corner of his bed, across from his trunk-segment nightstand. His treehouse had windows on three sides, the exception being behind his bed. It was centered on that wall so he could wake up and see out toward the highway and down it, both east and west. None of them had glass, so he'd found thick cloth and made curtains instead. And for when the wind threatened to blow and keep them open, he had the necessary parts and made fixture points to keep them drawn.

It was a fine life. When he was cold, his friend had helped him pulley that small wood-burner up. (The leaves supplied its first few meals, and thereafter he scrounged up twigs and sticks from the same woody field-splotches that raised small game for him.) When he was hot, the wind cooled him. When he was thirsty and out of water, he made a trip out to Great Lake St. Mary's. On the rare occasion he had no maintenance to do, and nothing of momentary interest to read, he had Willie's railyard to poke around for entertainment. He didn't go to school. Hadn't since running away. He had a friend, a place, and if ever he grew

11

sad, always he had the knowledge to gaze out over the cars and trucks and SUVs, all zooming by without much care for him, and knew that he was free from being one of them.

It was all he needed.

And sometimes his friend visited him. It happened less so during the school year, and more often during the summer. That very girl visited and helped drive the IRS men away. Hanging the rabbit on one of the curtain fixtures by the trap pull, she answered Len about her curfew.

"I'm not entirely sure. Since it's a school night, he'll probably be satisfied if I'm back by dark."

Len was sitting in the window frame, making sure the men didn't just use the exit and come back around again. "How was school?"

She laughed. "What do you care?" He loved how smooth her voice was. It reminded him of his mom.

Len shrugged. "Figured I'd extend the courtesy."

"Where'd you put the spit last?"

Realizing the rabbit was for sooner rather than later, Len jumped down from his post. He stood on his bed, stretching upward to throw open the hatch in the ceiling, so any smoke could escape. "It should be across the bed there, by the heater. Try looking – *damn*, he's a plump one. Where'd you snag him?"

She was too busy climbing past Len.

"Claire."

The girl turned, a blank expression about her face. "What?"

The hatch door clunked as it swung over and came to rest on the roof. "Where'd this one come from?"

"Oh," Claire said, returning to her search. "He's actually been digging around in my dad's garden. I left the trap this morning, but it was my dad that pulled the line."

Len eyed the kill. "Damn fine work. Unfortunate for the furry little bastard, but…"

Claire had the spit, and Len helped her set it up (after pushing the bag of leaves out of the way) at the foot of the bed. Claire offered to clean it if Len agreed to rotate it during cooking.

"So, those men that came today, what do you think they want?"

The question made Len gaze out a window. "I don't rightly know," he said, "but I have my guesses."

"And they are?"

"*Their* explanation was that they needed to contact me for 'tax purposes.' What exactly that would entail, I'm not sure and frankly speaking I don't care to know." He threw away a schnitzel of wood from a chunk he was carving. "I assume that whatever they wanted, it involved taking me back to my family."

"Do you think they know where you are? Or maybe those guys are going to tell them?"

Len eyed her squarely. "What I'm more interested in finding out is how in God's name those men found me." Claire nodded. "But as for my family," Len said, "I know they don't know where I am. Not yet, or at least not recently enough to be here already."

"You think they'd come if they had an idea where to go?"

"Oh, I'm *sure* they would. Remember Claire, I didn't go out on the best of circumstances."

She laughed. "Does any kid that runs away? Here, check that the skin's all gone."

Len sat back, closing his eyes. "Nah, I trust you. You always do a good job. What do you want for a go-with?"

"You have go-withs?"

"But of course." Len rolled off his bed and threw open a door of his cabinet, stuffed in the corner between the heater and the highway. From it, he retrieved three cans of vegetables. "Peas and carrots?"

"They're not expired, are they?" Claire asked.

Len flipped the can for a glance. "Not for a month yet."

Claire shrugged. The sky was turning orange. When the rabbit finished cooking, they cooked the vegetables in one of the pots Len had, giving the juices a chance to settle. Len thanked Claire again for the charity, but she waved him off. They continued on about boys Claire liked at school, her plans for Prom, whether Len would like to go. Len had laughed at that, called their peers a bunch of hump-dancing, musically tasteless bastards with no real concept of much of anything. Claire had seen it coming, but Len remembered how she'd laughed anyway and nearly choked on a leg. The sun sank, ever farther, and there showed no sign of the IRS men. Satisfied, and knowing Claire's father would want her back soon, the two of them made mutual farewells. With just enough light hanging around and a bow slung across her back, an Asian-Indian girl descended the plank rungs of an inhabited tree. She charted course across an ordinary Ohio field while the beans were still small. Len held a mirror out a window until Claire, now hardly more than a dot-sized silhouette, waved back to show she was fine.

Len turned in not long after. He drew the curtains, fixed them in place, read a chapter of *Sherlock Holmes* by candlelight and was done.

After a breakfast of oatmeal, Len foraged the highway. He would sell blown tire pieces for the rubber and whatever metal he could get as scrap. Luckily for him, there was a man within a couple hours' walk that bought such things in the small amounts Len could carry, and didn't ask questions. That man, Bobby if Len remembered right, was a convenient bastard. Len couldn't say much for Bobby's brains, but he had to admit the fat idiot's cash came in handy when push came to shove. It wasn't painfully far from Willie's, either, and Claire was waiting at the treehouse when Len got back with what he'd decided was enough haul for one day.

They snuck in to the freight yard from one end, where the tracks choked down to three. Immediately on the other side of the steel and rust-orange walls, though, they scampered off like intertwined tournament brackets. There was at least a football field's worth of nothing but parallel track, mostly empty, with the occasional curvature where a car would join or divulge from another way. Len sometimes wondered how Willie kept track of it all. The yard itself wasn't cluttered, but was dirty nonetheless. Some small, oil-rainbowed puddles were scattered to and fro. Len and Claire had to be careful to avoid them. Colors varied little.

The cars were mostly brown, save their graffiti (the leavenings, Len always whispered to Claire, of hopeless bastards who probably would have been better off apprenticing themselves to tattoo shops). Much of the rail were the grey of steel, some parts black from wear or rusted red. The walls were all rusted, crusty, and splotched over between orange and red with brown trim. Len imagined few people saw this side of the yard, though. Perhaps halfway through the yard, one side of the wall bore, like a cyst, a cement rise whereupon stood the office. That, Len and Claire knew, was the command post of poor, bitter, bent-over, white-bearded, conductor-wannabe Willie Euski.

The rail yard ran between a small river and a neighbor highway of Len's. He could see from the sidewalk of a nearby overpass to make an educated guess on whether Willie was out and about on any given day, although the risk always remained the old man was awake, and not napping, in the office. Len had to check before entering the yard, because the office windows were a cliché kind of dirty, as though from a run-down gas station in classic Hickville. Len wouldn't be able to see in them from the floor of the yard. God knew how Willie saw *out* of them to conduct business.

For the moment, the coast was clear. Len and Claire walked casually into the rail yard, toward the cars, which today were all packed together toward the far end.

"Do you ever think of breaking open one of these cars and taking something valuable before Willie knows, let alone can do anything about it?" Claire asked from over Len's shoulder.

"Why would I do such a thing?"

"Maybe you need something in one of them."

"Not likely," said Len. "A lot of cars and fuel comes through most of here. It's nothing I can put to use."

"But say there was something, that you could make serious use of."

Len turned toward her. "Then I guess some rich bastard's missing out that day, eh? Usually though I can find useful enough stuff in the open cars."

15

"Like this one?"

"Yeah," Len said, and hopped inside. "Remember, if this thing starts moving all over the place, wait until we're out of the yard to bail. We don't want –"

"...to jump into the path of another car or land and get chopped up, I know, Len." Claire stood up, having joined Len on the platform of the car's floor. "I swear, you'll make a great parent someday."

"Hey," Len said. "Let's not drop that p-bomb. That means I'd have to really get involved with one of our bastardous peers."

"Nobody said anything about our peers," Claire said. "Just let a cougar prowl her way around and hope menopause doesn't sucker punch the zygote."

"The what?"

"Oh, right. Sorry, Len, I forgot."

"Oh," Len said. "Something you learned in school?" Claire nodded. Len dismissed her apologetic face. It was hard sometimes for Claire to know what she could talk about and have Len keep up. Len always forgave her, though.

"So," she said, "what do you want to do?"

Len already had his whittling knife and his work in progress out and was finding a place to sit. "I want to think," he said, and when Claire asked what about, he said "I don't know how much longer I want to stay in the treehouse."

"Do you mean how much longer you can afford to stay in the treehouse?"

"How do you mean?"

Claire paced and gesticulated while Len sat and whittled with a leg dangling out the car. "Well, think about it," she said. Len shot her a dry look, which made her laugh. "You'll be of age before too long here. There are some legal things you have to take care of once you turn 18."

Throwing a schnitzel away, Len said "I'm not worried about that stuff."

"Well, you might need to be," Claire said. "I know for one thing the Selective Service wants you to register with them. If you don't, it's illegal."

"Not. Worried. About it," Len said, not taking his eyes off his creation. "I for one am not volunteering for some angry, small-dick bastard to scream in my face so I can fight a war I didn't sign up for."

"I guess that's why they want you to sign up."

"What else is important about my turning 18?"

"I don't know," Claire said. "Driver's license, legal adulthood, the ability to enter into contracts, not to mention a slew of new jobs you could legally do."

"And become just another bastard driving that highway in the lane next to another bastard driving that highway on our way to a building full of bastards who get to interact with other bastards so we can all make another bastard money, in the hopes and prayer said rich bastard will stop being a gigantic bastard long enough to cut me a check so I can have a tiny bit of the notes with some dead bastard on it, after I went and made that same rich bastard way more money than he's bothering to give me. Is that what you want for me?"

"No, but –"

"Listen," Len said. "You know that stuff doesn't interest me. If I turn 18 living in that treehouse, then it happens. So what? I just don't know if I want to relocate, or something."

Claire deflated at the idea. "Where… where would you move?"

"I'm not sure. It would have to be somewhere still where my family would have a hard time finding me."

"Is that it, Len? You think they're close?"

"Not close," Len said, "but I'm getting antsy. I don't know if I just need a change in scenery, or what, but my gut's telling me it's just been too damn long since I've done something to throw them off."

"Well, you moved into Ohio. I'm not sure there's much else you can do to throw them off."

"How long, though, before they start thinking of moving their search outside the state?" Len asked. "Ohio isn't entirely far, even if we are closer to Indiana. Do you think two states' cushion would be better?"

"I wouldn't be able to visit you," Claire said. "And it would be hard for me to help you get set up once you get there. You'd have to start all over. Build another treehouse."

Len stopped carving. "I don't know what it is. I don't even know if I should stay or go. I mean, what if they're just driving one day and they pass by and wonder what in the hell a treehouse of all things is doing alongside that highway?"

"Now you're thinking about the wildly improbable. Calm down."

"I'm trying to," Len said. "I just…"

Claire went to him and placed a hand on his shoulder. "It'll be okay, Len. I think those guys visiting yesterday just threw you for a loop."

"I still wonder how they found me."

"Maybe, once you're 18, and they come back, you can sign them to a contract where you agree to help them for their tax purposes. In return, they promise not to disclose your location to your family."

"Would I be able to do that?"

Claire climbed down from the car. "One can hope. Come," she said, "I see something shiny over here. I just want to see what it is."

Len came along, but it was only a puddle. There was no oil in it, though, and they found that odd. There was a shimmering coming off the water for an instant, and then it was gone. Then both of them jumped.

"Git!"

"Run," Len said.

"Naw, don't go doin' that way," Willie shouted. "Git back to yer own place!"

Len saw the old man from a stone's throw. "I can do fine on my own, thanks."

"But there's something goings-on at yer little treehouse," Willie said.

"Nice try," Len said. "Come now, Willie, you can't expect me to believe that."

The feeble old man hobbled over with an atmosphere about him that Len wasn't accustomed to. Usually he would wave his arms or shoot the wall next to him with his shotgun, trying to frighten him off, but this time Willie was just tenderly reaching out to him. Claire stayed right by Len's side, and Willie kept pointing over both their heads. "Oh come on now, how many times have I shooed you away with stupider things than that? If ye don' believe me, take a look fer yerself!" Willie said.

A claw clamped on Len's shoulder and spun him around. Willie pointied his whole arm over the boy's shoulder, where they could see, over some distance, a length of highway near Len's place. It took effort, but Len knew Willie wasn't joking. He knew because in the distance, standing between Len and his treehouse, was a familiar black Honda. Farther away still, yet not quite out of view, Len and Claire both saw two men in trench coats walking the shoulder. They exchanged looks. Willie was glad to release them from the yard.

Chapter Three

"Excuse me," Len said, marching up behind the men as they neared the rungs. They ignored or didn't hear him, and he seized the skinny white man by the scruff of the neck and yanked. Standing, face to face, with the subdued man, Len spoke as clearly as he could muster. "Maybe I wasn't clear before," he said. "Neither of you are welcome here, and I suggest you get lost."

The Steve Harvey lookalike was already three rungs off the ground. Claire unshouldered her bow and loosed an arrow. It stuck a couple of feet above the man's head, and he stopped climbing. Len released the skinny one, who stumbled forward from Len's outstretched arm as his friend came back to the base of the tree.

The four of them stood facing each other in pairs. The IRS men ignored Len and Claire's battle-ready poses and simply resumed the air of businessmen.

The mustached one made to start. "Mr. Campbell —"

"Cram it," Len said, barely loud enough for him to hear. He pointed down the road. "Get going down that road. I don't ever want to see you again."

"We're not looking for trouble," the mustached one said. "We just want to talk. That's it."

"All I want is to be left alone," Len said. "That's it. That's how it's going to be."

"Perhaps it would be better if we introduced ourselves, first," Len thought the skinny one said, and his mustached partner nodded.

With an exchange of looks, Len asked Claire. She looked at him in return, and then at the men.

"My name is Wallace James," the Steve Harvey lookalike said, "and my associate here, by a strange coincidence shares your first name." Len's face tightened even further. He scowled, his face falling scarlet. "We work out of a tax office based closer to Columbus," the mustached one continued, "and had received an e-mail about extended no-file and partial-file cases. Going down the list, your extended absence was reason for investigation – the case we now find ourselves in."

"Leonard Humphrey," the skinny white man said. He took a step forward, extending his hand. "Pleased to make your acquaintance, Leonard Camp –"

"MY NAME IS NOT LEONARD you deaf bastard," Len said, and when he paced backward, Claire reached for an arrow. Leonard put his foot back in line. Len returned abreast Claire.

Leonard and Wallace exchanged looks. "Well, whatever your name is," the skinny one said, stepping forward again and producing a file, "I have some documents here that say you have a family back in Pennsylvania. Would you, perhaps, care to comment?"

Len squinted, eyed back and forth between the two men and the file. The arm he used to point down the road he now used to reach for the file as he and Leonard drew steps toward each other. In the closing feet, the skinny white man closed the file and, with the same hand, handed it over to Len.

Len flung it into traffic.

The IRS man watched it fly, spewing pages, not realizing how he left his own mouth agape. When he turned back to Len, the boy was glaring. Before he could do anything or find anything to say, Len marched past him, bumping him shoulder to shoulder with such force that he fell to the ground. When Len came to Wallace, guarding the rungs, he stopped.

"Move," Len said.

The man did not move.

"Claire?" Len called over his shoulder. There was a small clacking noise, and when Len stepped out of the way, Wallace saw that the Indian girl had him lined up for a shot. "Now," said Len, "if you'd be so kind."

The mustached man did not take terribly long in his decision, and casually stepped aside. Len began to climb. Before the man could move to come up after him, Claire loosed an arrow that struck abreast of Wallace, springing to rest like a doorstop. She then climbed the rungs as well, making sure to retrieve her arrow from the trunk. Len slammed the trapdoor. The sound of the lock came not long thereafter.

On the ground, the men regrouped and craned their necks skyward. The green-outlined head poked out the window. "Leonard, please, hear us out!" the skinny man said.

Len laughed. "You're *trying* to lose another windshield, aren't you?"

"Come now, Mr. Campbell —"

"That's not my name, you stupid bastard," Len said, almost entertained. He dangled a chunk of concrete out the window. "Now, do we need to review what happens when you don't go away?"

It was Wallace's turn to laugh. "Nice try, Young Man, but our car's parked well down the road this time; I doubt very much you could throw that so far."

There came a pause, during which the only sounds were of passing traffic.

"Fair enough," Len said from within the treehouse, barely audible over the wind and traffic.

The whole top half of Len appeared in the window this time, and the rubble came straight for Wallace's bushy mustache. Barely recognizing the action in time, the man dove toward the cattails as the cape of his trench coat billowed in his wake. Thinking himself safe, Wallace screamed when the head-sized piece of concrete bounced off the ground where he'd been standing but an instant before and bounced, once more, off his shin. It rolled into the ditch.

The skinny white man dragged his cursing comrade out of the weeds, trying to put at least a little distance between them and the treehouse. Len stood in the window frame. Claire whispered over his shoulder. "Do you want me to shoot another one?"

"No," Len said. "I think I've all the punctuation I need." He called out to Wallace and Leonard. "Now GO! And if I see you drive this way on your way out, I'm still taking out your windows!"

22

"But Len," Claire said, "they won't have a choice but to drive this way, or they'll be facing oncoming traffic at a hundred miles an hour."

"I told you I had all the punctuation needed, didn't I?"

They peered out again. Wallace was on one foot, glaring at Len as Len had, so shortly ago, glared at his companion. With Leonard's help, he hobbled down the shoulder and out of sight. A few minutes later, the black Honda approached in the farthest lane. The skinny one, Len saw, was driving and trying to play tricks with his speed, so Len wouldn't be able to properly time a throw. Len launched one like a Molotov cocktail anyway, and missed. The chunk of pavement bounced off the center of the lane, rebounded off the median, and smashed the windshield in a high-pitched crash of sound. The Steve Harvey lookalike flipped him off as they drove out of sight.

"I'm beginning to think they're not going to leave you alone, my friend," Claire said.

Len harrumphed. "I'm beginning to think you're right."

Claire propped herself in the window. "So, any ideas about what you're going to do about it?"

Len thought about it. "Before any of that, I owe Willie an apology. Shall we?"

$\mathscr{L}$

Willie was tinkering with what looked like a generator near the yard office when Len and Claire returned. When he caught them walking in out of the corner of his eye, he wiped his hands on a rag and told them to go away.

"Git! Isn't yer precious treehouse under siege?" He waved his rag like a warning flag.

Len waited until they were close enough to not need to shout. "Actually, no," he said, planting his feet and, by effect, Claire. "And for that, I owe you."

"Say what now?"

"I owe you a debt of gratitude, Willie. If you hadn't said something, I might not have anything right now. You saved me."

Willie spat out some tobacco. "I know you too well, little mister Len. What is this about?"

"Nothing," Len said. "I merely wanted you to know that I thank you for helping me."

"Well it's the last time," Willie said, picking up his wrench and returning to work. "Now git."

Len glanced at Claire and smiled. "You know it's not that simple, Willie," he said. Willie stopped working, slowly set the wrench down, looked at Len. Spat. There was no porch-side pot and no ding.

In the time it took Willie to shuffle up the ramp to his office and retrieve the shotgun from its mysterious depths, Len and Claire were in the herd of railcars. By the time the old man had it loaded and came within shooting distance of where they'd been, they were on top of the cars, leaping from one to the other like a Bond villains. Willie hobbled on the ground after them, and they chased themselves toward the other end of the railyard. Buckshot sang off metal, but it was several cars behind them. They'd found their game.

During the fun, Len stutter-stepped once and wound up hanging off the edge of a car. Willie was about to turn a corner and find him there, fully susceptible to a load of shot that neither of them was sure he'd really fire *at* Len. Claire pulled Len up in time, though, and the chase kept on.

The two of them sprinted out the other end of the railyard and put half a football field's distance between themselves and it. Willie emerged from the herd of cars and stood there, in the gap between the walls. They walked a few more feet to satisfy him, and he vanished from whence he came. The sky began to turn. With perhaps an hour of decent light left and nothing but her own two feet, Claire wouldn't make it back before dark.

They caught their breath, foreheads dirty with grit and sweat. When they caught up with themselves and stopped laughing, Claire vowed to head home. "My dad's going to kill me," she said.

"School night?"

Claire nodded. "Don't you keep track anymore?"

Len broke forward in a small, renewed bout of laughter. "Why would I?"

Their conversation wound down. They said their goodbyes and Claire headed home. Len looked around to sense where he was; he couldn't remember the last time he had been on the far side of the raiyard. A simple bridge stood not far upriver.

Len remained by the river in the remaining light and saw a thing and remembered an idea. He peered back, saw Claire turn a corner to walk around the railyard, and faced forward himself.

"Yeah... you should have one," Len said.

Chapter Four

Len planted his feet where the bridge ended. He stood as a rat before a maze. A few feet farther and he'd be at an intersection, where one road led one way and its temporary mate led another, to ignore each other forever more. He grinned, and then frowned, at the idea. Whether it was against their wills, he didn't know.

What was he up against? He wondered. The convenience store sat on his left, kitty-corner from a dive of a dollar store. A Mom-and-Pop body shop and a sandwich shop filled the other corners and made the intersection a family. Len paid little attention to those extras. He took a long, deep breath. He held it for a moment instead of just letting it go. Then, sneakers blazing a trail, he walked out of his own skin.

Nobody was on the road. A few parked cars sat along the curb but, for the most part, Len had the evening and this chunk of the city to himself. He turned to keep on his own side of the street at the intersection, and devoted his attention to the in-and-out with the red and grey banner reading Buckeye Party & Lotto.

It had changed remarkably little since his previous visit. Neon greeted his approach from underneath the eave, but he found it a little difficult to cut across the empty parking lot. He felt as though the street lamps were accusatory spotlights, as though Wallace might have control of them somewhere, and was ready to pick Len out of a line in which he was already alone. Len didn't care for the dead light those streetlamps cast. He didn't like the way they just splashed some visibility on the asphalt and left it there. "To Hell with the consequences," he could hear them saying. And somewhere, deep down inside of him, he could feel the air rattle ever so subtly as they said "To Hell with Len," too.

It was only dusk. They'd just woken up, and he could get by without them. He skirted around their light.

The door rang a chime for the cashier in the back, and Len accidentally made eye contact with him. As Len had dearly hoped against, it was the same cashier as from his previous visit. From behind the protective glass, the cashier suddenly forgot to chew his gum and his magazine sagged in his hands. Len broke off the engagement and disappeared down the nearest of the one-way, kindergartner-sized aisles.

There was no one else in the store. Len looked up and saw a rounded mirror, and saw the cashier trying to keep track of him in it. The streetlamps had friends. Or perhaps they worked for the young cashier who, once upon a time, had nearly made a decent attempt to be Len's friend.

It had been an awkward attempt at idle conversation. Not terribly long after erecting his treehouse, Len had wandered over to Buckeye Party & Lotto and found the very same cashier minding the register. Newly hired and barely 18, the kid was an absolute tool in Len's book. He was clean-shaven. He kept his yellow hair far too short to do anything with. He read magazines about famous people whose activities – and the feckless articles obsessed with them – didn't really matter. He listened to the music the television told him to. He wasted his time. Then he tried to act like he was on the same level as Len. Green-haired even back then, Len had made a small effort to be polite and wound up scoffing it out. The more the cashier talked, the more dearly Len wanted to punch him. When it became evident to Len that a near-peer such as he could have little if anything of interest to offer in a conversation, Len immediately began giving the bare-minimum replies. Yet the cashier persisted, delving into ever-further degrading topics and the deeper the stupidity of the subject went, as it did with such speed and enthusiasm, so Len's desire graduated: from wanting to punch the cashier in the arm, to the face, to the mouth, to the throat, and soon Len would have enjoyed an outright kick well out of bounds… if only it guaranteed to silence the annoying bastard. There was a gap in memory for that episode, and Len forgot exactly why, but the cashier – whose name Len could not recall despite the nametag and the day's generous given quality time – had yelled at Len on his way out.

Now, over two years later, the reunion. Len combed the aisles as well as he could without re-entering the cashier's field of vision. He knew the kid wasn't reading his magazine any more, either; he knew because he knew enough about magazines like that and that people like that cashier didn't read them, but glanced more at pictures than anything else, which meant they turned pages fairly often. Len heard no rustling of pages. He listened for other sounds, though few came.

He wound his way, trying not to duck and make things look worse than they were. He tried not to dive and roll or dart and spin like a SWAT officer. Although he was successful, it offered no help. He looked in the candy aisle and browsed the end displays, but his prize appeared at none of them.

"Need help finding something?" the cashier said.

Len was surprised by the treaty on the kid's voice. "Not just yet," he said. He didn't dare check the rounded mirror again. Deciding it was time to improvise, he faked a quick potty dance for good measure and hopped to the bathroom.

A motion detector told the light and fan to go. Len sneered at the fan as he tried to ignore the pee in the grout troughs at the base of the toilet. The red-tiled bathroom was as cliché a gas station bathroom (minus the gas) as Len had ever seen. It was another reason to rethink his game plan and split.

He tried to think of where else his target might be, and thought of two. He hoped the second would not be necessary, and almost took another deep breath before abandoning the sanctuary. Remembering the puddle, he thought better of it. Why hadn't any of it gone down the drain in the center of the floor? Some incompetent bastard had failed the grout job, from the looks of it. Elevation had been foiled.

At last, the smell smacked him. It was the boost he needed. Len opened the door.

Glancing both ways to see if the cashier was waiting in ambush, Len realized two things. First, that the cashier was still in his assigned place. Second, that his quarry was at hand. For all his trouble, he had missed an inconspicuous display hanging on

28

the patch of wall between the store's restrooms. It seemed like an odd place. He grabbed a sample anyway.

At the sound of paper rustling, Len felt the cashier react. There was nothing wrong with what he was doing, he told himself, and as if to vindicate his attempts at self-comfort, another customer entered. That person – male or female, Len didn't know or care – went straight for the counter. With the cashier occupied, Len perused the maps.

The first he'd picked up was a dud. In truth, he had grabbed it at random for sheer excitement over simply finding the display. He realized now it was a North American atlas. That was too broad. He slipped it back amongst its twins. Thumbing through the other pamphlet-style maps, Len came up on an Ohio map. It was much closer to what he needed. On it, he traced his finger over his routes to the cemetery, Willie's railyard, Great Lake St. Mary's, and even the approximate location of his treehouse.

That map, however, was very similar to one he already had, waiting patiently beneath his bed for when next he would need of it. He replaced the Ohio map, and selected an Indiana one instead. He searched for a Pennsylvania map and hoped perhaps for a regional one involving all three states, maybe even Michigan, Kentucky, and West Virginia, but did not have such luck. It did not take long for Len to see the map as good enough. Flipping it over, he checked the price.

The cashier finished with the one customer, but just as the funny feeling of being watched returned to nag the back of Len's head, a new customer passed the old one through the door. This one, clearly a man by his voice, took the cashier's attention without delay. Len took the opportunity and returned focus to the map. There, in the lower right-hand corner, was a bar code and a price.

He stuffed the map under his arm and raided his pocket. Exactly how much Bobby had given him, he didn't know. He counted it in his palm, lest the cashier try to become his friend again.

Len was well over a dollar short. "Damn it, Bobby!" he said under his breath. "How much of a cheap bastard can you be…" He stuffed the money back in his pocket, even though he knew he'd have to deal with it in ball form later, which he detested.

Len checked the mirror; the cashier was finishing the transaction with the more boisterous customer. They were making small talk successfully, and on the inside Len was waving his finger in celebration. While he was still sure the yellow-haired cashier had forgotten about him, Len took and held another deep breath for clarity before pinning the map to his ribs, on the far side of his body from the cashier, and crouched where he would be even more difficult to see.

Nearer the door, the cashier saw Len in flashes as the angles of the aisles revealed the boy's presence. Frame by frame, Len saw the cashier transform from complacent, to confused, to surprised, to assertive.

The door chime was the final betrayer.

"Hey you, stop!"

Len booked it. Guilt had no hold on him. He'd left what money he had in the map's place on the display. It was all he could do in recompense.

A block or so away already, the sound of police sirens began to wail. Len knew he had to disappear. He would not spend the night in his treehouse. Wallace could appear and use his shin to add charges to Len's offenses list. The record could become a flag for his family. They might come. Who knew when he could see Claire next under such circumstances?

Len didn't even have to think about it. He didn't even have to put real effort in. His legs churned up momentum like a steam locomotive. The map pumped in rhythm with the arm which held it like a shop clamp, the folding crisp enough that it didn't betray him and flap and flop open in the wind. There existed nothing of Len's world except the sidewalk, the corner of the building, more sidewalk, the grass, whatever few square inches of ground his feet struck. Each step lasted him seven feet or more. Each launched him forward like a rabbit. Not even Willie's shotgun could make him run that fast. Not anything of Len's own will could make him run that fast.

And before Len knew it, he plunged into the river and in three superhuman strokes, came to the other side. He scrambled from all-fours to a dead sprint as equal to staying on one's feet when hanging on to an ATV. His feet barely touched the ground each time, yet flew him forward with the grace and certainty of a gazelle. He didn't know how long he ran. He didn't know how far he ran. But at some point just before dark, Len came out of that instinct-driven dash at the base of his tree. Hardly out of breath, he thought of the map for the first time in at least ten minutes. Its pages were soaked together. Wasting no time in cursing the luck, he folded it over gently and placed it in his back pocket.

Once he was secure on the other side of the trapdoor, Len unfurled the map across the floor and fed his heater some leaves. The integrity of the ink was still mostly there. The finer print was fuzzy and mostly indistinguishable, but Len reasoned that if they were so small, they couldn't have been vastly important. At least, not for his purposes. He pinned the still-soggy paper on his wall, as nearly in line with his Ohio map as he could muster.

Heart still pounding, his tunnel vision began to dull. As it did, he noticed the troubling extent of the water damage. By the time the map was dry, the crinkling left over would distort the scales. It was at that point that Len cursed Bobby again, fully aloud, for no one out there could hear him. It was loud in his treehouse though, and sometimes Len just needed that to vent. Later, perhaps, when next he had the opportunity to speak with Claire, Len thought perhaps they could brainstorm together on how to make up for the distortions. Len didn't think Claire would like the means, but if there was anything Len truly understood, it was "You gotta do what you gotta do."

"You gotta do what you gotta do," he said.

Sounds of police grew stronger. They were on the highway. Len's attention spanned their way. He would have to budget what

31

time he had, he knew, even though his budget was by no means well-defined. He rushed as well as he could.

Drawing the curtains, fastening them shut, dimming his lights, and pressing himself into his bed just as deeply as he could, Len waited. He waited as the sirens grew louder, clearer, until the drone of the tires was loud enough to join. Their engines were going, Len heard. Wherever they thought he was, they were wasting no time getting there. With sirens bearing down on him and his treehouse, drawing ever closer, Len glanced at his pocket knife. It made him wonder what it was like to have a sibling.

But, knowing he needed to be better, Len had to do something more. Still striving to make himself small and hoping his bed would simply absorb him flat, he grabbed his knife and his half-whittled block and shaved at it like a madman.

On the other side of the curtains, cop cars cruised by. It was a squad of one, two, three-four, five-six. Len lost count. He flicked some schnitzels away so they couldn't interfere with his carving. He brushed a couple more from the blanket, by his ribs. Sometime after he became sure that the police were looking elsewhere, Len knew he was sleepy and was coherent enough still to place the wood and knife on his nightstand. He didn't remember it, but that's where they were in the morning.

Chapter Five

Len's eyes opened to a lock of green coursed over his face. He knew right away that he was awake, and instinctively clenched up, pressing himself again into his bed. He re-opened one eye, tuned an ear as far as he could listen. There were no police sirens. He lifted his head, and listened the other way. He heard the sound of rubber rolling merrily along pavement, the heavy jetstream of a semi waft on the shoulder and nearly knock down all the grass in its wake, and the occasional, quick burrumph as a less-than-attentive driver migrated into the shoulder's sound strips and jolted back into his or her lane. He heard only the standard highway noises.

He sprang out of bed and started his day. He kept the curtains drawn and fed the heater.

In the afternoon, he was standing between the heater and the front window when he heard the trapdoor behind him echo a small, familiar tune (of four eighth notes followed by two quarters, to be precise). "You can come up," he said.

Claire crawled through and locked the trapdoor. Len heard her sit on the bed. He waited a moment, wondering perhaps if she was just getting settled, setting her backpack on the ground or opening it to retrieve something, but nothing gave it away. "Hello," he said over his shoulder.

"What did you do?" Claire asked.

Len stopped what he was doing and faced his friend. Before he could ask the matter, Claire pointed not at him, but over his shoulder. "And what is that?"

Len glanced. "It's a map. What of it? Hello, by the way. Did you have a nice couple of days without me?"

Claire stomped over to him. "You need to be more careful, Len." She produced an inner fold of a newspaper. "I circled it."

Len accepted the leaf. It didn't take long to find Claire's meaning.

Following Strange Theft, Local Party Store Left with Questions

The subtitle Len found amusing. Although the suspect was on security camera, the police had not only failed to catch him, but had no idea who the person's identity was.

But then it hit Len what the article was probably, actually, about. He read.

A local convenience store, Buckeye Party & Lotto, is searching for answers today after a queer robbery Saturday evening. The robbery left the store short only a map, although authorities told its management to check inventory to make sure that report is true.

The cashier on duty described the suspect as a light-skinned male in late adolescence and maybe his early 20s, of medium height and green hair. He was last seen fleeing the scene of the crime.

The cashier said he thought the suspect looked familiar, but could not place him or give a name.

The robbery is strange, officers said, because the suspect showed no interest in the cash register.

"It's like all he cared about was getting that map," Officer Clasby, a three-year veteran of the force and Wapakoneta native, said. "What's even weirder is that, on top of not robbing the store for money, he left some behind instead."

The cashier witness confirmed the detail, saying a few dollars and loose change was found approximately where the stolen map sat on display. After counting it, he said, he confirmed it was fairly close to the map's price before tax.

The suspect was last seen leaving the convenience store. The cashier did not chase, he said, because he said the suspect looked familiar but may have been dangerous.

Wapakoneta police ask that anyone with information step forward and contact their offices.

Len handed the newspaper back to Claire. Claire shook her head. "Keep it," she said. "You'd better hope your family doesn't see that."

Len laughed. "Yes, like they'll get ahold of a small local newspaper from a state away, and search its back stories for some vague details about me," he said. "Besides, I can't be the only green-haired kid in the tri-state area."

Claire offered a more critical look. "You're the only one *I've* seen. And it's still a gigantic red flag."

"But how many people are honestly going to peruse the back pages of a small, out-of-state newspaper for something like this?"

"I'm just trying to look out for you, Len," Claire said through her teeth.

"Okay, okay," Len said. "Thank you, I guess, damn." He allowed a pause for Claire to settle. Then he tossed the paper onto his bed and returned to the maps. "How did you find that article, anyway?"

He knew Claire shrugged even with his back turned. "My dad found it, actually."

"Since when does Almighty Subhail read the newspaper?"

Claire shrugged again. "If he has time at breakfast, which this morning he did. I was packing up to come here when he told me about the story. 'This suspect sounds an awful lot like that Len you hang out with,' he told me. I asked him what he was talking about and he handed me the section."

"And he still let you come here?"

"I guess he figures as long as you don't start showing up at our house and stealing from us, you're all right," Claire said. "Besides, you weren't exactly described as violent in that article, now were you?"

Len admitted she had a point.

"So what's all this?" Claire asked, waving a hand over Len's maps. Len had pushpins, string, and sticky notes spread about, mostly splintering west into Indiana from his cozy spot on 33.

Len went a long time without saying anything. He peered around at Claire, at the maps, and around the treehouse but wasn't exactly sure where to start. At last he plunked himself down on his bed and looked Claire stone in the face. "I don't know whether to stay or go," he said, "but until I decide one way or another, I need to protect this place better."

Claire's brow lowered. "Why's that?" she asked, looking out the front window.

Len nodded. "They haven't been back," he said. "Not formally, anyway. But I have noticed them still driving by. Wallace is the driver, most often."

"You remember their names?"

"Sometimes it's hard not to, when you're in a hard place," said Len. "Memory sometimes acts like a recording device, and during those moments I knew my livelihood was on the line. The black man, the one with the mustache, is named Wallace and the lanky bastard is –"

"Leonard, yes, I remember that one."

Claire's sentence interrupted Len's thought. "I thought you said…"

But Claire waved him off. "Once you started getting into it more, you jogged my memory. It's fine, I remember. Anyway, you said they've been driving by but not stopping. What on Earth for?"

"I don't know, although I have a few theories."

Claire leaned against the nearest wall. "Tax purposes?"

They both laughed.

"In all seriousness," Len said when they were done and settled, "whatever their motive, they clearly don't understand what I'm demanding of them."

"Oh, I don't think that's true," Claire said.

"No?"

"Nah. At this point, Wallace might just be doing this out of spite. I honestly kind of doubt that his manager would want him stalking a minor by camping a stretch of highway."

"So what do you think it's about? Vengeance for his ankle? It'll heal. His windshields? They've been replaced. Maybe even by his boss or his boss's boss somewhere up the ladder. I'm not worried about that. What I am worried about, however, is what they'll do now that they know I won't come quietly."

36

"Come on, Len, I really doubt SWAT is going to get forcefully involved just because a teenager doesn't want to go politely with a couple of strangers. For that matter, I also doubt that they'd get involved because he doesn't want to file tax paperwork."

Len stood, went to the window. "That whole tax thing might be a ruse. Long story short, bottom line of it all, they aren't leaving me alone and I need to do something about that."

"I assume contacting the police yourself is out of the question?" Claire said. Len shot her a smug look. "All right, then, so it's up to us. What's to do about it?"

"You have a half-day at school tomorrow, right?"

"Yeah. I'll shoot over here as soon as I get home, then," Claire said, and made for the trapdoor.

"No," Len said. "Meet me above Willie's."

"If he knows you and gives you a warning shot, what will *I* get if I just show up and say I'm meeting a friend?"

"No," Len said. "The rise near it. Meet me there."

A perplexed Claire tried for a moment to understand. By the end of the same moment, she disappeared with a shrug and a shake of her head beneath the falling trapdoor.

$\mathscr{L}$

Cars rushed by beneath their feet. They couldn't see them, but they knew they were there. The river flowed on their left. Len imagined himself and Claire as monarchs looking out over a courtyard full of loyal subjects. From here, they could see their courtyard and the treasures of the kingdom. Len stepped back from the chain-link fencing.

"What do you see?" Len asked of Claire, who stood on the curb behind him, on the cynical-looking side of stolid.

She released a long breath, finally uncrossing her arms. "I see a whole lot of junk, all of which the yardkeeper should have cleaned up by now. What happens if the cars need to move with some of that junk in the way?"

Len, alight by smile, gazed back over the whole of Willie's rail yard, which they could see almost as perfectly as though it were a football field and they had good seats behind a field goal. He pointed to a shiny abandoned shape in the corner. "It already happens," he said. "Willie isn't so good at bending over and doesn't have a young apprentice to help him out, so mostly it just sits around, waiting to either get destroyed like that hunk of junk or, by me, made into a useful little bastard."

"And what would you have done with a dented oil pan?" asked Claire.

Len shrugged, but asked her to scout the yard from their perch anyway. There were items, salvageable and not, littered throughout the rail yard as faithfully as the oily puddles. They could hear the metal sliding and slams as Willie closed cars in the distance. Claire squinted to be sure of some things she picked out, but did not move from her spot. Len half-danced from place to place, making a visor of his hand, doing all he could to see.

After a quarter of an hour, Len parked himself abreast his friend, who noticed and met his look. "Well?" Claire said.

Len, still beaming, nodded. "We'll wait until nightfall."

"And you know what you're going to do with half of this stuff? Already?"

Len offered a definitive nod. Then, only to Claire's facially expressive surprise, he pointed over his shoulder. "That too, if it comes to it," Len said. Behind them, perhaps a half-mile down the way, was a junkyard. It was Billy's.

"Well, let's get a move on," Claire said. She started walking off the bridge, so as to head for the choke point entrance of the rail yard.

"Whoa, whoa, not yet," Len said. Claire turned. "Willie's still out there. Wait until he's gone."

"Len, that probably won't be until nightfall."

"It's the weekend."

Claire came back, took another survey from afar. She forced a smile and, with bored eyes, looked at Len. "You'd better map out to yourself where all of these things are. Unless, of course, you've got some night vision you haven't told me about."

Len told her she was a smart bastard.

They killed time together. The sun sank, and night fell, and right on cue, they slipped into the railyard.

A few lights were on. Wherever Willie was, he was being very, very quiet. Len and Claire half-crouched as they jogged along from track to track, trying to make out what shapes were what where the light played tricks. This was especially true for objects hidden in the shadows of cars, where a curtain seemed to always hang; if you were in the light, your eyes could not penetrate the border to within the shade, but if you were in the shadow, you could lurk and wait as you pleased.

Beneath the first car, quite near the entrance, Claire pointed out a shape. Len waved her off, saying it would be better to get it on the way out. Not knowing how much time they'd have, they kept moving.

Some forty yards ahead to their right, there came a soft thump. Claire, jumpy already, darted behind Len. They waited for a moment, across the way from the rise and the office, where the lights struggled to reach. They'd passed a few isolated cars already, but they were all closed.

Seven full, deep breaths after the thumping noise came and nothing appeared from the darkness between the railcars, Len and Claire tiptoed farther into the railyard. The herd from before had a few heretics now. Some were in pairs, others alone. A majority of the cluster remained as before, which Len guessed to be about sixty percent, and there were probably about four small clusters spread about the tracks. As he and Claire neared one of these clusters along the unheeding wall, nearest the herd, another thump came from the same area as before. The thump, however, was not what they heard; rather, there was a single, softly singing pound on metal. Claire sank next to their railcar's wheel, trying to make herself one with the shadow. Len darted closer to the car as well, but remained standing and peered around the end.

There was nothing. The uneven end of the herd lined along parallel tracks, staring toward the entrance like soldiers in a line. For Len, it was even a little majestic to see such a lineup from the side, even if it was at their feet.

Len conveyed to Claire, by a touch on the shoulder and waves of his hands, that he was going to go out a little farther, into the light and look around the other long end of the railcar. He would be right back. Claire nodded.

Len went around the corner, over the tracks, and poked his head past the corner. He looked back at the entrance and much of the yard. Another noise came, and he sank back, keeping only his eyes out.

There was something moving, and his eyes locked on it of their own accord. Off in the distance, emerging from the shadow of the far wall, walking up the ramp from the very same choke-point entrance as Len and Claire, went bent-over old Willie, spinning his key ring on one finger. Whistling away, the yardkeeper locked up his office and vanished into the night. Len released the breath he only then realized he'd been holding.

"It's good," Len whispered over his shoulder. "He's gone."

And after a moment, Claire appeared. Onward they went.

The height of railcars, and the angles and locations of the lights atop the walls and office, made the herd almost completely blocked from sight. Just as Len and Claire hid themselves among their ranks, there came another of those dull thumps. It was low. It was closer than ever. It was behind them. It came short, definitively, and just on the other side of the same railcar as the two of them crept by.

Even with Willie gone, they were not alone. Len had to grab Claire by the shoulders to keep her from abandoning the mission at a full sprint. After all, she had the collection bag.

"Don't be a sissy bastard!" Len said at the lowest possible volume. Even eight inches from her ears, Claire barely heard him. "Let's get the jump on this guy before he does the same to us! Now, we're going to get down low, crawl underneath to the other side of this car, and take him down. Got it?"

A wide-eyed Claire nodded, and when Len released her, got a hold of herself. On the count of three, the two of them got down on their bellies and bear-crawled beneath the car. They didn't see anyone's shoes. Claire tapped Len's foot, and Len craned back to read her lips. "Did we not hear him walk away?"

Len didn't know, but turned forward again anyway. When he did, something brushed his face. He reeled, moving to all fours, and ponged his head on the metal underbelly of the railcar. All the railyard must have heard. He collapsed back onto his belly, stifling a curse over the sharp explosion of pain.

Nursing the back of his head with one hand, Len lifted his face and saw, of all the things in the world, the shape of a cat, the light beyond the far end of the car its background.

It meowed a question at him.

"It's just a cat," Claire said at normal volume. She rolled back out from beneath the car and sat up. "It's just a cat!" She lost herself in laughter until Len remembered himself and rejoined her. The cat followed suit.

They watched it emerge from beneath the car, walk up to them, and sit. "Meow," it said.

"Sneaky little bastard," Len said, "you scared me half to death. I probably woke half the neighborhood smacking my head." He pointed an accusatory finger to the ground beneath the car as he spoke to the cat. Then he and Claire exchanged looks and laughed, trying to be fairly quiet, before resuming their search of the yard. The cat, whom Claire named Becky, tagged along.

It wasn't long thereafter that they started running across useful objects. This area of the railyard had been too far for them to see, so they figured they would start from the far end, clarify the identities of the junk, and work their way into familiar ground.

"Got a couple of good-sized rocks over here," Claire said, and Len threw them in the bag.

"I just found a box of nails," Len said, and threw them in the bag.

"This is kind of strange," Claire said, and Len asked what. "There are some wooden stakes spilled over here." They shrugged and put them in the bag.

So on and so forth they went, collecting and rejecting all manner of things. They came across broken bottles, a hubcap, two gutted cassettes, three disposable pens (two a bit mangled but functional, the third too soaked-through to write), spare inches of twine, sharp rocks, dull rocks, tiny rocks, gravel, a stick, and even a spare tire. On their way out, they checked beneath the first car from before. Becky loved on Claire's shoulder when she held herself in plank.

"Looks like it might be a wadded-up tarp," she said.

"Grab it."

With several hours to spare before dawn, the two friends carried their haul out from the railyard and back to the sidewalk. Under cover of night, and from the overlooking distance, the lights weren't nearly as foreboding. They offered, instead, almost a sense of safety. Len wondered to himself if that was just because he was no longer there. Becky loved against his ankle.

L

"So," Claire said, "do you want to try the junkyard still?"

Len shook his head. "It's late. You go on home; I'll sort through there on my own."

"Nonsense, you stubborn bastard," Claire said. "It's the weekend."

Len looked at her.

L

Len lost track of what time of night it must have been, but they eventually came to the dirt parking lot of Billy's junkyard. He looked around while Claire rested with the bag of salvageables from Willie's. The door was locked, the gates were closed, and the walls stood much too high for them, even one boosting the other, to reach over.

"Do you want to try the lock?" Claire asked when Len returned.

Len shook his head in the low light. "We don't have anything to break it. Not unless you picked something up back there that I didn't see?"

Claire shook her head, averting his gaze.

Len waved it all down. "That's fine. I'll just make a trip over here tomorrow."

"What do you want to do about her?" Claire asked as Becky wove around her feet.

Len didn't know. "Screw it," he said. "I'm about ready to call it a night. Let's head back, get some food in us." Becky agreed.

"Yeah," Len said, "You too."

On the hike back, they took turns with the sack. Len realized how heavy it was. He figured he could make fine defenses out of some of them, and what he couldn't quite finish, there was always Billy's junkyard.

"Well, maybe not always," he said.

"What was that?" Claire asked.

"Nothing," Len said. "Just thinking to myself."

They were about half a mile down the shoulder from the tree. Len guessed it was between 1 and 2 in the morning.

"So, you know what you're going to do?" Claire asked.

Len heaved the bag back up toward his shoulders. "Wait until we get there, this thing's already trying to slip without my talking," Len said. Becky jogged ahead a little and meowed.

For the last hundred feet or so, Claire took control of the bag. Len went first up the ladder and dug out the old pulley contraption from beneath his bed. Claire waited at the base with Becky until Len was able to sort out the knot of rope and rods and doohickeys. Less than ten minutes later, he attached it to the outside of the window above the ladder. Claire tied the bag to the rope and then helped Len pull it up from within the

43

treehouse. When they were done, Becky was all alone outside, wondering why she'd been left behind. Len and Claire poked their heads out and looked at her.

"Couldn't you carry her up?" Len asked.

"I can't climb your jacked-up ladder with one arm, Len. What are we going to do?"

Len thought. It didn't take long. He retrieved another piece for the pulley: a very sturdy wooden plank that served as a crude elevator. Claire went back down the ladder, helped Becky onto it, and they were both surprised that she was smart enough to understand her ride. At the top, Len held the board from swinging and she hopped the gap. He disassembled the pulley, drew the curtains, and threw open the hatch.

"Len."

"Hm?"

Claire handed him a ball of paper. "It was lying on your bed," she said.

Len uncrumpled the letter. It was from Wallace and Leonard.

"What is it?" Claire asked.

"Nothing new," Len said. "I don't want to talk about it right now."

"Okay…"

"Here," Len said, trying to occupy himself, "I'll start sorting through all this stuff. Can you go catch something for a nice dinner? I'll have stuff ready when you get back."

Claire was surprised by the question. "Yeah," she said anyway. "Be back in a few. On one condition; when I get back, let me know what you plan on doing with some of this stuff." She pointed to the letter as he moved for the trapdoor. "I want to know if I can help out more."

Len broke eye contact, nodded. Claire left and Becky meowed, asking Len where on Earth their friend intended to go.

Some period of time later – still well before dawn – Claire returned not with a kill, but a pack of chicken from her own family's freezer. Len had the spit ready, having expected another rabbit or the like, but easily made do with the actual. They ate a meal, complete with vegetables and snack cakes for dessert. They even gave Becky some chicken, leaving her full, warm, and purring in Len's lap while he talked. The goods from the railyard were stacked neatly around the highway side of the treehouse, hidden beneath windowsill level so Wallace and Leonard would never be able to see.

"It also gives me less of a chance to see those ugly bastards' faces, since I can't get quite as close to the window now."

Claire laughed. "Lucky you."

"Anyway, I had a few plans on what to do with all this stuff. Those wooden stakes are going to be part of the final touch," Len said.

"What's that?"

"I'm going to leave a thin tripwire around in the grass so I'll know they're here if, for example, they come while I'm asleep."

"Will you let me know where it is?"

"Of course," Len said, "but you need to memorize it really well once I do, because I need you act like it's not really even there." Claire opened her mouth to speak a couple of times, as though she had a question but answered it herself but then had another question, and wasn't sure whether to ask it. "If they see you very purposefully stepping over something they can't see," Len said, "then they'll know it's there."

Claire nodded her understanding.

"But that won't come until the end. I want to set up everything else, first," Len said. "That box of nails will come in handy. I can hide those underneath the gravel along the shoulder, take out their tires if they decide it's safe to park near here while I'm away or asleep. I can drop that hubcap down the trapdoor if they decide it's cool to climb up. Then, while they're occupied with that, I'll throw some oil down on the rungs so they're too slick to climb."

"What about the spare tire and the cassettes? Do you have ideas for those, too?"

45

"Well absolutely. I'm going to get some more rope and attach the tire just underneath the treehouse like a volleyball. They'll have to get past that, too, as it swings for them. And it'll stay with them, too, because the rope should wrap around the trunk and bring it up as they go along."

"And the cassettes?"

Len wasn't entirely sure about those. "I can use the pens we found to rotate those, but the filmy parts themselves I haven't decided. There are a few things I can use them for, mostly in conjunction with the rocks we found."

"What," Claire asked, "you're not going to just throw rocks at them and tell them to go away?"

Fighting off a small bout of laughter, Len said no. "If they come again, I'll have to make sure I leave an impression."

"I think you did that last time when you took out their windshield and busted the one's shin."

"Not enough, obviously," Len said. "But I should find a way to get at that shin, because it should still be a tender area. I just wish I had a better concept of how much time there'll be before they show up again."

"Well, keep in mind there's still really no guarantee that they're even going to be back with force," Claire said. Becky spread her toes in a satisfying stretch.

Len petted her. He looked over Claire's head, at the maps. "That's true. I still need to have a last resort, though."

"How do you mean?" Claire asked. She saw Len looking over her head and glanced that way. "Oh," she said. "What about Michigan?"

"Seems a little far, doesn't it?"

Claire shrugged. "Well, it's closer than this place is to Pennsylvania."

Len's expression slanted as he chewed. "No, I think Indiana is the better option if it comes to it. I might want to deal with Wallace and Leonard, first, though."

There was a pause. "I'd deal with them before they deal with you," Claire said.

Len made a series of small, rapid nods. "Yeah," he said, and took a deep breath. "I think what I'm going to do is prepare the treehouse in case they come, and come hard. I can't start making preparations for one thing if I'm not prepared for the other when that 'other' can swoop down at any moment."

Claire's face turned sullen. "Do you... do you know where in Indiana you would go? I mean, aren't you going to scout the countryside a bit before you commit to leaving?"

Len met her eyes, but broke off. He looked over at his maps from right where he was, tracing the string running from pushpin to pushpin, sticky notes here and there. "I don't know."

Chapter Six

It took three days for Len to properly affix the loot, scavenge and buy spare parts, and test some of them. Four days passed before he admitted to being anywhere close to ready, however; a beautifully rainy day kept him from his work, and in particular kept him from establishing the stakes for the final tripwire.

Monday, Claire asked her father about a pet. It did not take much for Subhail to agree so long as Claire took proper care of whatever it was, and that it wasn't anything outrageous. Thus, Becky was saved confinement to the treehouse and escaped the following day's rain from within the coziness of the Mehtas' ranch-style house.

All day the second day, while the rain fell, hissing faintly on the road, Len couldn't help but be on edge. As much as he wanted to continue preparations, there was little he could do strictly within the treehouse. The rain, albeit calm, could still compromise his rope and other materials he had. It could make his hands slippery and cause things to fall, perhaps on his head, perhaps to the ground, which only awaited the opportunity to damage things. (The heartless bastard!) He already had to periodically change out his curtains because of it. Sure, he thought to himself, it made the grass smell good, and it mixed things up as far as the highway ambience went, but couldn't it have fallen on a more convenient day? Len cursed the lot of pattering raindrops on the roof as irritating bastards.

He stayed in that day, keeping the front window open. He wasn't entirely sure, but he thought he saw Wallace. It made him wonder about Leonard.

Looking in his mirror, for he had the spare time, Len realized he was just about due for a re-dye. He hoped he would have the spare time and money in the coming days to touch up his green. He tried not to worry about it. To kill time, he read. When he tired of *The Catcher in the Rye* for its inability to interest him, he whittled. The schnitzels formed an anthill-like lump on the floorboard.

Claire appeared fieldside on the third day. She unshouldered a roll of rope and let it plop to the ground. "Any headway?"

Len was standing on a rung just below the trapdoor, trying to secure his tire-volleyball trap. "Kind of," he said. "What I really need is a more secure way to fasten this."

"Can't you tie it to the other side of the trapdoor somehow so when you open it this just falls out, and then you can throw it to get it started going around?"

Len stopped what he was doing and stared at Claire. He examined the trapdoor and the tire. "I can try," he said. "But then what do I do with this platform?"

"I'm sure you'll think of something," Claire said. She tried to make herself busy. "You know, Becky misses you."

Len threw the tire up into the treehouse. "Does she?"

"Yeah," Claire said, "I can just tell, you know, the way she acts. She keeps meowing at me and the second I get up, she tries to show me toward the door."

"Can you pass me a hammer?" Len asked.

Claire gazed up at her friend, who kept looking at the trapdoor from different angles. She grabbed the only hammer she saw, one of several hand tools casually strewn across the grass just beyond the shoulder of the highway, and she placed it in Len's outstretched hand.

By the end of the fourth day after scavenging Willie's railyard, Len had a number of traps ready. He gave Claire a tour of it. Should Wallace and Leonard have challenged Len again, there counted seven tack strips hidden among the gravel of the shoulder, what amounted to three quarts of motor oil uncorked on string for the rungs, and strategically placed fields of particularly sharp, upturned rocks in the grass which could cause an instinctual retraction of step, if they didn't cut the person's foot outright. Len had the hubcap attached to the pulley, which he had modified and attached to the side window once more, so that he could puppeteer its height as it swung at anything below. He had attached plywood shutters to backup the curtain ones, and both repaired and reinforced the trapdoor. For good measure, he made some good knots in a small length of rope and suspended it in the middle of his treehouse so he could climb up the hatch and throw rocks and cement chunks from up there, if it came to it. He also told Claire about the cassette film as part of a couple of bludgeons-on-a-string, so he could whirl them around over his head and swing something at the IRS men again and again and again. If nothing else, it meant he would never run out of ammo. And if worse came to absolute worst, he had his carving knife. It stayed on his nightstand for now.

Claire saw the hatch-rope firsthand as it rested, a few knots slack across the foot of Len's bed. "Won't that be uncomfortable while you sleep? Right between your feet and all?"

The corners of Len's mouth flipped down as he shook his head. "Nah," he said, but cocked his head at it. "Even if it does, it's a small price to pay for the added failsafe position."

"So," Claire said, "tripwire goes up tomorrow?"

"Yes ma'am," Len said.

"You do good work, Len."

"Thank you," he said. "Sticks and stones, y'know?"

"Sticks and stones," Claire said with a nod and her hands on her hips.

"And a few little surprises."

"What was that?" Claire asked.

"Nothing," Len said. "I could use a break, though. Let's head out to the lake, skip rocks, something like that."

Claire checked the sun, and then shrugged. "The last few days haven't exactly been relaxing for you, have they?" He shook his head. "Not good stuff, that's for sure." Len shot her a look from beneath his flattened brow. Claire laughed. "I have a little time yet," she said. "Okay."

ℒ

Truth be told, Great Lake St. Mary's was closer than either Willie's or Billy's or Buckeye Party & Lotto. Len had a specific point along the road where they slipped into the brush. In fact, he had a secluded patch of grassy bank that was his refuge. Len brought Claire to the hidden paradise for the first time that day. It took Claire's breath away.

There they were, walking along through trees, and suddenly Len called to stop. Pushing half of a bush aside, he revealed a clearing next to the water, with waves gently crashing on the rocky surface below where the grass couldn't dominate. It was a good two-foot drop and to Len, it felt like a bulwark against any nosy swimmer that might like to have a word with him. So far, none had even noticed that this hiding place even existed.

Len strolled onto the strip, took a breath amongst the mist, and plopped down. He hugged his knees. Claire joined him. The two of them sat together there in the gloaming, and the lake hissed at them in the best way. Claire flicked her gaze this way and that to make conversation, but what she saw rode into her mouth like a demonic knight and slaughtered her words like the starving serfs they were.

Len was smiling. It was the deepest, most peaceful, most appreciative smile Claire had ever seen from anybody.

"I like to come out here sometimes," Len said. "Sometimes I just think, but a lot of the time I just let my mind go blank. You know, let it do what it will."

It took a moment before Claire knew what to say. "Which is it this time?"

"I think it's a little bit of both," Len said. "I'd just let my mind wander, but, well, you know."

"It'll be okay, Len."

Len just looked at her.

"I mean it," Claire said.

A long while passed. The sun threatened last call, but they remained where they were. A slight mist accented the air and a refreshing, albeit mild, breeze was coming straight at them. The air smelled so clean here, it made Claire wonder aloud what she took in regularly. But Len didn't seem so impressed by the comparison. Staring out over the lake, Len happened upon an idea.

51

"Does Subhail have a gun?" he asked.

Claire shifted. "Yes," she said, a little too soon to avoid surprising herself. "Do you want me to lend it to you for this?"

There was a pause, but Claire could tell it wasn't there for Len to think. "No," Len said. "I don't need it. And don't bring it if I need your help!"

Claire shifted her whole body to face her friend. "Why not?"

Len continued to stare over the lake. "Because," he said, "I'm not impressed with them."

"What? Len, what does that have anything to do with whether you need one to defend yourself?"

Len eyed her, and went right back to the lake. He didn't say anything. Claire edged closer. "Len, I'm telling you. If you need me to get your back, I've got it. You know that."

Len saw her say that, and made himself nod. He gazed up at the sky, taking a deep breath. Then he nodded more.

"So, I'll ask again," Claire said, returning to the more comfortable position, "would you like to borrow my father's gun?"

Len lay back, making a pillow with his interlaced palms. "Nope."

Claire digested the answer, and gazed out at the lake herself. Half of a laugh escaped beneath her breath and she shook her head, ponytail whipping either ear, before she too lay back. Together, the two friends watched the clouds. There were a few white, flat-bottomed, fluffy-top ones. There were also a lot of choppy, misty, formation ones. Despite their greater numbers, Len and Claire noticed them second.

"Although," Len said out of nowhere, "it should come as no surprise to me: I can't shake this feeling that all these preparations aren't for nothing."

"Isn't that why you started them in the first place?" Claire asked. "It seems pretty silly otherwise."

"I suppose so," Len said. "But this isn't like before. It's only gotten worse the last few days. It's been really, particularly bad since the other day. That rain set me back, Claire."

"It's one day."

Len got up on his side. "And what if having that one day back would show me a bit of rope that's slack? What if it would have given me the clarity of thought to improve one of my traps before it was so late that it's already set up? What if —"

"Stop."

"But —"

"Stop, Len."

Len just stared at her. The complacent smile was gone; Claire believed it was hidden somewhere behind his blank eyes. With telepathy, Len could have told her she was right.

Len released a heavy breath. "You're right. I can't worry about that. Besides, the treehouse is mostly ready now. By the time Wallace and Leonard were even to punch in tomorrow morning for their 9-to-5 and make their way to my place, I'd have the tripwire set and ready and good to go. You're right," he said, lying back down, "I'm overthinking it. I need to relax."

Claire's arms opened wide, indicating the lake. "What else of a place to start?" Both of them stared at the clear blue sky directly overhead, so Claire did not see how Len did not look convinced. "Let me ask you something," she said. Len hummed the approval to proceed. "What did you ever do with the tarp and glass?"

"You mean from Willie's?" Len asked. Claire hummed a yes. "I have them rigged together next to the front window, in case those bastards try to lob something nasty at me. I figure a grenade can't go up thirty feet and still penetrate a good nylon tarp, right?"

"Good God, Len! Why would they have grenades?"

"I don't expect anything good of people. You know that," Len said. Before Claire could interject, he kept going. "As for the glass, there's a slight slack in the trap the way I hung it, but if I pull it taut to cover the window, it'll release it all and if those persistent bastards are standing where they were before, then they'd better get ready to dive. Still, for all that, I can't shake this feeling."

Claire expelled her breath. "It's probably just your gut trying to stay focused on Wallace and Leonard, making sure they don't get the drop on you," she said. "You're clever enough; just take care of your business and you'll be fine. You always have been."

Len's eyes sank, but he nodded. "Yeah."

ℒ

"Hey Len?"

"Yeah?"

"If you're setting up the tripwire first thing tomorrow, does that mean you'll be setting out for first looks at Indiana tomorrow, too?"

"That's the plan," Len said.

It took a moment to sink in. "I'll miss you."

"I'm not gone yet," Len said. That seemed to satisfy her, and he caught himself saying it again. "I'm not gone just yet."

"What was that?"

"Nothing," he said.

Claire barely had enough light to get home. They made do. In the waters of the lake they left behind, the waves rolled on.

Chapter Seven

It was exceptionally foggy the next day; so much so that when Len stirred, his treehouse was rife with it. He could see nothing but the gray. He felt quite rested, for such thick fog had stifled the traffic outside which, on any normal day, would wake him up once or twice. Surely, however, when Len could barely see his hand in front of his face, it could not be safe to drive and, bastard tools as they were, at least the everyday commuters had sense enough this morning.

He sat up, thirsty out of his mind. His throat burned from a dryness he'd never known. How long had it been since he'd last had something to drink? He didn't know. As he tried to remember, he rubbed the sleep from his eyes. And suddenly, there was no sleep to rub.

He blinked it away. The layers of gray fog shifted around him, permeating every bit of his inner sanctum. He coughed, and began to choke. A small black dot popped out from the fog, landing in his lap. It was a metal canister. Len thought it looked an awful lot like a spray paint can. But that idea was short lived.

"Why is the front window open?" he tried to ask. The fog harpooned the words from his mouth, incinerating them, sloshing what felt like acid around inside his cheeks, going for his throat. His eyes widened. And they burned.

His arms jerked up to rub the burning away, but he clenched them at the last moment. Curled up on the bed in the fetal position, Len clawed the canister away, tossing it anywhere but his bed. He heard it clunk against the wooden floor and begin to hiss. The fog descended on the unoccupied space where he'd been sitting up. It billowed down on him.

Len tried to breathe, but retched instead. Knowing now he had to move for his life, he held his breath. His gut protested and, with his lungs, eyes, throat, and chest ablaze, he forced himself to roll off the bed. He shot out one arm to search beneath the bed. He didn't dare open his eyes again.

His hand found the spit; he threw it aside. It clunked and clattered along to the far wall. His hand closed around a baseball bat; that too he flicked out of the way. His diaphragm stabbed him in a cramped-up spasm, demanding oxygen. The arm flailed around in darkness.

Len retched again, and he nearly had to rest his head in it afterward. Please, he thought to himself, where is it? WHERE IS IT? I can't let her find me here! I can't let this be it! *Where is it?*

His fingers brushed something that felt elastic. He grabbed it, turned it around in his fingers and scowled. It was a fat rubber band. He cursed aloud, rolled onto his back, and yanked on it, elbows flaring. It snapped, and clipped his hands. The sting forced him to take a breath; he found perhaps the only half-fogged pocket of air in the treehouse. Fire touched his lungs, but there was oxygen there, too. He shot his hand beneath the bed one last time.

Right in the same neighborhood, his fingers brushed something else. It was soft, maybe an elastic strap of some kind. He grabbed it, felt its shape. It was good.

After flipping onto his back, Len slipped the gas mask over his face. The strap rested above his ears. He waited a moment, and the stinging eased. He adjusted it to perfection, and what stinging lingered, left him. The fog fell back, and was unable to come within an inch of his face. He took just a breath or two – enough that his entire body stopped hurting like one big Charlie horse – and crawled over to the open front window. He set himself against the highway wall.

Under his own, heavy breaths, he thought he heard people talking outside. He had no idea what they were saying. He would have to calm down. Now that he could breathe, it didn't take long to collect himself.

His eyes crossed the border between wood and window. The fog was not as pervasive as he thought; though it coursed out the window and his vision wasn't clear of it even from the window, he could see flashing red and blue lights somewhere in the beyond. Man-shaped shadows stood and paced all over the place. Len quickly understood then what thirty people were doing just standing on the highway. He pressed himself back under cover of his bulwark.

What now? Len thought. What next?

"What next?" Len said to himself. An idea came, and his vision snapped-to accordingly.

The trapdoor. He needed to make sure it was locked.

"Hurry, while we still have the drop on him," said a voice below Len. They were at the rungs! He scrambled on all fours to the trapdoor, and flipped the lock. Whether they were climbing yet, he didn't know, but the time had come.

In his head, Len ran over his battle plan one more time. Though he hadn't prepared for dozens of people, he had prepared for Wallace and Leonard to "bring company." While he retrieved his bat, the trapdoor shuttered.

"It's locked!" Leonard shouted.

A big, clear voice cut through the fog. "Mr. Leonard Campbell," said a police officer through a megaphone, "please exit your treehouse calmly or allow these men to enter peaceably."

Len scoffed. "No deal," he muttered. He gripped the baseball bat, stuffed his hammer in a loop of his pants, and fished his hand through the fog until it bumped into the rope hanging from the hatch. Until the tear gas dissipated, he knew it would be nigh impossible to puppeteer the hubcap properly, so that window would remain shuttered; with Wallace and Leonard just beneath him, they had at least a temporary shelter and would have to wait. What would be best, Len decided, would be to understand what he was up against, and throw up a defense against it. The roof had his answer. He clambered through to the ceiling.

The gathered police watched as a square of wood swung open on the top of the treehouse, and the shape of a boy emerged like a sailor emerging from a submarine. He stood tall, escaping the fog from below, bat in hand, shield on face. Shoulders back, head held high, Len gazed out over the lot of them.

He saw one of the fat police officers, the one with the megaphone, raise the blasted cone to his mouth. "Leonard Camp–"

The officer dove inside his cruiser. A can lid glanced off of the door he'd been using for cover. As it spun to rest on the pavement, the can lid seemed to laugh at its own dirty work: a modest grey cut that marred the door. Len had rows of the lids lined up – his improvised shuriken. He stashed the baseball bat at his free hip and, careful not to cut himself, readied three more can lids between his fingers.

"I told you people to leave me alone!" Len said. "If you need me to make that point any clearer, BE MY GUEST!"

Again, a voice rose from beneath the treehouse. "Len, this is serious now," Leonard said. "Please just come quietly and I promise we won't hurt you."

Len's focus drained but for that of the tax agent. It sounded like the skinny man was still just below the trapdoor. Without another instant's thought, Len hopped back down through the hatch without need of his hands. He poked his head out the window overlooking the ladder and, seeing the tail of Leonard's coat, swung out. Like a gymnast, he swung out from his bedroom freely onto the ladder just below Leonard and, when nearly there, committed all his weight not to the rungs, but to Leonard's coattails. Just as soon as his grip had the desired effect and yanked Leonard from the rungs into free fall with Len, Len let go and reached instead for the rungs with both hands. Ten full feet below, Leonard landed, flat on his back. By the time the man realized what happened, Len had already scrambled up the rungs. Leonard looked up and saw him just below the trapdoor, next to the tire's nest.

Len peered down, and his eyes met Wallace's. He wrapped one arm around the tire, armpit-deep, and yanked. He rode the tire around the trunk of his tree once, twice, and on the third go-round, lined up Wallace with both feet. He too flew to the ground.

Len didn't waste time; in the same spin, he dismounted perpendicular to the highway shoulder. Already in full sprint, he unsheathed his hammer and made for the police minions. He probably should have felt pain as the wooden baseball bat smoked his calf with each stride, but he didn't.

The megaphone cop was back out of his car, and straight ahead. Before either of them really knew it, Len was on top of him, and Len's hammer scattered the megaphone's parts through the air. He grabbed the door by the exterior handle and batter-rammed the officer back into his own car.

All the other officers drew. Two fired out of instinct; one at about one o'clock, the other at nine. The officer at nine o'clock was two cars away, and his bullets hit metal, wailing as they ricocheted. The other cop was very close, and Len, finding himself between two closely parked cars, ducked. The one o'clock officer's bullet hit the trunk of the car on Len's right, and Len could think of nothing else to defend himself except to charge the man. In one motion, he took his hammer through the man's wrist – relieving him of his firearm – and then dispatched the man himself with an uppercut-like swing. Len about-faced and made to sprint for the next attacker when he saw the recently-beaten officer's gun lying on the pavement. He slid into it like home base, and it skittered away. Len made for the nine o'clock cop.

Some sort of sense came over that officer, for he'd traded his gun for his taser. Len saw that – and the fact that he was in the line of fire – and just managed to get a hand on the weapon as the officer fired. The wires soared well wide of both of them, and shocked another cop entirely on the other side of that cruiser. While the taser-holding officer registered what he'd done, Len grounded him with a hammer across the face.

The rest of them were done playing games. All around him, the officers aimed, and fired. Len took to the cover of the nearest cruiser.

Heart screaming, he pressed himself flat against the ground as bullets flew over his head and whistled off of his shelter. He dared open his eyes at foot level, and saw beyond the bellies of several cruisers, the feet of his attackers. He had an idea.

Bear-crawling from one car to another as not to be seen, Len approached the nearest shoes. From beneath that car, he waited for the shots to relax, and then quell. As the officers began to wonder where he'd gone, he latched two hands around his target's ankles. The cop jumped, recoiled, and dove down to catch Len beneath the cruiser. But when he did, there was no one there. He rose to one knee, confused.

In full battle cry, Len vaulted off of the trunk of the cruiser and hammered that cop unconscious with one blow. The cop's partner, standing right there beside him, Len took in the next, flowing swing. As that victim fell aside, another cop came into view a stone's throw away. His and Len's eyes met, and the officer leveled his gun at the boy. Len chucked his hammer at the man and leaned aside. The gun shot before the hammer clipped the man's throat, but Len was already – barely – out of the way.

Clutching his Adam's apple, the officer fell to his knees as the hammer clanged to the ground.

Enough was enough. Len found his way out from the cluster of cops and cruisers and sprinted back to the treehouse. In the grass, still recovering, were Wallace and Leonard. Len leapt over both of them, but his foot caught on something mid-air.

Wallace had him by the ankle. The fall knocked Len's breath away, but he didn't need any coaching to rip his bat from his belt loop – tearing it from its stitching in his haste – and clunking Wallace over the head with it. Though it didn't knock the man out, it did stun him long enough for Len to wrench free. He scrambled to his feet and hurried up the crude rungs.

He tried the trapdoor. It didn't budge.

'Still locked!' Looking around at the scene, Len saw that what police remained were closing in, entering the grass from the shoulder, guns drawn. They were in no rush to get him, but they knew he was cornering himself. Wallace was nearly back on his feet.

If he couldn't get back in the treehouse, he was finished. Wallace might ship him back to Pennsylvania. Would he exact a personal revenge beforehand? Would Len be killed outright, here and now?

"No…" Awkwardly positioning himself at the top of his ladder, Len squeezed a foot into the empty tire's nest. He lifted his face to the underbelly of his treehouse and launched himself straight out from the trunk of the tree. As soon as he saw blue sky, he brought his arms forward like lightning.

By some miracle, they found the frame of the window. The act of holding on yanked Len out into open space and drained him of strength while stretching his arms and denying them want to flex, but he held. With all the might he could find, he hauled himself up through the same window he'd exited. Hand by hand, forearm by forearm by registered armpit, he gained purchase. With several swings of his weight, Len managed to grab and claw until from the waist up, he teetered on the windowsill. With one, final, completely ungraceful devotion of weight, he toppled back into his treehouse.

Below, the police were talking to each other. Len didn't bother trying to understand them. He unlocked the trapdoor and opened it, making sure to catch the strings with it. As raucous plumes of white gas billowed from above, small falls of motor oil glubbed down through the opening, coating the heads and feet of those below. Some of it coated the plank rungs and, Len was happy to see, several rungs became soaked enough that they only offered an inch or two of unoiled surface, with several – often consecutively – needing to be skipped entirely. How he'd clean it off later he neither knew nor cared.

One of the officers he'd dispatched earlier – Len knew because of the welt on his face – fired. Len saw at the last instant and dodged. Beforehand, he'd noticed that some of the officers were debating whether to try to get up to the treehouse anyway. Len decided to rid them of the idea.

He locked the trapdoor again.

In his cupboard on the far side of the treehouse, he retrieved a box of matches and, from the top of three shelves, a few fireworks. From the shelf below that, he snatched all the batteries he owned, and then he retrieved his carving knife.

Len shuttered all the windows and opened the ceiling hatch. In the thinner fog, it was much easier to see what he was doing. He reached up and placed everything he would need on the roof and then rose above his unlit room. Once again, he looked out over the battlefield.

There were officers still on the road. Len used leftover cassette guts to attach batteries to some bottle rockets, and aimed the fireworks at the cars. With four good shots of fire and acid, Len made the cops disperse and think twice about firing at him. They couldn't see him when he stayed on his belly anyway; he made use of that.

The flank worked – the cops approaching the ladder realized and returned to the road. Where Wallace and Leonard were, Len didn't know, but he figured at that point that his hubcap-pulley on the left of the treehouse was not going to come into play. He barely wasted a thought on it.

He held off the attack by frisbeeing sharp can lids and dropping back down before anyone could line him up and fire. He punctured batteries and chucked them at the ground below so they would explode or leak acid. He fired minor fireworks, both the harmless noisemakers and the potential burners. He was sure to smash a couple of windshields with his reserves of concrete pieces. Five times that morning the cops thought he was done and tried to move in or wait him out, only for Len to continue again. Three times he caught stray officers trying to flank him; he rewarded and surprised the naïve bastards by letting battery-firework grenades and pavement chunks just ahead of their paths. At one point, Len even taunted the officers by pitching the chunks to himself and batting them into their ranks.

It was just about noon. The police were just about ready to give up. They shouted pleas at Len. Len had none of it. Finally, to Len's right, he heard the IRS men shouting at the officers.

"That's enough!" Wallace said. He was moving. From cover, Len strapped one of his last batteries to some fireworks. He slipped halfway back down the hatch. "This'll go on all day if we keep this up," he heard Wallace say. "Can we call for a chopper?"

An unfamiliar voice, probably a police officer, said something. Len didn't know what. He listened for where they were.

He found it: dead ahead. He cracked the front shutter slowly, so no one would notice, and then he lit the grenade and flicked it as far directly forward as he could.

There was an explosion. There were screams. There wasn't gunfire.

"Wallace!" Leonard shouted, somewhere to the right of the treehouse. "Are you okay!" Len didn't think he'd moved.

"Damn it!" Wallace shouted. Through the sliver of an opening Len saw Wallace hobble back to about the same spot as where they met earlier. Len guessed he felt safe there, and supposed it was his own fault for concentrating so much on the officers in the street.

"I'm done!" the unfamiliar-probably-cop voice shouted. "We can't keep this up, Mr. James! This kid's dug in and dug in good! We'll be here all day at the rate he's going!"

"What are you saying, Jim?" Wallace asked.

"I'm saying I'm done!" Jim said. A car door slammed, but Len didn't hear an engine start.

"So, what, you're leaving us here with it?"

"You go get him yourself, and then maybe – maybe – I'll try to slap some cuffs on him."

A pause came then. "Useless piece of…" Wallace grumbled to Leonard.

Within the nearly lightless treehouse, Len smiled. He waited just a moment, and then unlocked the trapdoor. A small serving of light washed against the wooden boards, flicks of dust highlighted in the rays. Len descended only the first few rungs before remembering the oil; he grabbed the rope, with the tire somewhere at the other end below, and used that instead.

He still had the baseball bat, though with its original hilt snapped, Len had it borrow the hammer's place. He unsheathed it as he turned to find Wallace and Leonard in the grass before him.

Leonard's back was still convulsing; he wasn't going anywhere. A few feet beyond him, though, Len saw Wallace favoring his bad ankle. Len marched straight toward him.

Wallace watched the green-haired adamant come. In the closing distance, he held out both arms, showing his palms. "Please, now, Mr. Campbell –"

But Len smote him across the face. One of Wallace's hands instinctively covered that cheek as the other reached out for the ground. Defeated, the man's cold eyes glared into Len's as the boy stood over him. "We only wanted to help!"

"I know," Len said. "That's why I didn't just kill you bastards outright." He reassured his grip and carefully knocked him out.

Wallace's companion stared on like a helpless animal as his back continued to spasm underneath him. "Of all things, where did you get a gas mask?!" he asked as Len strode his way.

"Don't worry about it," Len told him, and fast-forwarded the full-named nuisance on to when next he woke.

Some hours later, Len found himself alone with the mess. He took stock.

The rungs would take some doing, but could be cleaned; getting the sharp rocks out of the grass would be easy, but time-consuming (and Len caught himself ready to curse them for having turned out so useless); the remaining tear gas would eventually dissipate from his room, especially if he fanned it away; the burn marks from his makeshift grenades, both on and off the pavement, he decided he would keep; the concrete blocks were simply a matter of re-foraging. Save a few bullet marks in his tree and the planks of his treehouse, he came out fairly well. "That wasn't so bad," he said.

However, just in case Wallace and Leonard returned again (*Thick bastards as they are*, Len thought), he decided to reset leftover precautions and set up the tripwire by evening's end.

So he was, hunkered down, as he fiddled with the wire round a stake at the grass's edge. Traffic began to resume not long beforehand, and this was after he'd given Wallace the courtesy of an ambulance – even if it was using the man's own phone. The paramedics had insisted Len accompany them but, after their earlier tango, Len needed only punctuate an expression at megaphone-police-officer-Jim to say his presence wasn't necessary. After the police chief turned to the re-conscious Wallace, who nodded, he confirmed there was no need for anyone to bother Len any more. Len grinned as he made sure the stake stood in tall enough grass so as to be hard to notice.

Far too late, Len realized he wasn't alone. Someone was walking toward him, no more than ten feet to his back. Cursing himself for failing to hear sooner, he flipped up to his feet. He half hoped it was just Claire coming to his belated rescue.

It was not; rather, Len knew not the peer that stood before him. His brow furled automatically as he beheld the kid. The teenage male, with his overswung gait and loose, oversized faux-skater's clothing – including, of course, a ball cap worn backwards – made Len plant his feet.

"What do you want," Len said as the newcomer closed the distance. His hand went to his hip and hammer.

"Dude, that was crazy!" the contemporary said. "Don't worry, I got it all on video!" He produced a phone.

Len shot a hand forth and took two steps to close out the gap. "Give me that," he said. The contemporary jerked back at Len's sudden advance, yanking the phone to safety. Len continued forward, beckoning with his fingers. "Give it here."

"What for, man?" the contemporary asked. He relaxed.

"Just – just give it to me. Come on, give it here."

"No way, Man. This could go viral; I at least have to show it to the news or something, y'know?"

Len's eyes widened. His mouth shrank. "You insidious, false-conformist bastard, I said GIVE IT HERE!" He advanced again and grabbed for the phone. He had to rob this kid of it, throw the stupid contraption against the ground and smash it and stomp it and hammer it and burn it and bake it and throw it and soak it and rip it apart until there was nothing more substantial to bear its witness than the schnitzels Len reaped from his carving!

His contemporary retreated again, and again, and kept the phone out of Len's reach. "Chill out!" he said, but Len kept moving forward.

They played that game for half a dozen steps before the kid took off. Len's first instinct was to catch his wrists or chase him, and he made several paces to do so. However, doubt called his name, and he peered back at his home. When he turned back, his contemporary was jumping into his car. The sight of it forced Len to look back at the treehouse again.

"Indiana, here I come," he said.

With the remaining light, Len made preparations to head out before dawn. From what batteries he had left, he found one to match his obnoxious alarm clock. He affixed its ticking majesty on the nightstand. He didn't bother whittling before sleep. Instead, he debated whether to leave a note for Claire. Sometime the next day, he would realize that he drifted off before coming to a conclusion.

END PART ONE

Chapter Eight

A thirty-something-year-old, African-American woman with thick, well-groomed hair sat at a desk. Len didn't know her. She wore a suit jacket, because she had to consider herself on the formal side of things. She was a professional, after all!

She had some paper in front of her. She didn't look at them at first but, and this was the dirty little secret, when the monitor bothered with pre-recorded footage, she could afford to read what she didn't remember off the top of her head. She knew she only had to get the ball rolling. With a few minutes to spare before the eleven o'clock news, central Ohio's favorite anchor, Loretta Heller, reviewed the introduction.

The camera guy asked if she was set. She asked him to stop bothering her so she could concentrate. He apologized and concentrated on the camera. Thirty seconds, Mrs. Heller.

There wasn't time to really practice the paragraph she'd just read but, since she wrote it, it wasn't a big deal. She sat up straight, let her co-anchor sip some water, and the guy behind the cameras counted her in.

"Good evening. I'm Loretta Heller, and welcome to the 11 o'clock news.

"The FDA is issuing a recall tonight after traces of non-amiable proteins were detected in beef shipments out of Europe and Mexico. A spokesperson for the FDA said the inspections failed after it was determined that the meats were not only packaged incorrectly, but were discolored. Retailers have been urged to repeal the brand from shelves, with the manufacturing company responsible to soon provide details to consumers who may have already purchased the compromised meat. We'll have more to come as the story develops.

"Our top story tonight comes from just off the peaceful highways between Great Lake St. Mary's and Lima, as law enforcement shut down US-33 for most of the day. The stoppage was used to set up a blockade of over a dozen police cruisers, all focused, on this:"

The news signal shifted to footage taken by an unsteady hand. The central point of the shot included the cop cars as they gathered in "the courtyard" before a treehouse along the side of a highway. The tree had what looked like crude wooden rungs leading up to it. Men were lying on the ground. Viewers heard explosions.

"A curious bystander supplied our station with footage taken by cell phone," Loretta Heller told viewers, "showing the battle scene that raged this morning as police accompanied IRS agents Wallace James and Leonard Humphrey to the alleged home of one Leonard Campbell of Pennsylvania – the subject of a three-year Amber Alert."

The feed interrupted the footage of Len's defense for a moment, showing Len's old picture from his Pennsylvanian state ID.

"Although the owner of the treehouse is difficult to see in the amateur footage, his identity is made clear from the sounds as explosions and screams erupt from among the police officers. Reports of fireworks and punctured and broken batteries came from every officer from the scene, who also detailed accounts of attacks in which the boy used a hammer in numerous assaults on the officers themselves."

The Contemporary's footage was interrupted again as the station rolled a snippet of an interview with the police chief and his drooping gut.

"We weren't sure *what* we'd find or have to contend with when we came here today," Jim said. "Next thing we know, the kid's riding a tire down like goddamn Tarzan, kicking people off his ladder and attacking the rest of us by hammer, ducking and dodging the whole time!"

"Were any officers killed in these attacks?" the on-the-streets, reporting version of Loretta Heller asked.

"No," the Chief said, "but it's funny you ask that. The kid had some odd sorts of defense mechanisms up. Maybe he didn't think to get a gun from somewhere, maybe he's just working with what he's got. I don't know."

"Is this child in custody, to be reunited with his family in Pennsylvania after what must have been a long, scary, and grueling few years on his own?"

The Chief shook his head. "No," he said. "We received orders to back off. S'far as I know, he's still in that treehouse."

The footage returned to the modern Loretta Heller, who suddenly dropped her need to punctuate words she thought viewers might find shocking and newsworthy.

"The treehouse's resident was described as a male adolescent, with green hair and somewhere between five and a half and six feet tall. Although authorities aren't one hundred percent certain it's Pennsylvania's long-lost Leonard Campbell, they're trying to get in contact with the child's family to see if this might finally be him. On to you, Bill."

The locals saw, and wondered. *'How interesting!'* they thought. Many of them turned to each other or to their spouses and said things like, "I recognize that bit of highway! Why, I drive by there every morning! What reason could they have to stage something like that? That kid doesn't hurt anyone by living there, does he?"

Others thought differently, saying things akin to "Three years? Oh my – but it's so good they might finally be able to reunite that poor boy with his family. I hope they see this. I know I'd be just so relieved to know my little boy's safe and sound."

Still others saw and found the story intriguing, wondering what, in the first place, would keep such a kid from simply returning to his family. And the rest of the viewers didn't think that treehouse-living, police-attacking kid was Leonard Campbell at all, because they figured after being missing for three years, the real Leonard Campbell was almost certainly dead and rotting in a wall or basement somewhere.

As for Loretta Heller, it was more or less just another day reporting news. She was thankful she had something else to report for a change, instead of the usual murder and mayhem. When she and Bill finished out the eleven o'clock news, they stacked their papers and went home.

Chapter Nine

Bad dreams perturbed Len's sleep. They forced him to relive the attack, and the defense – to feel the impact of steel on bone as he drove the hammer through one of the officer's chins, and had the impactic bolt ride up his arm, jarring his shoulder and rebounding his wrist away from the man's face as it flew, reeling, the other way. Again he felt his sneakers hit the ground like pistons as he ran between cop cruisers, felt the tail end of one absorb the thrust of his step as he leapt off the back bumper to pounce on the cop he'd distracted. In one dream, he could even see the officer that could have ended him, and watched in bullet time as the shot flew past his head. The police tried to flush him out of the treehouse, away from his home, and for what? "Stupid bastards," Len muttered in his sleep. Below, purely through dream knowledge, Len knew exactly where the gun he'd kicked had stopped. He felt it sit there, calling out to him, whispering his right to wield it after having defeated its master.

He screamed at the cops while he bashed away at their gun-holding wrists. "Ignorant bastards!" he said, seeing himself grab the taser-wielding cop's wrist. The taser hit one of the officer's comrades. "Stupid bastards!" "Cocky bastards!" "Bastards!" "Bastards!" "*Bastards!*"

And Len relived the moment when he knocked Wallace and Leonard unconscious. "We're just trying to help!" Wallace said, as if any such thing would reassure the young man standing over him.

Some time after he woke up, Len would realize what he said next wasn't at all what he'd really told Mr. James. "You can't fool me, you government bastards," he said in the dream. "You work for them or you don't realize the good you do them. Either way, you're evil to me." Dream-Wallace moved to ask Dream-Len what he was talking about, but was asleep in the grass before the word could climb his throat.

Dream-Leonard asked about the gas mask. The image of Bobby and his junkyard flashed for an instant, but Dream-Len told Dream-Leonard not to worry about it.

And then the dream, as curious a thing as Len ever saw, rewound.

"You work for them or you don't realize the good you do them," Dream-Len told Dream-Wallace.

But who was "them?"

Who were "they?"

An earth-darkening thunderstorm shook the dream and, amidst an earthquake that rattled time forward, erased the scene around the treehouse as Len defended it. Len stood in the front window, peering down over his courtyard. But he was no longer king. Traffic hesitated to pass by and skirted around the edge when it did, for standing on the border between the grass and the highway shoulder stood a woman.

The dream needed, nor made, no effort to dress the woman up like a dribble-chinned vampire or a snarling, ravenous zombie. It presented her just as Len remembered. She and Len stood and glared into each other's eyes with the most solid recognition in the world. Three years hadn't made a difference. Len saw the molten intent in the woman's eyes. He hoped she saw the cornered viper in his.

She was every inch of six feet tall, with no curves to speak of. She'd filled those spaces with muscle and dressed in a sweatervest and slacks. Her hair was conventionally beautiful in her faked brunette curls that landed on her shoulders like a mane and framed her stocky, rectangular face. Dress shoes adorned her feet, but they had no shine to them. They were as dead and black as her heart. She stood before him, fists at her sides, face dour. Len remembered her as the cliché middle school dike-lesbian gym teacher dressed up for Easter brunch, and there she was.

It made Len never want to dream again.

Such ended what might have been the most organized dream Len ever had. By his standards, though, it wasn't a dream. There was no mistake; it was a nightmare. A "fucking bastard nightmare," he would say not long after waking up.

Len clipped out of sleep. He blinked, waking up on his side. He didn't spring awake, bolting upright in bed with a cold sweat

71

and a scream of her name. No; instead he opened his eyes to the real world, where he was safe. Because he'd been safe for three years, a full state away from that cold bastard... with the intent, today, to make it two.

He blinked again, and then sat up. Rubbing his eyes, again he found no sleep to rub from them. Despite his sixth ultra-detailed nightmare about Jodie since leaving Pennsylvania, he felt rested. He gave it a moment, and realized he felt overly rested. And there was way too much sunlight seeping into his treehouse. It was the wrong shade of orange, too. In fact, as Len thought about it, he realized it was downright yellow.

His eyes grew wide. He'd overslept. He'd overslept *a lot*. He snatched his alarm clock from the nightstand. In all his tiredness the previous night he managed to set the time, but had neglected to set it to actually go off.

He chucked the bastard across the room, threw the covers from his legs and began getting dressed. As he did, he realized people were speaking outside. A sigh of relief escaped him, for he recognized one of the voices as Claire's.

What was more, Claire did not sound distressed. She chatted pleasantly with whomever else was out there, be it Wallace and Leonard or perhaps her dad. Len didn't know – he was concentrated on the sanctuary of Claire's presence.

The window to the right of Len's bed opened, and the green-haired youth leaned out. Before he could say a word, though, Claire broke conversation with her partner – whom Len's window frame hid from view – and looked relieved. "There you are!" she said. "I was beginning to get worried - did you just now wake up or something?"

"Yeah," Len said. "Where have you been the last couple days?"

Claire glanced toward the street. "Fishing trip with Dad," she said. Len nodded casually. "I saw the news!" Claire added, making Len's heart skip a beat. "Are you completely insane?"

Len opened his mouth to say something, but thought better of it. He shrugged. "I held them off, didn't I?"

Claire, smiling, shook her head. "Anyway," she said once she was done (a chuckle snuck up on Len over it), "can I come up?"

"Like you even have to ask," Len said. He disappeared from the window for just a moment to make sure the trapdoor was unlocked. "You'll have to pardon the mess, though. I'm trying to get everything packed up."

Len re-locked the trapdoor as soon as Claire came up. After a moment to breathe and think and wake up a little bit, he switched into a mode where he zipped around and all about the treehouse. He moved things, unlatched the pulley from the left window, began stuffing his backpack for the road.

"Are you okay?"

"Yeah, sure, fine," Len said. "It's just, I remembered something and now I gotta get ready and pack up and hopefully I'll see you and if not then have a good life and it's been fun but I've really got to make sure I get out of here because things aren't going that great or working out anymore out here and in the wake of that –"

"Len!"

Len quit. Huffing and puffing, he stood before Claire, who sat on the foot of his bed. "Yeah. What?" His eyes darted to and fro, planning his next twenty moves as soon as Claire gave him leave to flit further.

"Are you okay?"

"Fantastic why do you ask?"

Claire looked at him, not quite sure what to think. She stood up and paced the room. "You know, when I saw that news report, I was worried about you. And I felt bad that I wasn't able to come and help you."

That distracted Len, who stopped shaking from his anxiety long enough to return the curious look. "Help? I thought we discussed all that before it even happened."

"We did," Claire said, "but I still feel like I should have been here."

"It's okay," Len said. "I held them off, didn't I?" He placed a hand on Claire's shoulder.

73

Claire didn't brush it away, but her head glided away just as if she had. "That's not the point," she said, sighing. "My point is that you really could have gotten hurt and I feel responsible that you had to take that risk."

"And what if you'd helped and gotten hurt yourself? Then *I'm* the one who feels terrible."

"Would've been my own fault," Claire grumbled.

Len resumed packing, but calmly. Claire watched him do it. "In any case, it all worked out and I'm fine and you're fine. Sometimes it's best to accept things the way they went, even if they don't go as planned, because in the end, you can see God made sure you made it out all right."

Claire smiled. "I think that's a good way to go."

The return to peace of mind did Len good, and allowed him to focus again. As he stuffed a shirt into his packing, he turned his head toward Claire. "Hey, did Wallace or Leonard decide to be stupid enough to visit me again?"

"No, why?"

"I just wondered," Len said. "I heard you talking with someone out there when I woke up."

"Oh, sorry about that," Claire said.

"No, no, it's no trouble," Len said. "My alarm didn't go off so it was actually nice that you got my day started. Yesterday wasn't all that good, if you know what I mean."

"What," Claire said, "afraid they were going to attack again so soon?"

"No!" Len said. "I just didn't have a very good day."

Claire didn't dig further. As Len continued packing, his friend went to the window. "You know," she said, "maybe today will be a better day."

"How do you figure?"

"Well, your mother came to see you."

Len froze. "What?"

Claire was still peering out the window, and hadn't seen Len's reaction. "I just said that your mother came by to check up on you."

Len wheeled around, flipped Claire from the window and grabbed her by both shoulders. "Tell me you're lying!"

"What?" Claire asked, her face a wild contortion of confusion and fear.

"Tell me you're lying! Tell me she isn't here!"

"Yeah," Claire said. "Yeah, she's right, right out there," she said, nodding toward the window.

Len threw her aside, more forcefully than he intended. He snatched a chunk of concrete automatically. Millions of lights stormed up in Len's mind, each a possibility of how Claire might be mistaken, each an identity for the newcomer. They flooded his judgment and blinded him. Words left him. He stood in the window, jaw ajar, hands stupid, expression blank. His feet retreated upon themselves, and he hoped against God that any of those lights, any one of those possibilities at all, would be true except for one. "Just one, God," Len almost mumbled. "Just let that one just not be true…"

One voice mounted the crowd long enough for Len to snap out of it. "It's been this long," the voice said, "there's no way. The trail is cold! The trail is cold."

A second voice snuck up on the optimist and, with a hundred thousand buddies, lynched it. In lieu of their victim, the multitudes threw a chorus at Len: "It's true! It's true!" A football stadium's worth of hockey fans chanted at the forefront of his mind. They mocked him. They waved black banners. A huge victory flag crowd-surfed, passing from one hand to another.

They dragged the limp, blue-faced optimist off the edge of Len's brain, where it fell into a black void, kicking and screaming and vanishing into nothing. In the face of this waking nightmare, Len found a way back to the real world and saw Claire who, thank God, was still standing there. Heart racing, Len turned his head slowly toward the road.

He dropped his weapon, stole across the room and peered around the shutters.

There she was.

Chapter Ten

"What did she tell you?" Len asked, though it sounded very nearly like a contented statement of acceptance.

"What do you mea–?"

"What did she tell you?"

Claire showed her hands, retreating a couple of steps. "Calm down," she said to Len's turned back, for the owner of the treehouse didn't dare rip his gaze from the woman outside. "She's here to help."

"No, she's not," Len said. He snatched his chunk of pavement from the floor and leaned out the window. "Filling the world with more lies, I see."

"Leonard?" called a woman's voice. It grated against his ears to the point that Len nearly pawed at them to make sure blood wasn't gushing out. He watched instead as the curveless, sweatervested Jodie walked into view. And then her cowboy voice made more words. "Thank goodness!" she said. "I've been looking all over for you, and to think that after all this time –"

"Leave."

"Len!" Claire said, pulling her friend's wrist, and with it a chunk of concrete, down. "What's wrong with you? She just saw you fend off the cops on the news and made her way down here so she can take you back home. Then you'll be safe and sound."

Just as she let go, Len snatched Claire's wrist in return. He spoke just loud enough for his friend to hear and made his lips move as little as possible while Jodie stood below. "Listen," he said. "I don't know what she told you, but this –" he pointed out the window "–is not a good thing."

Claire yanked her hand free. "How isn't it?" she asked. "You could finally go back home with your parents, where the cops will be on standby to actually help you. You'll get to catch up on old times! And you won't even have to go into Indiana. She told me herself, Len. She already told me what you told me."

Len glanced at Jodie, but as soon as he confirmed she was still there, his brow sank, flattening into an eave. "And what exactly did I tell you already?" he asked. 'Choose your next words carefully, you bastardess.'

Claire ignored the glare. "She understands that, in the past, there's been tension between you and your parents. She gets that. But she also said that, seeing you in such trouble on the news, where you're cornered and the very people that should be protecting you are trying to hurt you... it was too much for her *not* to change her tune," she said. "She wants to put the past behind your family, start fresh."

Len scoffed, eyeing out the window again. "That last part I'll believe," he told Claire, "but just because it's new, doesn't mean it's good."

"Ah," Claire said. "No use fixing things that aren't broken, right?"

"Not what I mean," Len said. "She may want to put a shitty track record in the past, but she'll replace it with one just as bad. Worse, probably."

"But think about it, Len!" Claire said, and one of Len's feet shifted onto its heel by itself. "If your family says they're ready to change their tune, I mean, I know you – you're headstrong enough that you'd be able to call them on it if they veered from it, you know, make them stick with it. And once you guys go down that road, and become a complete and healthy family again, Len, you can have those days back when your mom would tuck you in at night or you went on a road trip for some quality time with your dad... I guess what I'm trying to say, is, I wouldn't pass that up. Not the opportunity for it anyway."

A clear, contorted look somewhere between disgust, contempt, and pity surfaced on Len's face. "You have no idea what you're talking about."

By the look on Claire's face then, Len could see she didn't like that remark very much. It didn't matter. Lest the day turn worse, Len returned his attention to the woman in the courtyard. He glanced at Claire before continuing. "My friend says you're here looking out for my safety," he said.

"That's true, Leonard, and you know it," said Jodie.

77

Len looked very amused at that. He sat on the windowsill, turning his weapon over in his hands. "She also told me, based on the nice little conversation the two of you had while I was asleep over here, that you'd like to take me back to Pennsylvania."

"Of course, Honey!"

Len exchanged looks with Claire, who didn't get it. "Did you also tell her about yesterday?"

Claire's attention snapped-to. "What happened yesterday?"

"What's there to tell?" Jodie asked. Her voice filled the treehouse as Len and Claire looked at each other.

"Didn't fill you in on that one, eh?" Len said using his inside voice. Claire didn't reply in words; she was too lost.

"Oh, I should think you owe her a great deal more and better explanation than whatever it is you told her," Len said. Jodie began to say something, but her first syllable cut off when she hopped one foot out of the way. A piece of concrete rolled downhill.

Claire watched it happen. "Len!"

"Relax," Len said.

"How can I relax?! You just threw a clump of sidewalk at your mother! Stop it!"

"I suppose," Len called out the window, "that you also didn't tell her what's waiting back in Pennsylvania if I go with you. Neglecting basic facts, I'm sure."

"There are two sides to every story, Leonard. You know that," Jodie said. That got Len to his feet again.

"The bruises were the only side I ever saw!"

"And were you ever in the room when all that took place?"

Len didn't have a reply for that. He peered back at Claire, who was of no help. Instead, then, Len attached a battery to another small firework and loosed it on Jodie, who dove out of the way.

"*Leonard!*"

"Not my name, Bitch," Len said under his breath. He fired another. It fired well wide, but everyone got the point. "You're not welcome here, Lady," he said. "I'm not going *to tell you* AGAIN!"

"Len, this is insane. Let her up. We can talk this out," Claire said. She leaned past him, toward Jodie. "Come on up, Ma'am, let's get this whole thing ironed out."

Next thing anyone knew, Len had Claire pinned to the wall by the collar. "Don't you dare let that thing up here! I understand you're just trying to help, I do Claire, but you've got to also understand that right now, I just need you to *listen to me* and help me get her to go away!"

Claire shoved him off. "Can't you see you're hurting her feelings? Why don't you let her up? For God's sake, this is your *mother* we're talking about!"

Stomach sinking, Len jumped back, ready to unleash another firework contraption. It missed completely; Jodie had vanished from view. In the corner of his vision, Len saw Claire move, and then heard the trapdoor unlatch. Then he heard the creak of shifting wood.

He wheeled around, eyes huge. Shoving Claire over his bed, he fiddled with the lock, his fingers suddenly numb and stupid, until he heard the woman's head clunk up against it. After making certain, again, that the entrance was absolutely, positively, one hundred percent and totally locked, Len sat on it and told her to go away some more. She wouldn't move.

"If you don't get away from this treehouse in ten seconds," Len shouted into the open air, "I will unlatch it. You should know, though, that when I do, I'm going to shove a metal rod through your face and my friend will do the same with her BOW AND ARROW!"

Claire shook her head vigorously, and the two of them whispered objections back and forth. In the end, Claire remained unwilling to bring harm to Len's guest.

The woman didn't say anything. Several unending seconds of silence passed. Near the end of his personal ten-count, Len gestured at Claire to ready her bow and hand him part of the cooking spit. Just as Len prepared to stand, however, the noise of creaking wood began to descend from the other side of the trapdoor.

She didn't leave. But she did return to the ground. Claire, by then, was up again and at the window, and it was she that told Len of Jodie's return there.

Len joined Claire in the window. He could see the oil over half of each of her hands; she must have used two or three fingers at a time to wipe off each rung and used the remaining, non-oiled fingers like pincers to climb. "Do you have your phone on you?" he asked Claire. She checked her pockets and nodded. "Good," Len said. "Call 911."

Claire didn't take out her phone. "Why?" she asked.

Len's jaw flopped open for a second, but he remembered himself and gestured out the window. "She can't be here," he said. "I need her to get out of here. I can't throw anything fast enough to hit her and you won't just freaking shoot her, and she's not going to leave on her own. Until she's out of here, I can't make any attempt at Indiana."

"Now hold on for a minute, Len –"

"No, *you* hold on for a minute! I did not just hide out here for the last three years and take every precaution I could, just to be found out here and dragged back to Hell!"

Claire flinched. "What?"

"I'm not going back to Pennsylvania," Len said. "Not with her, not with anybody! Now call 911 so they can get her out of here."

"Len, just think about it for a moment," Claire said, and Len twitched at the exasperated parent in her voice. "You'll be okay. You're turning 18 soon, so whatever she takes you back to, you can leave on your own in a couple of months anyway. I say go with her, and in a little while I'll see you."

"Claire! That is not what this is!"

"Then I'm confused," Claire said, slacking her arms.

Len couldn't help but sigh. He looked down at the woman. "You're not leaving, are you?"

She stared back. "I am leaving, Leonard," she said. "But not without you. Let's go home."

Len flung his arms wide. "Done!" he said, and did his best cordial wave. "Ta-ta, now."

She shook her head. "No, that's not what I mean and you know it, Sweetheart. Please, now, it'll do everybody good back home to see you're okay after fighting the police and being out on the street for three years. Wouldn't you like to see the family's happy face again? Wouldn't you like to be safe again?"

Len stepped back from the window. He looked at Claire. Claire looked at him.

"Yeah," Len told her. "I would." He turned to Claire, who peeled herself off the bed and rejoined Len at the window. "I'd love it, in fact…"

Suddenly Len's hands were on Claire's back, stripping the Indian archer of her bow and arrow. It took Claire a moment to realize what he was doing, another to resist, and one more for Len to win and shove Claire back, who accidentally landed on the nightstand. Len's belongings scattered. Then, right before Jodie's eyes, Len made clean eye contact with her as he stared down the shaft of an arrow.

All the confused shock flushed from Jodie's face. A shade of calmer waters replaced it. There wasn't much understanding there, but Len saw some. He saw a seed and a pot to grow it in. She opened her mouth with a counterpoint, but just as quickly gave it up as a bad job. It was she that broke eye contact, turning away slowly as she left. Len released the shot once she was gone, so as not to dry-fire the bow. He'd barely turned around when Claire snatched it from his hands.

As Len collected himself on the windowsill, Claire paced the front of the treehouse. The deepest scowl Len had ever seen her have was on her face. At least full five minutes passed without a word from either of them. It felt longer, for Len counted his heartbeats as it calmed down during those quiet, pulsing moments.

"Happy?" Claire finally yelled.

Len didn't jump at the sudden noise. He didn't say anything, either. Claire continued to pace, but went on. "So you're headed off to Indiana, now, are you?" she asked. "Gonna blaze a trail on your own? Don't need me, I see. Just looking for resources and backup and when I don't offer it, you turn on me! All you had to do was hear her out!"

Len stared at the floor.

Claire got a little closer. "And you know, after all this time I thought I really knew you, Len. I thought I did. Honest. But the shit you just pulled? Where did that even come from? Pulling explosives on your family – I know you've said you don't like them before, but I never expected anything like this. And to be completely honest, I can't be a part of this any more if that's how you're going to treat your family, whether you've got beef with them or not."

"She really sold you on all that, didn't she?" Len said.

"Hey, I'm not the one stealing weapons from the girl that's trying to make peace!"

"You're not the one trying not to die!"

"You weren't going to die, Len! Don't you see that? She's still your MOTHER! She still wants the best for you and even three years later she's still willing to cross state lines just to come make sure you're okay!"

Then Len was in Claire's face. "It must be nice living that naïve," Len said.

"What's that supposed to mean?"

"It means she sold you a bullshit sob story, and you bought the whole stupid thing like a gullible little bastardess."

"Give me one reason I shouldn't take one of these arrows and stab you in the gut right now," Claire said.

Something came over Len at that moment, and he backpedaled to the windowsill. "Hold on," he said. Len took long breaths and, through a scrunched-up face and a bad taste in her mouth, Claire did not attack. She waited, and became statuesque.

The sun sank a couple of degrees, and the clouds shifted over it. A sheet of overcast threatened to hurt Len and Claire's ability to mark the hour, should they have left the treehouse.

"Okay," Len said at last. "You weren't here yesterday."

"So?"

"So... she was here yesterday, too."

That caught Claire's attention. "What did she want then – or say she wanted?"

Len said: "When my alarm didn't go off yesterday morning, I found her standing out there on the shoulder, just glaring at me. My stomach absolutely flipped over, Claire. I'd bet I turned completely white in the face. I could barely stand. And the entire time she just stared at me, didn't say a word."

"So what'd you do...?"

"I told her that I didn't know how she found me, but to rest assured that she wouldn't find me again. I told her she should leave right then if she didn't want to get hurt, and instead of saying anything, even so much as asking what I was going to do about it if she didn't, she just... walked away."

"She left?" Claire asked. "Just like that?"

"Disappeared right into the cattails. As true a snake in the grass as I ever saw. I knew she'd be back."

Claire digested the new information. She leaned against the front wall. "Why didn't she offer to take you back home yesterday?"

"Because that's not what she wants," Len said. They exchanged looks.

"So what *does* she want?"

Len opened his mouth to say something, but then thought better of it. He did this several times in that moment, each stringing Claire along until, about the ninth or tenth time, he simply lifted himself from the windowsill and opened the trapdoor.

"Len?" Claire asked after him. "Len!"

Len tied a rope around the hubcap and offered to let Claire leave the treehouse first. She obliged, and once on the ground Len acted like they were bidding each other a simple goodnight.

Before Claire knew it, Len was already a hundred feet farther along the shoulder. Not sure what was happening or exactly what had just happened, Claire could only think to follow her friend. She lost time in wondering how to latch the trapdoor from the outside. *Only Len knows anything about how to do stuff with his treehouse,* she thought, and realized she hadn't heard the latch when Len came down. Still calling after him, Claire jogged along behind Len. Acknowledgement did not come. A mile and a half later, Claire just hoped the treehouse would be okay.

Chapter Eleven

Claire pursued Len as he absentmindedly made his way into the woods. Beyond the protection of the canopy, a light rain began to fall. Len's and Claire's clothes became darkened with scattered spots where the water wetted the material, but they were not soaked. As the sky fed her this snack, the waters of Great Lake St. Mary's churned. A wind – certainly stronger than a mere breeze – shoved small waves against the rocks, and across the way Len could see some foam slide down the rocks once its carrier fell away. But no sooner did that water subside and the foam lose its grip that the next wave-in-formation took the frontliner's place. It reminded Len of musketeer warfare, when ready men swapped place with those who'd just fired.

It wasn't nasty-looking weather, though it did look as though to foretell a light storm within the hour. Len saw the last of a crashing wave fall back behind the edge as he emerged from the trees and sat down in his isolated spot. He felt better, even with the grass bowing in a wave of their own as each gust blew through. He set the hubcap aside. Unbeknownst to him, Claire watched him about fifteen feet within the trees.

Len whittled. Each crashing wave, as well as the sky's scattered attempts at rain, made a fine mist that hit him again and again. Notwithstanding the reflexive scowl he made as each gust hit him, he ignored it all. The wind, blowing into him, made the schnitzels land in a wave of his pants and so accumulated in his lap.

A large leaf dumped water when Claire had to push it aside to enter the small clearing. Instantly, Len's head snapped to see who it was, and he just as quickly stuffed his knife and project once he realized the company.

"You... said she was there yesterday," Claire said. "Why wouldn't she come back the next day to take you home?"

Len eyed her. Claire stayed on the edge of the clearing with her hands in her pockets, almost daring to rock back and forth on her heels. The wind would likely, barely, knock her over if she did, so she refrained.

A larger than normal wave hit the rocky cliff. Its crest mounted the edge and, scattered vertically by the wind, spattered Len on one side. It made him take a step and wince. "Why do you even care?" he asked.

"Because," Claire said. "I'm your friend. And that woman's your family. It… matters to me that families stick together."

Len marched up on her, gumming his lip. "Claire, you listen to me and you listen good," he said, inches from his friend's face. "As far as I'm concerned, she might as well not be my family anymore."

"I…"

"So drop it," Len said, and backed off.

About a minute passed. Len just stared out over the lake, thinking as hard as he could.

"No," Claire said. And Len turned around. The polite anger management and sternness he'd practiced a moment earlier looked prime to collapse.

"Claire…"

"No!" Claire said. "It's *my* turn to talk! I'm just trying to figure out what exactly the hell is going on here! Why don't you go home, Len?" she asked. "Why don't you go home with your mother and let things start to get easy again? For God's sake, dude, you live in a wooden treefort along a highway! You scavenge, barely get by, you're not in school, you don't have a job, you don't hang out with any friends, you just subsist from day to day and week to week and month to month! You've made a hard life for yourself and, honestly? I can't figure out why you won't let it go!"

Len stood there and took it, along with the beating wind as it picked up and the waves' mist beginning to soak his back.

"Sure, life can be rough for some kids," Claire said. "We know this. Puberty sucks. You get into arguments with your parents. Home doesn't look so great anymore. Kids run away. I get that. And eventually, you take a step back and look at what you've done and decide enough is enough and you come back home!

"But now you're out here by yourself, damn near killing police and getting shot at and when, finally, after three years of worrying her heart out, your poor mother comes all the way from Pennsylvania to come and rescue you – and take you back to a place where you can have a roof over your head without rain dripping from the ceiling, where she can provide for you a hot meal whenever you need it instead of hoping we can find something or busting open a can like we're trying to ride out a freaking nuclear winter – instead of giving in and letting whatever argument it was be done and in the past, you throw concrete at her and fire explosives and acid at her!

"And of course, after all *I've done* to help you and spent time away from *my* own mother and father and warm cozy house and clean, fresh meals, you decide the ONE TIME I don't offer help – never mind that I tried being a mediator and family counselor to patch up your messed up life – the one God-*blessed* time I refuse to help for whatever reason it is, you take what you want from me and steal my bow and arrow so you can tell that woman to leave you to your makeshift life! What the hell's wrong with you, Len? What the *hell* is your problem? Go home with her, Len! Go find your mother and tell her you're ready to make it work and go back to your family and GO HOME!"

"I AM HOME!!"

Claire stopped talking.

"I AM HOME!

"God, Claire! You think I *like* scraping by and hoping I can find enough stuff here and there to make it work? You think I enjoy freezing in the winter when I run out of wood and there's too much snow on the ground for you to come help or for me to go chop some? You think I wouldn't like to be a cozy little bastard like you with your comfortable, middle-class family and warm bed and bedtime stories and college savings and shit?

"You know, *you've* got a future ahead of you, all cut and clean and laid out for you to check off as you go. And I'm happy for

87

you, I really am. And yeah, it'd be nice to know I could just fucking go back to the days when my parents could be there for me and life was worry-free and hunky-dory and I could get my education and make something of myself. Gee, that'd really be swell. But you know what? THOSE CARDS AREN'T IN MY HAND.

"So no," Len said, "I won't go back." He shook his head, almost as a spasm, when he said it. "I won't go back and put up with all those clean-cut bastards with degrees at the front of the class telling us what to do. I won't go back and act like another drop-out bastard trying to pull his life together. I don't want to be like that, Claire, because I don't want to deal with my family. I have my reasons, and you need to let it go. And why won't you respect that? Hm? Sorry I'm not a trust fund bastard like you where my stoic Indian daddy can buy me whatever I need except a fucking emotional connection!"

Claire didn't like that, but why should Len have cared?

"Sorry my family's not worth going back to. You know, I really don't care what she told you back there. I don't. Really. And you know why, Claire? You know *why* I could give a shit about her and every other stupid, poor, lazy, rich, existing bastard back in Pennsylvania? Because that woman is a liar, and liars do one thing pretty exceptionally well, and that's *lie*. Anything cutesy and pro-family and positive-in-intent she told you about her plans for me is a fucking *lie*, Claire. Hell, you're the closest thing I have or want to family, and I'd love nothing more than to keep going as it is. But then this bitch's gotta waltz back in to my life and drive me to find a new hiding spot where I can start from scratch and hope I don't see her for another three years. You think I like any of that?"

"Well, no, but –"

"But shit. What I have out here is golden for me compared to what's waiting when I get back. Yeah, she might fill your head with all these visions of just wanting me back home safe and sound and away from bullets flying at my head, but that was a *lie*. She might tell you how much she loves me and just wants the best for me, but that's *a lie*. She might even tell you about all these wonderful, cute little things I did as a kid to win you over and convince you I need or should have her in my life, but those'd be lies, just as well. Being my mother? That might as well be a lie, too!

"So I'll tell you again," Len said. "Drop it."

Then Claire took a step forward. "Well it's an awful nice sense of urgency you've got over all of this," she said. "I must say, you're playing her game quite well."

Len made a calculated few shakes of his head. "There's no game involved, man."

Claire shrugged. "Feels like one to me. Real casual, no rush to escape out from beneath her. I gotta say, if this is some sort of emergency, you're handling it extremely well. I don't see you, for example... carjacking someone on the freeway the instant you see her or, say, robbing that party store again for long-term bus fare or, even, digging a hole in the ground and waiting it out. If I had to guess, I'd say you're not nearly as worried about all this as you should be, if what you're telling me is true."

"Don't even play at that," Len said. "You know I'd be honest and straight with you about this."

"And yet," said Claire, "you seem bent on keeping me in the dark on most of it."

"Because you don't need to be worrying about it," Len said. He seemed very pleased with himself.

"Hmph. We'll see about that, too."

"Leave," Len said. He pointed back into the brush. The gusts and mist kept on and kept on. Both of them were soaked. "*You* go home. I've got better things to do."

Claire held back the urge to spit at Len. In that moment, she thought even of perhaps tackling Len, right then and there, or shoving him into the lake. That rock face was too high for a swimmer to mount, and maybe Len would drown in the semi-stormy water. "You know what," she said, "I've got better things to do than try to be nice to assholes anyway."

Len didn't say anything. He just averted Claire's gaze and turned back toward the lake. Edging halfway back into the trees, Claire realized Len had nothing more to say. She went the rest of the way into the woods, and left.

Len shivered, crossed his arms, and stared across the lake.

And after a while, with the already diminished light running the rest of the way out, Len knew he had to follow Claire's lead. It wasn't the respite he'd needed, coming out to the lake, but he hoped that wouldn't cost him. 'Indiana,' he thought. 'I have to get to Indiana.'

Claire didn't know her way home without cutting across the field from Len's treehouse. Len watched from a good distance – nearly close enough figure to out whether you recognize someone or not, but too far to really make anything they say unless they shout – as Claire stopped at the treehouse for a few moments.

'To think,' Claire thought as she went, 'for so long, I've been able to look out my living room window and see that funny little treehouse just before the tree line and smile about it. But now? Now I guess I'm glad that window's got blinds.'

Claire moved on, past the cattails and fence. She made her way to the field, wet as it was, and tried not to get too much mud everywhere.

Several moments later, Len arrived at the treehouse, too. He was glad it was intact. He glanced about for sign of Jodie, but didn't see her. He smiled. Before heading up, he looked into the field and saw a dot shifting about – Claire, no doubt. And despite the treehouse looking to be in good order, Len realized that he really didn't like what he saw.

Chapter Twelve

Claire lived on an acre of land that sat three quarters of a mile from Len's treehouse. A field separated them, accented with small patches of trees. The farmers had been through and upturned the dirt, and so as Claire made her way back to her family's single-story home in near-darkness, she had to be very careful not to twist her ankle. To her right, maybe a hundred feet away as she came to the midpoint of the field, was the small patch of forestation where she caught the animals – rabbits included – that she ate with Len. There were other patches like it ahead, upwards of a mile away and framing the neighbor's property. Beyond that, a much bigger swath of trees made a rural skyline, but that was another mile-worth of farmland past her house.

As the young Indian bowwoman trudged over the ruts between clumps of dirt the size of basketballs, her shoes made clomping noises. Her bow bounced off her back as she went, making an almost rhythmic clunking noise. It was all very sloppy, but it held together. Within a few minutes, she would be home, bid her father goodnight (who was undoubtedly waiting up to see her return safely), and go to bed.

In the meantime, Claire tried to make sense of Len's behavior, the way they'd treated each other. 'Where had any of that come from?' she wondered. Nothing had ever come between them, and a pebble in Claire's gut made her worry that perhaps, strangely, that was exactly the problem.

She looked up from the ground and saw that Subhail had the garage lights on. 'Good,' Claire thought. It gave her direction in the night. She stopped to reshoulder her bow and make sure nothing had dropped off during her hike.

As soon as she was done affixing everything, a distinct feeling of being watched struck her, nearly driving her to panic. To ward off a possible coyote, Claire shouted. She didn't hear anything scamper away. She glanced one way, and then the other. She looked over among the trees and among them. Nothing.

Claire walked on, keeping her eyes on the ground so she could avoid tripping. A couple of times she had to change course to avert holes she knew would be better to avoid, but she was careful to keep straight for home. That awful feeling ran icy fingers on the back of his neck.

Just to make sure an unwise animal wasn't following her, she stopped and did a full 360.

She froze halfway. Jodie was a short distance behind her. Suddenly, Claire felt like a sheriff in a wild west shootout.

Her bow was out and knocked. She looked down the shaft of her shot and made eye contact with the woman at the same time.

"I thought I made myself clear," she said as calmly as she could. "I don't fire warning shots. Why are you following me?"

"Aren't you Len's friend?" asked Jodie. "Maybe you could help me reason with him."

"Stay right there!" Claire said, for Jodie had taken a step. "I don't want to get involved any more than I have to, Lady."

"Please, call me Jo," she said.

Claire looked at her, wondering whether to shake her head or fire. Instead she nodded, stage right. "Leave me alone," he said. "Go now, or I shoot."

"Come, now, Young Lady," Jodie began to say. Instead of leaving, she took another foreboding step forward and, thinking just enough to realize that, Claire fired.

But the woman dodged.

And then she ran. And suddenly Claire saw Jodie was coming for her.

Without time to try again, Claire turned and ran as well.

She ran so fast she was nearly floating. Without the luxury of time to tee up each step, Claire had to simply carry herself away. Her feet caught no holes, and she thanked God for that in the back of her mind. As she ran over the open field, she had no time to put her bow away. It arced at her side as her arms pumped. She heard Jodie gaining on her. Not daring to look back and see just how close the woman was, not even to gauge whether she could get home before Jodie got to her, Claire instead exaggerated one of her pumping arms to retrieve an arrow from over her shoulder. Two strides later, she flipped it in her hand so the head pointed backwards.

She made it another twenty, maybe thirty feet before she dared glance back to see where Jodie was. When she did, she was dismayed to see Jodie nearly upon her. 'My God,' she thought, 'this bitch can *run*!' Far from home still, Claire did the only thing she could do to buy time.

She hit the brakes for but an instant, turning herself and thrusting the arrow with all her might, hoping to disable Jodie with a solid backhand stab. Jodie dodged, though, ('Of course she dodged,' Claire had the flash of time to think) grabbing Claire's wrist on its way by and using the girl's own momentum to tackle her to the ground.

And just like that, Claire found herself pinned and, for all she knew, doomed.

"I'm not playing games anymore," Jodie said. Claire tried to wriggle free, but Jodie's knees had her thighs pinned. Her wrists were in the iron chains of the woman's hands, and there was no escape. Sharp pain in Claire's thighs kept her from forming sentences.

"Get off!"

"Ah-ah-ah!" Jodie said, making the small adjustments to quell the girl's wrestlings as they came. "Now, before this all gets too unpleasant, you're going to help me take Len back home."

Claire stopped squirming for a moment. "And why should I do that?" She fought off the temptation to spit.

"I don't expect you to have any idea of what's at stake," Jodie said, "so let me be very clear. I'm in repo mode. And I need Len to come home."

'Well that's a hell of a way to put it.' "Your son is not a car, you deranged witch! Now get off of me!"

"Of course he's not a car. Sit still! But I need you to help me on this, because the dear boy won't listen to his mother. There are people back home that are... let's call them worried. And I

93

need to show them that there's nothing to worry about." Jodie's pace quickened, her voice nearly turning shrill. "Now, he doesn't have to like it, but he needs to come home! I want my peace of mind back!"

Claire heard the sick crack of breaking bone, and suddenly the weight on her fell off to the side. She looked up.

"Len!"

Len was standing over her. He offered a hand, and they grabbed each other's forearms so Claire could regain her feet.

They looked down. Jodie lay in the field unconscious. A small trickle of blood ran from her temple and down her cheek. And that was all right. "Are you okay?" Len asked. His chest heaved.

Claire nodded, catching her breath. "I think so," she said. "What the fuck is wrong with this woman?"

"You tell me," Len said. "She's a sick one though, isn't she?"

"Hold on!" Claire said, using her whole arm to help Len retreat with her. The teens reeled back a few steps, for Jodie stirred. Within the same couple of breaths, Len and Claire saw her rise to her feet. She touched her head, saw the blood, and glared.

But she didn't say anything. At least not at first. Len and Claire planted themselves, poised to run or pounce. Jodie stood, a Roman pillar in the midnight field. Len stood, armed with a chunk of pavement. Claire stood, aiming her bow. They each weighed their chances – even between themselves, for fear that the other was still yet bitter. Jodie, unarmed, grew an expression that belied her need to improvise. She sized up her chances.

She must not have liked them, because she just stood up straight, turned, and walked away. She trudged away from both of them, headed in the same direction as the Hunting Grounds. It relieved Len to not see her cutting an intercept of his route back to the treehouse, and it relieved Claire not to see the woman try to attack them again.

It had to be an hour or so before they were certain she was gone, and not simply hiding in the trees like a panther. They walked toward the treehouse some, enough to see around the patch of woods. They saw a distant figure walking down the road by the light of street lamps. At last, the young friends turned to each other, though they could barely make each other out.

"I figured she might try something like this," Len said. "She'll do anything to get to me."

Claire puffed her cheeks. "So I guess that includes taking me as a hostage."

"Or tricking you into thinking it would help me," Len said. "I'd bet a lot that's how she got Wallace and Leonard to come knocking."

A pause came then that was anything but silent. "So what happens now?" Claire asked.

Len glanced at her, then back into the distance at Jodie. "Follow me," he said. "We're going back to the treehouse."

Claire looked on as Len had already begun walking. "But what about my family?"

"What do you mean?" Len asked.

"The bitch knows where I live, now," Claire said.

Len twisted about-face and rejoined her. Their eyes drifted off to the Mehtas' home in the distance. The garage light was still on. It reminded Len of a lighthouse during a great sea storm. But it was less majestic than that. It was just a lamp using some power so they could see from the middle of a huge patch of upturned dirt. To Len, it seemed unrefined, and yet totally welcoming as an island of surveyable refuge in an abyss of dirt and darkness.

It then reoccurred to him that the sun had long since set. "I have to lock up the treehouse again, and I can't do that from the outside. I'll meet you there. I need you to do me a favor, though."

"Anything," Claire said.

"Let your folks know you're spending the night with me – I don't care how upset they are or if you have school in the morning. Just let them know where you'll be, lock everything up and meet me back at my place. Tomorrow, we're going to start prep."

Claire looked between Len and home a couple of times. "Prep? For what?"

"Indiana," Len said, and when Claire looked, he was smiling. "What else?"

Claire couldn't help but smile a little, too. "And how exactly do you want to do this?"

"Off the top of my head?" Len asked. "It might be time to pay ol' Willie another visit. But before that, even, there's something I need to talk to you about."

Claire looked into his eyes. "Okay," she said. Len stared back as resolute as usual, but his heart warmed that Claire looked a little hurt that he even needed to ask. When at last his friend nodded, Len nodded back even more firmly, and the two split into the night.

Claire made sure to leave a note for Subhail – surely he would be furious on such short notice – and locked up the house and the garage and all the windows. She rendezvoused with Len in the treehouse, appearing in the window first instead of simply knocking on the trapdoor. They spent the night up there, discussing the necessary but also making sure to find time for listening to the sloppy, wonderful sound of midnight traffic on wet roads.

Chapter Thirteen

"Claire, you've been a good friend to me all this time. I know I haven't been completely forward with you about how I got here or why, and I appreciate that you haven't pried. It means the world to me to have you here, now."

Claire sat cross-legged before him. Len sat on the edge of the bed, where he could look up and see out the front window. He concentrated on Claire, though.

"I owe you a debt," Len said. "For everything you've done for me, you deserve at least to know, especially now with what might happen, how things got this way."

Claire watched him, saying nothing.

Len took his time, taking breaths, mostly avoiding eye contact. He leaned over and retrieved his whittling project. He scraped bits off as he continued.

"You know I'm originally from Pennsylvania. You know green isn't my natural hair color. Thanks to those IRS bastards, you know my given name," Len said. He expected Claire to say that name, but she kept silent. "Thank you for not repeating it," Len said. Claire smiled.

"I'm just trying to think, what do you know and what you don't know," Len said. "I guess I'll start where it began.

"We lived in the Philadelphia metropolitan area. It wasn't strictly urban, but we were close enough to the city proper to be near the main things we needed without the highest crime rate. I'm sure less obvious crimes happened, but this was back when I was just a kid, mind you. There was probably a drug dealer somewhere in the neighborhood, but where we lived was actually a neat and clean suburb. I lived there as far back as I can remember, with my parents. I'm an only child.

"My mom worked in a daycare. She loved kids. Probably still does. She always wore the prettiest casual dresses with yellows and blues and flowers on them, and her voice could swoon a god. She had silky blond hair and clean blue eyes, and a smile that must have made men's hearts melt. I loved her," he said. He pressed his knife through a knot in the wood and harrumphed. "Still do."

Len peered up from his carving. Claire looked curious, but kept listening. Len ran his knife along the wood some more.

"When I was really, really little, and I mean little enough to be a cute little bastard in my mom's daycare, I was. She and I had a ton of mother-son time. We bonded a lot. But every day, when the kids went home, she and I had to as well. Home was an entirely different story.

"The curb appeal was outstanding, I'm sure. My parents took pride in it. Inside, the décor was nice and groomed and coif and whatever you want to call it. It was sterile. You could hardly tell a kid lived there, let alone a five-year-old. I say five because that's when I remember first distinctly hearing what made home so ugly. Behind the scenes, my parents fought. They fought a lot.

"And my mom always lost. I'm not sure why they fought so much, and I'm not sure why it took me until I was five to understand why my mom would have regular black eyes and bruises, or why it took until I was five to at least remember hearing the ruckus, but that's when all that clicked. Shortly after graduating to kindergarten and leaving my mom behind in daycare all by herself, I came to learn that the woman who'd borne me was a habitual victim of domestic violence.

"What was worse," Len said, pausing in his carving and staring past Claire's shoulder, "was that she never did anything about it. I could see it in her face – she knew it was wrong, and she knew it shouldn't have been happening. Hell, she knew I shouldn't see it and yet she made every attempt to cover up the bruises in public. She was an expert at it. But I saw it. I saw it every day after they were done fighting.

"Sometimes they fought more than once in a day. Usually there wasn't any reason for it. My mother would just call her into the room to 'help with something' and next thing you know, there's smacking and shrieking and desperate questions of 'why?' and, for the longest time, I just covered my ears." He picked his teeth for a moment and carved a little more. "I just covered my ears and fell over on my side, hung out in fetal position for a while.

"I mean, what was I going to do about it? I couldn't stand up to a grown-up three times my size! How was I supposed to stand up to an adult that beat up another adult?" Len made brief eye contact with Claire. "I still blame myself for it, Claire."

"Don't," was all Claire said.

Len considered that for a moment, staring off to one side. He continued whittling.

"So, for years that went on. I advanced up through the grades, made it out of elementary school. Every year I got more distance between my mom at daycare and my own classroom, and once I left Fifth Grade, all I ever saw of her was at home. By the time I was in high school and had projects to work on for class and meeting with classmates and tried an attempt at having friends outside of school, well, I almost never saw my mom except after a fight. Sometimes there was blood. Usually on her lip. She played it off like it was nothing. She made it her burden. Just hers.

"One day I decided to change that. I didn't pay attention for a minute in any of my classes. I spent the whole day thinking of exactly how I was going to finally stand up to that monster and free my mom from the torment and the fear and the pain and the blood and the screams and the tears and the helplessness, even if that helplessness was a choice she made – God knows why. I played through dozens of imaginary conversations in which I won handily every time. I pretended it broke out into a fight, where I finally took my mom's place, and of course, as in any imaginary fight like that, I emerged victorious and my mom and I lived happily ever after.

"And then I got home. I didn't say anything, and I waited. I waited for the two of them to get into a fight again. It took maybe an hour, and my mother called my mom into the next room.

"I stood up before my mom could. I shielded her with one of my hands, and made the bitch look at me instead. The words I'd practiced all day stopped in my throat, but I crammed them the rest of the way and told my bitch mother enough was enough. I told her just to try and take it out on me."

Len placed the whittling knife on his thigh. He sighed, and brushed schnitzels from his lap. "She won. I went to school the next day with a black eye and a broken arm.

"To this day, I have no idea what they ever actually fought about. Maybe it was money. Maybe it just fed on itself and had something to do with a long-ago fight that became about fighting where I could hear and one of them cared and the other one didn't and it just escalated and escalated. I really don't know, but it kept going, and it didn't stop.

"Sometimes, when Jodie was at work, my mom Dianne would take me on a bit of a road trip and we'd visit her brother's grave. It always brought her to tears, but there was something else in her eyes when she cried there. It wasn't until I visited it after running away that I thought back and realized it was comfort.

"Uncle Hank died a year or something after I was born, so I never got to meet him, but my mom always had something good to say about him. She talked to me for hours about how kind-hearted he was. That led to my coloring my hair. Green was Uncle Hank's favorite color. From what my mom told me about him, he was the kind of man that would have stood up to Jodie, and now that I think about it, probably did before he couldn't.

"Dianne never said how Uncle Hank died. There was enough tears and pain in our lives that I didn't figure to ask. No use opening old scars, right? In any case, we'd make that trip out a little less than once a month right up until I ran away.

"When I actually did it, none of it seemed real. I wondered how I would *stay* away, and the only way I could half-guarantee myself that was to make a lot of distance in not a lot of time."

"Do you ever feel bad about leaving your mom behind?" Claire asked.

Len glanced at her, then back at his carving. It took a minute, but he summoned his answer. "Not anymore," he said. "I tried to get her to come with me, but she was a cowardly bastard and refused to leave. So whatever befell her after I left, she deserved."

"Len…"

"Claire," Len said, and his hardened face disarmed Claire's concerned one. "What's done is done. I can do nothing for her now."

It was Claire's turn to sigh. "Do you ever wonder if she's still alive, at least? If she might somehow be okay?"

"I didn't think of that," Len said. "That's something, at least. If my mom is still alive and back in Pennsylvania, then any time Jodie spends here is time my mom spends safe from her."

A contented smile crept across Len's lips, but Claire didn't react to it. She let Len enjoy it, even though she was confident Len had no idea it was there.

"Anyway," Len said, "the first couple of times I tried running away didn't work. Jodie rewarded me by beating me. My mom was always there afterward to try to make things better, but by then it didn't really work. I knew there would be no end, and that made the wounds throb in other ways. I remember lying on the living room floor, spirit broken, as Dianne cradled my head in her lap. She sang to me, stroked my hair and I just stared at the ceiling with glassy eyes.

"I came to realize my first attempts were too obvious. I needed to be a cunning bastard, you see, and taking extended stays at friends' houses wasn't going to cut it. Simply walking as many blocks as my legs would carry me by nightfall wasn't going to cut it. Stealing a car and blazing a trail down the highway wasn't going to cut it.

"It took me four weeks of hard thinking to come up with something after that. Dianne wasn't going to the police, and I knew we'd both die if I tried, so in a way I don't blame my mom for not doing it. She began to grow calluses. The sharper angles that made her face glow just kind of rounded out, like Jodie's fists were sandpaper. That glow that I'd known as a toddler… it slowly and quietly vanished.

"And the day it was finally all gone, I waited for that bitch to make a milk run. I was cocked and ready to spring out the door. The longest two minutes of my life, I swear to you Claire, were listening to Jodie start that car and clear the block.

"Once she was gone, I had my route all mapped out in my head. On my way out, I damn near broke the screen door like football players busting through their cheerleaders' banner. I ran down the sidewalk, the opposite way that Jodie drove. I ran as fast as I could, until my side hurt and I just had to look down and breathe down my legs' necks as I made them go one after another. I watched them go, one after another, left right left right left right left right, as sidewalk flew by in the background. I don't know how long I ran like that. But that day, a panting, sweaty, unkempt sophomore arrived at a railyard and asked about a job. When the supervisor denied me on account of my age, I acted like I was leaving and waited until the bastard's back was turned.

"Then I hid in some cattails until a train headed out. I came sprinting out of those weeds for everything I had and bounded alongside the tracks. I grabbed for the train and hoisted myself up, held onto the ladder on the back for miles. By the time the engineer bothered to look around and see his stowaway, we were closer to Columbus than Philadelphia. He called the police to try to get me back home, but I was a ghost when they got there.

"It took me two days, but I managed to find my way back to the graveyard where Uncle Hank was buried. I figured, maybe if even in a life of pain and suffering, my dead relative could bring my mom some comfort and an anchor for sanity, maybe he could lead *me* vaguely in the right direction, too.

"But I couldn't hang around the graveyard itself. That would be way too obvious, and then Jodie and Dianne would've found me within a week. Maybe two. Either way, they'd've found me and then you and I would never have met.

"So I was in Ohio, I had a basis for direction, and I was out from beneath my mother. It was a good start. But I needed to set up shop away from that graveyard. I needed a place close enough to still use it as a point of reference without being so close that if my parents went there, they'd hone right in on me. I wandered northeast, hit Wapakoneta, and shot this way.

"And there was something about this place that told me it was perfect. There was a glow about it. This tree, in fact, just seemed to leave words on the wind that only I could hear. I saw her, and within a moment it all clicked. I knew this was where I could make a new home for myself, where my parents would never think to look, where I would be left alone and could make my way.

"Earlier in the day, I'd met that slob, Bobby. The circular bastard took pity on me, but also took advantage. He agreed to let me work for him in exchange for some supplies. I didn't want to get tied down with a permanent job; I just needed some shit to put something together. When it was done, I sometimes sold him scrap and used the money to buy food and all that. But within a month of arriving here in Ohio, I was able to lug the planks and nails over here, hiding them in the ditch so litter-retriever chain gangs wouldn't get them. I made this treehouse in those days, and I stayed here ever since.

"And every once in a while, I made my way to the graveyard and visited Uncle Hank. But never when it was light out. Never when I would be making myself easy to see. And I hoped, when I was there that even though there wasn't much light, maybe he could see my hair and know that I hadn't given up his fight."

They'd gone out and gotten another rabbit for dinner. It cooked on the spit, and with the sky as dark as the charred wafers of cardboard that float away from the bonfires that create them, Claire turned to Len, who stared into the fire. Or maybe something inside of it.

"So," he said, "what are you going to do now that she's found you?"

Len's eyes remained locked dead ahead. A long pause pounded like a Viking's war drum. "I can run. That's it." He looked at his new map on the wall, and Claire copied.

She digested that while turning the spit. She looked at Len for a moment, and then at the fire and the rabbit. In doing so, she suddenly became conscious of each revolution. Her lips made a smacking sound when she finally made to speak again.

"Why don't you do to her what you did for Wallace and Leonard and the cops?" she asked. She almost added that at least now Len wouldn't have to fear being subtle, for the media had already betrayed an alliance they'd never even had.

Len stared into the fire. "Not possible," he said. He flicked schnitzels from his carving into the fodder.

"How so? You just held off a hockey team's worth of armed, grown men like friggin' MacGyver."

"It's not the same," Len said.

"You're right," Claire said. "Much easier. Just one person to take care of this time. And you can probably get away with killing her, ending the nightmare right there."

"Drop it, Claire."

Claire stood for effect. "Len, do you realize what you did the other day? For God's sake, you used a *hammer* to disarm cops, kept them at bay with bottle rockets, batteries, and fucking tuna can lids! I think you can take your mother. One adult of any kind, for that matter. I saw the footage where you whapped Wallace to the ground with the bat and —"

"ENOUGH!"

Claire shrank. Len glanced her way as he sat back down, and even patted her leg so as not to seem too heated. With Claire seated and calm again, the scene returned to what it once was; they sat around the fire, and Len stared into it.

"It's not the same," Len said. Claire stared at him, but they did not exchange looks. As the tiny fire licked the air, it reflected in Len's eyes, and so it was that Claire could see both.

"Why?" Claire asked. She swallowed the frog in her throat. "Why isn't it the same, Len?"

"Because," Len said. "You can't really kill someone that's already dead inside."

"So you plan to run, then," Claire said. The resigned method irked her. Len could tell, because Claire never spoke her guesses like sentences.

"I can run, and sometimes I can hide," Len said, "and someday, her body'll give out and she'll keel over. And maybe, just maybe, her ghost won't haunt me."

Claire smiled. "You could hang out in a church for the rest of your life. I'm pretty sure zombies aren't allowed in those."

Their eyes met, and they laughed together – about that and other things – for the rest of the night. One of the corners of Len's mouth was still stuck, curved up, as he latched the trapdoor.

Chapter Fourteen

It was almost first light the next morning. Claire had gone for a quick check of the ranch, to make sure Jodie hadn't broken in or run a car through the living room. Len remained behind with the pronged part of the rabbit spit hidden up his sleeve in case his mother decided to attack him instead. Although Claire still had her bow, arrows, and hunting knife, Len kept an eye her way every few seconds in case of a repeat of the previous night.

He'd just finished wiping off the majority of oil from the rungs when Claire marched out from the cattails.

"Everything good then?" Len said, wiping his hands.

"Perfect," Claire said. "There's no sign of her, although my dad left a note of his own."

"Oh?"

"Yeah," Claire said, not producing the note itself. "It just said I'd better get it all sorted out quick. You know how he is about my hanging out with you."

Len nodded, hanging his head more than he realized. "Yeah…

"Anyway," he said, perking up, "did you come up with any more ideas about what we can look for today?"

Claire might not have had Subhail's note, but she did have the list they'd made up overnight and so was uncrumpling it from her pocket that very moment. "Nothing we can really expect to find," she said. "I mean, how long do you think you're gonna be gone before you find a new place?" Before Len could reply, she pointed the paper his way. The flapping sound made Len look. "And whatever it is we scrounge up, you had better call me when you get there so I know you got there all right!"

Len laughed. "I will. But I'll need your number."

Claire closed the gap, laughing harder. "You asshole," Claire said, shoving the list at Len's chest and mounting the rungs. She knew full well that Len had it memorized. Len smiled back.

"Hey, now that I think of it," Claire said from the trapdoor – for Len had just started his way up – "did you see any sign of Jodie while I was gone?"

"Not one, thank God," Len said after joining his friend in the treehouse proper. Claire nodded agreement as they each took a seat. "So you're all set to go, then?"

Claire glanced at the list again, mouthing the items and counting them off on her free hand. "I'm not sure," she said. "Are you planning on using a train again, or something else?"

Len shrugged. "Whatever works," he said.

"I - I get that," Claire said, "but you may only get one shot this time."

Len did not want a failed runaway attempt to set him back to square one, so he was glad Claire thought of it. "It may be to my advantage, then," he said, "if I take an extra day – ward her off as I need to, obviously with your help – and make sure whatever I do, I can do it right and it's going to work."

Claire set the list down. "How far do you have go?"

"How far is Indianapolis?"

Claire thought about it, but interrupted herself. "That big a city?" she asked. "I mean I know now she'll be looking for treehouses along the highway, but still you can't seriously think you'll lose her just by hiding in a crowd."

"No, no, not Indianapolis itself," Len said. "I was thinking somewhere within reach of it. You know, where I'm still relatively close to pilfer about for the stuff I need but not where I'm either drowning in the Bastard Sea, or not reducing the amount of area she has to comb."

"Actually, since you bring that point up," Claire said, "the city might not be such a bad bet after all." No sooner did she finish the sentence that Len sat up on the bed with a face set to argue the point, but Claire held up her hand to keep her turn. "Hear me out now. It might all be close together, but it's still a lot to search. It's dense, which could slow her down. And there's still plenty of places to hide and easy to get tangled, so even if she finds and chases you, there are tons of corners and places to disappear."

"Eh. There are also a lot of corners for her to suddenly appear from."

"Hm," Claire said. "Good point."

"So," Len said, "if I can find a place about as populated as this and hang low, then she has to comb through all the little, dot-on-the-map communities like it just to get a whiff of me. And if some dyke is poking around a small town asking people about a kid hardly anybody knows exists, well, aren't I more likely to see her coming and vanish?"

"And if you're just walking around the day that she comes into town and the two of you just happen to find each other at the same time?"

Len flattened his mouth. "That's a risk I take anywhere."

After nodding absently, Claire shrugged. "Fair enough. First stop is Willie's, then?" she asked. They exchanged looks, and mounted up.

The two of them trudged through the choke point entrance to Willie's by six o'clock. With a burlap sack, some plastic bags ready, and breakfast in their stomachs, they headed in. Immediately, they saw Willie standing in the office, manning some kind of block sticking out of the floor. It had all sorts of buttons and levers with knobs on them. The old man's own knobby elbows flew about in zany patterns with each crank and shift of the gears. There was enough fly shit and rust-colored filth on the windows, though, that they figured they could sneak in easily enough so long as he stayed distracted.

The railyard was full of sounds that morning; Willie had a small crew (who were far more likely to warn Willie of their presence) out among the tracks, helping make sure car-moving day went smoothly. All around them, Len and Claire heard metallic clangs as brakes dropped and hitches disengaged. Train engines shoved cars to and fro, making the wheeled rectangles float by right in front of their faces without anything to stop them. Len warned Claire how it was the exact kind of day that they needed to be extra careful, for to get in front of a shoved railcar was certain death without an engineer to cue the brakes – so much like simply being touched by an enemy in a classic arcade game.

Even as the scene morphed before their very eyes, Len didn't like the layout. They stood near the opposite wall from Willie, near the entrance. "Looks like we got most of anything worthwhile last time," he said.

Claire looked around a car as it moved, but there wasn't anything special on the other side. There was gravel, but gravel was everywhere, underfoot. There was some compacted, dusty dirt in patches where the gravel had fallen away, but those were scattered about here just as normally. "Well," she said, "it was also night. The day and light are both on our side this time. Plus," and Len exchanged looks with her at this point, "with the cars moving, we can redouble over areas and probably find some stuff we otherwise wouldn't."

Len peered back out over the yard and nodded. "Yeah, and with all the metal-hitting-metal sounds I'm hearing, maybe luck'll have some of that fall off where we can snatch it up and I can sell it to Bobby as scrap."

"True, though not that I would count on it," Claire said. "Did you want to maybe check by his place too today?"

"Whose? Bobby's?"

"Yeah."

Len's head made an off, figure-8-type swimming motion from side to side. "I really kinda doubt we'll find anything we need there," he said. "And even if we did, everything on his side of the fence has a price. I don't have a lot of money right now."

"All right then. Shall we?"

They started forward. Although the yard crew largely ignored them, it wasn't long before Willie stepped out of the office and shouted at them from the rise.

"HEY! GIT!" he screamed, though Len and Claire could barely hear him over distance and the sounds of a train stopping and the cars clacking together like big metal dominoes. He started saying something else, but Len had a lot of trouble making any of it out.

"I don' need no lawsuit when you young buggers get yer legs run over by a car!" Willie said. He continued to shout things, and it was cool to hear the reverberations as his voice bounced off the walls around them, then becoming fainter as he stopped shouting directly at them, and so the sound waves had to bounce off of the huge corrugated walls and railcars before it eventually, nonsensically, reached them. At some point, they figured, those shouts weren't at them, but maybe at the crew, and perhaps even weren't enough about Len and Claire anymore. They wound their way deeper among the herd of iron pill bugs.

The pickings were marginally better than Len thought. As the hours wore on without much yield, Len tried not to be discouraged. There hadn't been any sign of Jodie all day – something which Claire greatly appreciated, but Len couldn't help but find suspicious.

In the early afternoon they were halfway up the yard, on Willie's side, with numerous cars in between them and the yardmaster. The clunk of hitches and the squeals of brakes continued. They were taking a short break, walking between the cars and the wall.

"Pretty exciting so far," Claire said.

Len kicked a rock and scoffed. "Oh, just edge-of-my-seat stuff," he said. "They must have cleaned the tracks."

"That would make sense, I suppose," Claire said. "I mean, I know a lot of the stuff we've found wouldn't impede on the cars themselves moving, but if I'm one of those guys out there walking around and making sure not to get caught by one, I don't want to even worry about tripping up on something randomly in the yard."

Len grumbled.

"We can't blame the yardkeeper," Claire said. "He just doesn't want people getting hurt. Besides, maybe he got as bored as we are one day and occupied himself with cleanup."

"Doesn't help us now," Len said. "I just hope anything he tossed wouldn't have been useful to me – I wonder if we can find wherever he dumped it?"

Claire perked up and tore her eyes away. "Now there's an idea. But where would it be?"

"Hm," Len said. He stopped pacing to think. "I've been here enough to keep a map of the yard in my head and track myself in it. There's no room anywhere for a dumpster…" He swung on his heels and pointed at, but really through, the wall. "There might be one waterside, or," and he swung another ninety degrees toward the rise and office a few hundred feet down the wall, "Willie might have something in there that can clue us in on it."

Claire looked at each mention as Len thought aloud. "Why would Willie have a map of his own railyard?" she asked. "Surely he's been here long enough he knows it like the back of his hand."

Len stared off toward the office and shrugged. "Maybe there's a fire escape plan or some law makes him keep a map of it in there."

Claire looked that way then, too. "Huh," she said. "I hadn't thought of that."

So they tried it. Making sure to hide as best they could where neither Willie nor his crew could see them, they kept watch for an hour or two and waited for the old, boney man of many years and white hair to leave the office. Once they realized it was going to take a while, they allowed themselves some rest.

About an hour into their stake-out, Claire turned to Len out of the blue. "While we're waiting… tell me another story about before we met."

Len ducked his head back behind the railcar and sized her, and her question, up. After gumming his lip, he left the corner and sat next to Claire. "Switch me," he said, and she went to peer around the corner in his stead.

From the ground, as they waited, Len recanted the story of the week when he ran away.

Dianne was on the couch a couple of rooms over, tunnel-visioned and lost to her soap opera. Len waited at the landing above the basement stairs, his hand fully engulfing the fragile doorknob on the side door. That doorway led to their driveway, just beyond the gate to their garage and backyard. It was a simple a plan as any: leap the fence, listen for which way Jodie went, and run like hell in the total opposite direction.

That wasn't going to be enough, though. He knew that. Merely fourteen years old, he knew just running wasn't going to be enough – because he'd tried that already.

His thoughts flickered to Dianne and her latest in a long series of black eyes. A frog leapt into his throat and choked him, but he heaved it away and brought himself back to the door.

Meanwhile, the hum of gas burning in Jodie's idling engine wouldn't stop. It taunted him by, every dozen million years or so, slipping into a lower note. Maybe the dinosaurs wouldn't be completely extinct by the time the RPMs fell. Len didn't count on it.

Len stood in the darkness by the door, and began to worry that the beating of his heart, generating a pulse in his wrist, would soon cause the doorknob to vibrate and cause the entire door to rattle. That couldn't happen, Len thought, for then he would be caught, and punished. So he calmed himself, but his pulse pounded in his temples – and for a time lasting approximately the lifetime of a Hellenic god, he listened through it for his opportunity.

The car kept running, keeping still.

All the while, he forced himself to keep an ear in Dianne's direction. He couldn't let her hear him leave. The timing for his escape would have to be during a commercial break – but in that, too, rested his destiny. It wrung his stomach to admit it was entirely out of his hands.

If the break came too soon, and Jodie still hadn't taken off, then Len risked the click of the locks giving him away. He knew the first commercial of every break to be substantially louder than the dramatic whispering between lover-characters directly before it. If the break came too late, however, Len would be halfway down the driveway when Jodie pulled back in, and then there would be hell to pay.

"No – worse," Len almost said, but caught himself just in time. He hammered his jaw shut, nearly chomping his tongue in half as though with scissors. His teeth slammed together instead, and his breath held itself instantaneously.

He peered into the kitchen and tried to see over the counter as barely as he could from the shadow, to see if Dianne had heard the sound of bone on bone. Releasing his breath, for she hadn't flinched, he tried to calm himself down. 'Why does everything sound like the sun exploding when you're trying not to let your parents hear?' he wondered.

Suddenly he heard the rubber peeling off the pavement as the car pulled away. It took everything in him not to leap through the door, splintering it into twenty thousand pieces while he made a break for it right then and there.

But he held himself there. He not only stood there, he pressed his feet into the ground as hard as he could, desperately rooting himself to the spot. He couldn't move. Not yet. Not if he wanted to be free.

Then the car stopped, and Len's heart with it.

Controlling himself so as not to slam his head up against the wood, Len ever so gently pressed his ear to the door (and yet still not gently enough for his liking as he felt he could practically hear every, single, tiny hair fold over against the surface). What was going on out there?

Out on the street, another car passed by on the road. Then Jodie's back tires dropped off the curb, and then the front. Len heard her shift into drive, straighten out the wheels, and feed the engine gas. He could make out and count every small combustion

113

as she got up to speed. To his dying day, he remembered one hundred twenty-five.

Jodie was gone. For a little while. Len couldn't move yet, though. He waited even more. The sound of Jodie's engine became one with the background, forcing Len to the edge of panic. He thought he was going to have a heart attack.

Although nobody saw, he flushed white when an industrial aquarium of sound shattered, flooding the living room like a tsunami, flushing the uneasy quiet into nothingness.

It was Len's opportunity.

He moved, because he had to make it count.

And yet still, he took the full thirty seconds to turn the knob and make not a sound. The jailbreak was on.

For several minutes after that, the memory was largely a blur. Len remembered setting the screen door neatly back closed so it wouldn't clack and rebound and give him away. He remembered clearing the fence with one hand even though his running start was all of a pace and a half. He didn't remember turning from the driveway onto the sidewalk, though. Maybe he didn't do it that clean, and really sprinted across the neighbor's lawn. If he did, he didn't remember any of his neighbors raising hell over it, even if they saw him do it. So he ran for a while. He covered several blocks, passing house after house and understanding, not long into his flight, that no doubt Jodie had returned. How long would it be before she took attendance? How long did it take before she noticed Len wasn't there? How long would it be before she asked Dianne if she knew? How long before she accused Dianne of helping him escape? How long before she tried to beat the answer out of Dianne? How long before she beat Dianne for not knowing? How long before she beat Dianne for letting it happen?

Len didn't know. He tried not to think about it. He failed, and ran instead. That night, he acquired green hair dye for the first time.

Walking into a one-stop-shopping center whose name he couldn't recall, he assumed Jodie would put out a description for him before long, and so he would need to be prepared for that. He didn't want to be reeled back in like a yo-yo, so he located the vanity section of the store as quickly as he could. He got in and got out.

And he made himself disappear again. Part of him deeply wished that Jodie had been given the surveillance tapes from that store that evening, for Len hadn't been stupid enough not to put his hood up and try to conceal from the cameras what he had. Although he had the money to pay for it, he couldn't afford for there to be a sales record in the computer coinciding with the camera footage. That would be too easy for Jodie.

Len stole. For once, things were easy for him. Nobody came after him. The hair dye didn't set any alarms off. The world was none the wiser. A cashier or two was suspicious, but they had bigger problems, just like Len.

The occasional wispy cloud sat in the orange, gloaming sky when Len slipped behind the fence of the Philadelphian railyard about two hours later. He still had the hair dye, though had dumped the box to be rid of bulk. It sat, by that time, in his front pocket, which always reminded him of a queer kangaroo pouch. He wasn't sure why it always reminded him of that whenever he thought of a hoodie like that, but he did. It entertained Claire briefly to hear.

The yardmaster was actually a fairly good-looking woman named Erin, whom Len approximated at no more than twice his age. She was nice enough and, dressed in nomex coveralls, she looked the part for him to ask about helping out on the yard in exchange for some means of making distance. Erin had, of course, explained that the job was too dangerous for her to hire him before he was 18, and asked where his parents were. She'd gone "all shifty-eyed" when Len insisted it didn't matter and he didn't want to talk about it. That forced her to think about calling the police to let them know he was there, and that in turn forced Len to vanish.

The time he spent hiding in the cattails, just a couple stones' throws from Erin's office, wasn't anything like the time waiting at the side door. He patted down some cattails in a miniature crop circle while he waited, and didn't feel at all frustrated when, just as he'd gotten his nest exactly how he wanted it, his opportunity began its departure.

A train was on its way out, with the engine on the back. Erin couldn't see Len's hiding place from her office, and after studying the angle of a watchtower and control building in the yard, Len supposed that by the time he was sprinting gung-ho in the engine's wake, there wouldn't be anything she could do about it even if she *was* paying attention.

He took off like a bat out of hell. Again, God blessed him with an ease of path; he ran as fast as he could, then reached out and grabbed the ladder. His feet barely kept up, barely making contact with the rail ties before jolting back again. He got his other hand on the ladder too, and wasted no time in getting his feet off the fleeting ground.

Philadelphia flew by for a while, and then it all stood before him. Then it started to look smaller, and smaller, and smaller, until it was a big bunch of lights in the night. Fields took over on both sides, and Len had all of Pennsylvania to himself.

He wasn't to be satisfied. The engineer made a couple of stops for food and whatnot, and Len was sure to capitalize in parallel. A few days later, even Pennsylvania fell away. Len held onto that ladder for hours and hours and, in hindsight, he was surprised he hadn't gotten tired.

Forests whizzed by. The train went around curves, where Len could no longer look back and see the line of rail extend into infinity. He only ever got nervous when it went over water. He didn't count the days; he was too busy hanging on, too busy not being in Pennsylvania.

Eventually, Len's gut told him it was time to disembark. The engineer finally found him not long thereafter. Although that man gave no warning and immediately called for someone to pick up Len and take him home, Len had had much more time to find an out. By the time the police arrived, not knowing exactly who Len was except a young stowaway, he was nowhere to be found.

The rest, he told Claire, was about as simple as he'd said before. He made acquaintance with Bobby, built the treehouse, and began his life in Ohio.

"And I never looked back," Len said.

Claire nodded contently, and glanced around the side of the railcar again. "Hey," he said, "hey, wait! It looks like Willie's coming out for something."

Len got to his feet. "Which way is he going?"

"I can't tell yet. Just get ready."

It wasn't long before Willie was across the way from his office and thoroughly distracted. Len and Claire skulked up the ramp and pretty soon, Claire found herself closing the door behind both of them.

For as filthy as the office was with coffee spills, orange and black crud around the windows, papers strewn about, and in general looking like an abandoned, post-apocalyptic outpost, it smelled fine. There was even some quiet elevator music playing, and air conditioning. Len and Claire exchanged looks and shrugged. As soon as they looked about the room in search of some clue for the fabled fire escape plan, they found it. It was on the wall right in front of them.

"Looks like we can just head through there," Len said. There was a single door at the back of the rectangular space, which Len knew immediately was on the outer side of the yard wall. Only about half the office, he realized, was actually inside the yard and he'd never been between the yard and the river to notice.

Claire was already at the back door. "It's locked," she said.

"Then we'll go around," Len said. "We need to hurry; Willie's on his way back."

"Same side or different?"

"From the other way, entrance-side. We'll have to go back the way we came and take the long way around to avoid him."

Claire checked the map while Len made for the door through which they'd entered. "This says the dumpster is closer to the way we came in," he said.

"I'm glad you could find it," Len said, who'd felt too rushed to pin it down on the diagram. "Come on, let's go."

They slipped out with a moment to spare, and Willie went back to his office as if nothing had happened. The kids went back to their hiding place, as before, but had to move farther toward the back, for the railcar was elsewhere by the time they returned. They ventured a little out into the open to see where the crew was and where they were looking, so they could see which cars were likely moving next. One train, they saw, was headed right down the gut of the horde and out of the railyard altogether. As it snaked along, as happy as a crab to be complete, Len figured to move across the halfway point of the railyard – as the herd in the back looked about the same theme by then – and then walk along the wall back to their entrance, and out.

Halfway across the field, the train on its way out of the yard finally cleared their path.

"Hello," said Jodie. Like a bird, Len's head snapped her way. Whatever he'd been looking at before, he forgot. She'd been waiting on the other side of that train. Now, she stared straight at the two of them. Hardly the width of two rail tracks separated them. Then it was hardly one.

Len didn't have to waste time telling Claire to run. They took off toward the wrong end of the railyard, but Claire didn't make it far without turning around.

"Get off!" Len said, for Jodie had him by the collar. Before she could hold him tighter, as she came down from her run and stood, pulling him in where she could whisper something mad into his ear, he knew he had to do something.

He threw an elbow. It knicked the inside of hers, the arm holding him. The shock was enough to surprise her and release her grip, but she barely stumbled. While she was off balance, though, and before she could come after him and grab him by the hair, before she could run up alongside him and throw him into a train's wheels, Len did the only thing he could think or do in that instant to slow her down: he shoved her. He shoved her with both hands, not caring what he hit, not caring if he shoved her by the breasts, not caring when she tripped over the tracks where the complete train had been but half a moment earlier. He didn't care if she fell and broke her ankle. He didn't care about anything, just as long as his hands landed on something, anything at all, and exerted force on her to make her be farther away from *him*.

She didn't fall; her feet backpedaled as she stumbled back, but her heels did not catch on the rails around their feet. She and Len looked at each other, neither really believing what had just happened. Len turned and sprinted away alongside the complete train.

Len and Claire fled.

The game began on a board of shifting pieces. Alleyways abounded, parallel to one another except where tracks curved into each other, where cars would hop lines. The exit, the closer choke point to Buckeye Party & Lotto, was perhaps within Len and Claire's reach. Jodie, however, was taller than either, and in good shape. She ran after them and, before long, they would have to abandon their straight line. For the moment, at least, they were fine. For the evaporating moment.

Then Len noticed a junction ahead that connected the two tracks on either side of them. Though unoccupied at the moment, there was an otiose car pointed at it, and he could not see the crew to pass judgment whether to go for it or not. If he and Claire tried for it and it closed on them, they would be cornered. At the risk of tripping on junk or debris, Len scanned about for an alternative.

He found one: there were ladders on the sides of some of the beasts. Len tapped Claire on the shoulder mid-sprint and pointed. Claire nodded, then looked back, and ran even harder. It left Len a couple feet behind, who then also noticed Jodie right on their heels.

Before they knew it, their choice was upon them: the car ahead did in fact begin to shift over the curved bridge-section between tracks. They had to call it. Either they bounded for the end of the forming dead-end alley and hoped to squeeze through in time, or they vaulted onto the ladder as high as they could and tried to scramble up before Jodie could claw them by the ankle and drag them to a black fate.

Claire chose. She reached for the ladder first, but the instant she was on and held out a hand for Len, the car convulsed, breaking inertia and crawling toward the dead end. A hair's breadth behind him, Jodie pounced.

It was the break they needed. Len caught Claire's hand and was able to wriggle onto the ladder with her, tight squeeze as it was. Jodie fell on her face in the dirt, and her arm nearly landed in the path of the railcar's wheels. As she lifted her face and snarled, she saw the kids dangling in midair next to the car, floating away.

The two of them wasted no time in mounting the top of the car.

The car lurched again just as they gained their feet. They stumbled, nearly falling a story to each a broken leg, but they held. While they regained their balance on the still train – for it had linked hitch with the car that had formed the cap to the alley below – they looked back and were disheartened to see Jodie checking them from halfway up the ladder.

A new act in the game began. Len and Claire sprinted down the top of the train. Claire's bow clunked on her back with each stride. Len's shirt billowed out behind him. And barely a car's length behind them ran Jodie.

The leap between cars didn't seem like much. Momentum carried them from one to another. The hollow metal pounding that greeted each landing filled Len's ears. If it filled Willie's or his crew's, he didn't know. He hadn't the time to concern himself with them. He didn't have time to concern himself with anything except getting away from Jodie.

Len crashed headlong into a standstill Claire, sending both over the edge of the train's end. They landed, rolling over each other for dear life, in an eruption of dust and gravel that skittered from the blast site. When they regained their feet, Jodie stood where they'd just been, at the top of the last railcar. Len and

Claire were in a small clearing, surrounded by railcar links. The only gaps were the two ruts between three sets of tracks, and the empty bit of track where their link had run out. They were glad to have a way out, for Jodie was already on her way down.

Without bothering to exchange looks, Len and Claire made for the path on their left, back alongside the railcar chain toward the office's end of the yard. Jodie saw them coming closer and closer, making ready to skirt by her, but she would be damned if they were to give her such a small girth and she wasn't to complete the simple task of grounding her misbehaved child.

Poising on the ladder, the dyke leapt to them, soaring over their heads. Len and Claire ducked mid-sprint, never missing a beat.

The railcar on their left *ponged!* as Jodie flew into it, a full three feet from the ground, and rebounded into the dirt. They did not bother to glance back at the half-conscious shape left in the black and grey rocks and dust. They pulled a U-turn at the first opportunity, and ran on the far side of the cars from Jodie, back in the direction of the party store exit.

Jodie slowly got to her feet to the sound of their approaching footsteps, which quickly passed her on the other side of the car she'd nailed. Determined to walk it off, she shifted her jaw, rolled her neck (not without a dozen repugnant popping noises), and looked about for the nearest railcar ladder.

Len and Claire thought themselves nearly in the clear when a woman's running shadow presided over their own. They looked up and saw Jodie keeping pace atop the cars. Just as she ran abreast, an end to the chain forced her to stop and dismount.

They redoubled their efforts to run as hard and as fast as they could. Len himself commanded the individual strides of his legs. Up, and down, and out, and drawing it out, and putting all his might into stomping the ground so he could go farther.

Just then, they skidded to a stop. The train on its way out of the yard was blocking their path. At that moment, Len realized how tightly packed the exit was. Although the outbound train was the only one moving, every other track was occupied by at

121

least one car, and here they were packed so closely together that he and Claire would not be able to squeeze between. The field shifted around them, and the game did, too. Len dreaded to turn and check where Jodie was.

"End of the line, Leonard sweetie," Jodie said from what sounded like the top of a railcar. He turned and, to the gratitude of his racing heart, she still stood atop the end of the chain. "It's time to come home."

"And become another prescription-life bastard like all the other 'promising young men' my age? Screw you!"

"Len," Claire said, "do you have a plan or something? You know as well as I do that I can pull my bow on her all we like, but she's not afraid of the damn thing. We need to get out of here. Now!"

"I know, I know! Give me a minute!" Len said.

"We don't have a minute, Len!"

"Get out an arrow."

"What? That didn't work last time and –"

"Get out an arrow," Len said, and though Claire shook her head, she reached over her shoulder and retrieved one. She reached also for her bow, but Len waved her down. "No," he said, watching Jodie climb down to their level. "Get another one, and give it to me."

Jodie began walking casually over to them, foot by foot.

"Follow my lead," Len whispered, strafing along the moving train, out of the corner.

"Where do you think you're going?" Jodie asked as loudly as she could, perhaps as though she meant to entertain the Emperor and the Coliseum. Len and Claire held out the arrows like West Side switchblades, and Jodie laughed. She was too close for them to duck and run away; she had them cornered.

They moved farther along, but she walked closer. Len and Claire played her game of checkers. If they went left, she could move to her right and grab them. If they went right, she could move to her left and grab them, too. She was close enough then.

"NOW!" Len said. Claire made a break for it behind him. Jodie looked entertained, and moved to within arm's length of Len.

When she went to actually grab him, one of his feet was flat facing her. Using the side of his shoe, he kicked up an entire loose patch of gravel. Half of it hit her smack in the face and chest. Some dirt got in her eyes, but the surprise overall was enough that when she shook it off, Len had a two second head start. Shrieking, Jodie continued after him.

The only way out that didn't invite Jodie right back to the treehouse was to continue with the exit to the railyard. To do that, Len knew, he and Claire absolutely had to find a way atop the outbound train. Lost in the maze of shifting railcars and pursuant mothers, Len wasn't sure how they were going to do it, but a very long minute later, he did.

As the game wore on, with cars shifting and disconnecting and clashing together, Len and Claire found their ladder on the far end of the moving train, which at that point was only about a quarter of the way remaining in the yard. Wasting no time, they hopped up the ladder, careful not to get caught on the train's underbelly, and ran as low to the roof as they could. If they could avoid letting Jodie see them atop the getaway car, it was worth more than Len could rightly say. After all, he thought at least once before it was over, this was about Claire, Becky, and even Subhail, too.

As they rode the train, it neared the exit of the yard. The herd of cars remained scrambled and scattered behind them. They'd finally gotten a chance to take a breath.

Until they looked down the train again.

Jodie was there yet again, closing the gap. They were trapped. Len and Claire sprang to their feet, forsaking their thought to rest and ride out. Len's mother had found them, and now it was all but game over.

"Len!" Claire said, "What are we going to do?"

Len looked all about. The drop was too far to jump. The train had gained speed and now neither could they rush back to the end behind them and climb back down the ladder. The speed and tracks would twist their ankles or break their legs all the same.

In the closing instants before Jodie would have them, Claire did the only thing she could do and grabbed several arrows and wielded them as before, with the heads forward ready for stabbing. Len realized, though, that Jodie may have been on the train with them, but she was outside the boundary of the wall. No sooner did the thought brush against his brain that his eyes darted left. The wall was low enough, or the train high enough – what did it matter? – that if he and Claire had the luck to have the time to take the chance, they could take a leap of faith from the train and over the wall.

"We'll jump," Len told Claire, who looked at him like he was nuts. "We'll jump," Len said so only Claire could hear, "and we'll swim."

The sense came over Claire then. "Are you sure it's close enough on that side?"

"Yes," Len lied. "We'll dive over the wall and into the water, and disappear into the river."

They stood. Jodie waited a few car lengths away, laughing. At last, victory was hers! Her family would be complete again, and her happiness might finally resume. She clapped. Meanwhile, Len and Claire edged to the side of the train and waited, in a half-crouch, for their one chance to lose her.

Len's memory couldn't tell him for sure just how far the river actually was on the far side of the wall. He knew there was a river there, sure, but the width of the bank? In spite of himself, he took a deep breath and readied himself beside Claire.

As the ground whizzed by in a blur, and the wind licked through his hair, Len remained glad that his mother watched them from a distance.

'Here we go,' he thought. 'Here we go'.

Chapter Fifteen

Len's heart raced as fast as the ground flew by in the background. His pulse matched each blob of color as its details escaped him, and it very nearly matched the day when he last ran away from Jodie.

Crouching against the side of the railcar, he and Claire took one last look at each other. Len glanced Jodie's way, who he saw now scrunching her face. All too late, she realized they had a plan after all. Len took one last breath, and then the wall was close enough, for the briefest moment, to go for it.

For a clean minute, it seemed, Len hung weightless in the air above the rusty, wavy steel wall. The train chugged along somewhere vaguely behind him as he cleared empty space. And then, clothes billowing, arms held high, he was falling.

And he looked down, and the river was not below him.

He had not the time to exchange looks with Claire. From at least a ten-foot jump, the two crash-landed on the warbling, aluminum roof of the rail yard's exterior dumpster barn. They had, at least, the luck to land on a portion of the weak sheet that was supported underneath; else they surely would have fallen straight through, a full fifteen further feet to the ground, with only the metal and boot-stomped dirt to cushion their landing.

Len and Claire rolled amid the obnoxious *wop-wop-wop* of the roof as it bent and warped under their weight and sprung halfway back to shape as they moved on. Bearing the pain of impact, and the further, sudden weightlessness of a body-length freefall, they rolled right off the edge of the roof and hit the ground in a heap.

For the first several breaths, neither of them could move. As they lay there, stunned from shocks to their backs, they both tried rolling onto one side and propping themselves up. Slowly, and amidst no shortage of groans and retries, they twisted themselves into seated positions.

Len was on his knees, folded over on himself when he lifted his face to Claire. "Are you okay?" he asked.

Claire sat in a similar, uncomfortable position. "I think so," she said. "You?"

Len just nodded and held his sides. He looked to his left and saw the riverbank another ten feet off. "Damn it," he said.

Claire looked the same way. "Don't worry about it," she told Len, "we had to try. She was going to get us otherwise."

"We need to keep moving," Len said, shifting one leg, then the other, and making a careful attempt to stand. "She'll find a way down before too long. You need to get out of here."

"Me?" Claire said. "Len, I can't leave without you."

"It's me she's after!" Len said as Claire regained her feet. "This isn't about you, or us, it's about me and her. You go on home, Claire. I think I can lose her."

"Can you even walk?" she asked.

Although he winced and nursed the small of his back every inch of the way, Len managed to take a couple of baby steps and nodded. Claire grimaced.

"To hell with this," she said, "I'm getting my dad's gun."

"No!" Len said, holding out a hand as if to stop his friend. "No, we don't need that. I'll lure her away. You just go on home, Claire."

While Len stood there, bent over and waiting for the pain to recede, Claire looked at him a long time. The two of them paced circles in the dirt, trying to walk it off. The last of the train cleared the yard.

"I'll be fine," Len said. Claire left without another word. She followed the riverbank, outside the wall back to the other side of the yard, and from there made her way back home across the field.

Meanwhile, Len looked up the hill. He eyed the bridge, and meant to glance at the retreating train when he locked eyes with Jodie. She was still coming. She may have been atop a train that rolled into the distance, but she was still coming. Len gathered himself, holding his back and walking off a mild limp, and made up toward the bridge again. Every step stung, making him pant and frown the whole way.

After forever, he stood on one side of the bridge. He dared look down the hill. Jodie was hiking after him. He needed to move, and so crossed the bridge and once again found himself in the side parking lot of Buckeye Party & Lotto. By then, in a combination of natural recovery, adrenaline-induced instinct, and will, Len rounded the corner ('on the sidewalk even, like a good force-conformist bastard') and walked in like a normal human being.

"Shit," Len said when the cashier reflexively greeted the chime of the door. They locked eyes too, but before Len got too caught up in the cashier calling the cops, he glanced back. Jodie was strolling past the window. Whether she still had sight on him, he wasn't sure, but he wasn't about to wait in place and find out.

He faced forward and made his feet march on. The cashier finished up his transaction and, much to Len's dissatisfaction, that wound up being about one second after Jodie came in through the door.

"Hey you!" Len heard called halfway across the store. He ducked down so the kid wouldn't see his hair, but that was no use. "I see you over there," the cashier said. "You! With the green hair!"

"*Shit…*" Len said, and did the only thing he could do. He moved. Nearly in a run and crouched and hurt, he ducked into another aisle.

"Where?" he heard Jodie ask.

"Oh, you bitch. Be that good Samaritan," Len said under his breath.

He could practically see the cashier snap to the sound of her voice. "Oh," he said, "Hello. He's, uh, over there somewhere in the third aisle from you, looks like. Can you see him?"

"No," Jodie said, walking, "but let me look…

"Now, what did he do to you?" she asked the cashier. Len bit his tongue in the next aisle over from her, and made sure to duck into another.

"Stole from me – the little shit," the cashier said, but interrupted himself. "There he is!" he said. "I see him in the mirror! He just darted into the aisle two away from you."

"Okay," Jodie said, and moved his way. "Leonard… Leonard honey, come on out. Give this nice man his things back."

Len didn't dare say anything. He was glad, though, that she was stupid enough to keep talking. Using the sound of her voice to keep track, he made sure to sneak past her back into the aisle he'd just been in, and to do it from the opposite end.

He envisioned in his mind Jodie popping her head into that aisle with the same sick, fake smile that she fed Claire. Len pressed himself against the tip between aisles, trying not to squish the flimsy plastic packaging that would give him away and mouthing a curse at the rounded mirror on the ceiling.

Out of the corner of his eye, he saw the cashier lean over the counter. He was trapped.

"There he is!"

"Where?"

"Hiding right at the end there," the cashier said, but by then Len was on the move. "Stop him! He's going to steal another map from me!"

"I paid for it what I could, you unconsolated bastard!" Len said. He darted into the women's bathroom, for it was the one directly in front of him, and flipped the lock despite his sweaty, pulse-shaken hand. No sooner did he afford himself half a second's rest that the door shook on its hinges.

"Come out of there, Honey!" Jodie said, and slammed her whole weight against the door again. Len looked about in the tiny bathroom for something to use, but he had to settle for nothing. His only comfort was that an air fresher plug-in was doing its job.

"Hey, hey, hey!" he heard the cashier say outside. "Don't break the door! Damn."

"Oh," Jodie said. "Oh, I'm sorry," and Len heard the voice grow just a touch dimmer as she stepped away from the door and resumed politeness. He dared to press his ear against the door and listened as hard as his ears would let him.

"What are we going to do?" Jodie asked the cashier. "Do you have a key you could use?"

"Gragh! We used to," the cashier said, "but some of my coworkers were abusing it and so my manager keeps the only ones."

"Is your manager here?"

"Not today."

"Well can you call him?"

"Maybe. I have his number written down here somewhere." Len heard footsteps going farther away and knew the cashier was headed back to the counter. "He won't like the idea of swinging by here on his day off, but I think it'll be worth it once he sees why."

"Leonard, honey, won't you please come out now?" Jodie said into the other side of the door.

Len stood up straight and looked into the wooden blankness. "Choke on the dirt from your own grave," he said with such fierce smoothness that Jodie flinched. "Call the cops if you want!" he said, hoping the cashier could hear, "but I'm not going to be the one opening that door! If you think I'm going to go quietly, you're going to have one torn-apart bathroom by the end of the night!"

Then Len sat down, and although it felt quite strange to be wearing his jeans over his butt and not pulled down as he sat atop the throne, he couldn't smile over it. He eyed the door for a long time, in silence, not knowing what to do.

Chapter Sixteen

"You've got to be kidding me. This has got to be the absolute stupidest thing you've ever thought of."

"I don't care," Leonard said, "it's where we're going."

Wallace sprang forward in the passenger seat. "There is, literally, no point in this. Why do you insist?"

Leonard kept his eyes on the road, but he offered the courtesy of a shrug. "Because it's the right thing to do," he said. "Besides, we're almost there. It won't take long. We'll be back to the office in no time."

Wallace grumbled something, crossed his arms, and threw himself back into the seat. "Ow!" he said.

"The doctor told you to be careful with that thing," Leonard said as his cohort pawed at his neck brace.

Their little shuttle-shaped Honda came upon the site of Len's treehouse and pulled over, stopping fifty feet well short on its one side. Traffic hummed on their left as they walked up.

"Len?" Leonard called. "Len, buddy, are you there?"

The treehouse was still and silent.

"Well, that's it. Let's go," Wallace said. He swung his crutch around.

"Hold on," Leonard said, still peering up into the empty window holes. "I'm sure if we try to climb up he'll acknowledge our presence."

"Hmph," Wallace said, rooting himself to the spot. "You go on ahead, if you're so eager for another thrashing."

Leonard shot him a look and went up the first couple of rungs anyway. When nothing continued to happen, he stopped. He stared up into the treehouse, wondering why there was no shout of warning, no chunk of concrete coming at his head, no battle-raged teenager leaping out like a jungle monkey ready to bash heads. He stood here, looking up like a turkey in the rain.

"Satisfied?" Wallace said from the other side of the tree. "Come on, let's go. Oh, hold on, wait a minute."

Both of them turned at the sound of another person walking. Claire noticed the two of them as she came out from under the overpass. They all watched each other as she trudged into the grass and came within earshot and then within talking distance.

"What are you two doing here?" she asked. She had her bow out, but no arrow. Leonard and Wallace hadn't budged, which was a good sign.

"We were," Leonard began, but turned to Wallace for reassurance. "We were wondering where your friend Len is," he said.

Claire squinted at him. "Why? Don't you remember what happened the last time you bothered him?"

A look of understanding flushed Leonard's face as he nodded. "Yes, yes," he said, "that's actually why we're here. You see, in the wake of everything that went on, and all the injuries and damages to the car we sustained, we... well, we realize that it's really not worth all the trouble and to make sure Len wasn't looking over his shoulder for us the rest of his life, we thought we'd let him know that we've petitioned our office into allowing us to relinquish the case."

There came a pause as Claire considered that and eyed Leonard, with Wallace over his shoulder.

"Why are you calling him Len now?" she asked.

The question surprised Leonard, who glanced to Wallace for an answer. Wallace, however, was too far away to even hear the conversation. "I... just thought that is what he preferred? Isn't it?"

"It is," Claire said. "It's just strange that you so suddenly care. Unless he knocked some sense into the two of you when last you met?" She saw Leonard's bandaged hand automatically go to the patch of gauze on the side of his head. "I'll tell you what. I'll let Len know that."

"I'd really rather tell him in perso –"

"I'll let Len know that."

Leonard stared at her. "I... understand," he said with a bow. "We'll just be going now."

Claire stashed her bow. "Goodbye," she said.

"Thank you," Leonard said. "Goodbye." He turned and moved to point Wallace back to the car. Wallace, however, was preoccupied and staring down the road. It stopped Leonard in his tracks, too.

In fact, all three of them watched a pack of police cruisers in the distance. At first they were quiet, distant flashes of red and blue, but within a minute they were flying by – one, and two, then five, eight – as they wove in and out of the traffic that barely had time to register their presence before getting out of the way. Their sirens screamed and honked all the while.

Leonard and Claire both turned to each other, faces bunched up in basic questions, but couldn't think of anything to say or ask. Leonard looked down the road and watched as the cops rolled into the distance. Within another minute, they could not be heard over traffic. Their lights flashed over other cars, but that was it.

Chapter Seventeen

An hour of judgment loomed over Len as he sat, jailbird, in a claustrophobic bathroom and twiddled his thumbs. He would sooner breathe every last scrap of air in that tiny space than come out before the cashier's manager unlocked it from the outside or Jodie broke it from its very hinges. He heard them talking outside, though, and knew nothing good was about to happen.

"So that's your son in there?" the cashier asked.

"Yes," Jodie said. "I'm so glad that I finally found him, but I do wish he'd come out from there."

"Don't worry," said the cashier, "we'll flush him out." There came a pause before he continued. "My thing is, though, where have you been while he's been running amok? Did he run away from home or something?"

"I'm afraid so," Jodie said. "Heaven knows why, I just came home one day and he was gone!"

"Don't buy it," Len shouted through the door. "She's full of stories and not one of them is true!"

"Oh, please!" the cashier said. "Who am I gonna believe, Kid – the guy who keeps coming and stealing from me or the grown-ass adult trying to leash him and take him home?"

"Your funeral," Len said, back at a volume where only he could hear.

"Is your manager on the way, then?" Jodie asked. 'My God,' Len thought, 'they're just carrying on like I'm not even here!'

"Yeah, he said he's on his way," the cashier said. "Should be here in about twenty minutes or so. In the meantime…"

About that time, Len heard the rising sound of approaching sirens. He cursed again as he heard a jumble of them grow deafeningly loud, even through the door, and come no closer. No doubt, Len knew, they were in the parking lot. There sounded to be more than one of them, but he couldn't sort out the noise to make any sort of guess at the number. Outside, the doorbell chimed a couple of times, too far apart for people not to be holding the door for each other, and he heard the cashier greet police as they flooded in.

Someone knocked at the door. "Hello?" a man said. "My name is Officer Clasby. Young Man, are you in there?"

"Occupied," Len said.

"We need to talk to you," Clasby said. "Can you come out for us please?"

"Not if my mother's standing right there," Len said.

On the other side of the door, Clasby pulled his head from the door and gazed around at the others. Jodie returned his perplexed look, and then he knocked again. "Young Man, I don't have time to be playing games with you right now. This isn't funny; this is serious stuff."

"Don't talk to me like I'm eight you condescending bastard," Len said, and the relative calmness of the statement sent Clasby aback.

"Er – that's fine then," Clasby said. "Tell you what. I'll give you to the count of three, then. If you don't open up the door by the time I get to three, I'm not going to have much choice but to come in there anyway."

"I'll come out," Len said, "but first, I need you to help me."

"All right, what can I do?" Clasby asked.

"The woman standing beside you, her name is Jodie, correct?" Len said through the door.

Clasby turned to Jodie, who nodded. "That's right," he said.

"All right," Len said. "What I need you to do is very simple. Like I said, I'll come out, but you'll need to make her go away, first."

"Leonard, stop being so unreasonable!"

"I think we can do that, Young Man," Clasby said, and motioned for his partner to escort Jodie away from the bathroom.

"That's not what I mean," Len said, correctly predicting their misunderstanding. "I meant I need you to make her go away permanently, where she can't bother me anymore."

Clasby's face scrunched. "I'm not sure I have the power to do that, exactly. That's more up to the courts."

"No, no, you still aren't getting what I'm saying."

Clasby sighed. "Then how do you mean? I can make her wait on the side of the building until you're ready to talk this out with her, if that's what you need."

"Would you listen for a second, you misled bastard? I promise that I'll come out with my hands up and all that, all I need is for you to stand her up out there, pull out your gun and shoot her in the face."

"Leonard!"

"I can't do that, Young Man. Now please step away from the door. You've got until three."

That was fine. Len could tell when it was time to try something else. "Hey Cashier Guy!" he shouted, not knowing whether the cashier actually heard. "Are you going to berate the cops too when they shatter your door? So I took a map – I paid for it, at least in part! I'm not tearing your precious little gas station apart from the inside out!"

"One," Clasby said.

"So this is it, then," Len said to himself. "All the time and energy I invested, three years of being okay… and this is how it ends."

"Two!"

"I gave it a good run. There's that, at least," he said. "I had to try."

Len began to cry. He wondered how fate could let it happen, how life could let him get so far and do so well for so long, if only in the end he would be thrown right back into Jodie's arms. Why had he even bothered? But he had the answer: he had to try. And try he did. Three years of freedom had been his reward, but now he had to go back the Pennsylvania. That was that.

'At least Claire was right,' he thought. Before too long, assuming he survived the grand thrashing he would no doubt receive as soon as Jodie locked the front door back home, he would turn 18 and be able to venture into the world on his own.

He could ask the court for a restraining order as a legal adult. He could get a job and save up, buy a car and the gas to move across the country, where in an entire continent of states, cities, and people, it would take Jodie a lifetime to pin him down.

Right before Clasby finished his count, Len thought too of something else. There was a single bright side to Jodie dragging him back to Pennsylvania. He would see Dianne again. And maybe, somewhere deep down, she could see that it was possible to escape Jodie. He had at least shown her that.

Len smiled, a single tear trail on each cheek, when the cops bashed the lock and opened the door. He expected them to rush in and seize him, but they did no such thing. A stern-looking but nice female officer with her blond hair in a bun – red-headed Clasby's partner – just came in and held him by the arm, escorting him back onto the floor. She presented Len to his mother.

"Thank you," Jodie said, the officer returning her smile.

Len and Jodie looked at each other. She refused to drop her act of good mother, giving him a warm smile and rubbing his cheek. She even passed a hand through his hair, noting how badly he could have used a haircut. All the while, he glared and glared and glared.

Clasby approached. "Now, Mrs. Campbell, the fact remains that your son here did commit theft from this location," he said. "We have the video to prove it and if I wanted, I could probably get a search warrant for his treehouse and see the map there."

A couple of wrists presented themselves to the officer. "Then arrest me," Len said.

Clasby glanced at him out of the corner of his eye but otherwise ignored him. "I'm willing to make a deal, though. I read your file and what with this long Amber Alert coming to a happy ending, it'd probably be better if we just compensate the station for the map and the door and call it even."

"I think that sounds fair," Jodie said, pulling Len in close while they spoke. "Just send us a bill and I'll make sure to pay it – anything as long as my baby's safe." She smiled at Clasby, who nodded acknowledgement and moved on. A couple of other cops stood in front of the open bathroom with a notepad, detailing the repairs and other things.

"You're really buying this, aren't you?" Len asked a disappearing Clasby, leaning around Jodie to do so. "Hey! HEY! You bastard, I'm not done talking to you, GET BACK HERE!"

"Stop now, Leonard, you'll make a scene!" Jodie said, holding him by the shoulders.

"*Fuck* you!" he said, wriggling out of her grasp. "Just because everybody else's willing to go along with your bullshit stories doesn't mean I'm going to, too!"

"Come on now," she said, "let's go home."

He beat back her reaching hand. "No! Now get your hands off me and leave me alone!"

"Is there a problem?" a bald-shaven cop with the notepad said.

"Yeah, there's a problem," Len said, pointing at Jodie. "This lady's a monster and has no right to be a parent! My God, can't you get her for child endangerment or something?"

The cop seemed abnormally stoic about the whole thing. He just stood up straight and flipped his notepad shut. "I think you ought to go home with your mother and behave," he said.

Len's shoulders sank as his heart and hopes deflated. "Oh, go... kick rocks," he said. "Unhelpful bastard." He felt Jodie reach around his shoulders and turn him back toward the door. In the doorway, she stopped and grabbed a shoulder in each hand, got down on her haunches and looked right into his eyes. He could see that, with three cop cruisers still on-scene, she had no intention of looking like a bad parent.

"Leonard, I need you listen to me," she said. "It is very important that you come home with me."

Len spit in her eye. She flinched for only a moment and smiled on after wiping her face with one hand. "I don't think you understand why it is I've been trying so hard to find you and bring you back," she said, "but right now I need you to trust me because I love you and just want the best for you. Okay?"

Len leveled his chin, scowling, and mentally karate chopped every letter as it coursed from her lips. "You're the only one that believes that," he said. "Now I'll get in that car with you," he said, "what with the cops being right here to basically force us back together but you should know, that the instant we're clear of them, I don't care how fast we're going. You'd better have a child lock on every door, because otherwise I'll jump right out into traffic if I have to."

Her jaw fell open at that. Searching for words, she gazed off to the side but saw two approaching men that gave her reason to stand up straight.

"Officer James! Officer Humphrey! It's great to see you again!" she said. Len looked over his shoulder and, by that time, sure enough, the two men stood before them.

There was definitely something different about the two of them, and it took but an instant for Len to pinpoint it. While the men still wore their tan overcoats, Leonard had his hands stuffed in his pockets like he had something on his mind, and Wallace was leaning on a crutch. He also had a thick white neck brace, forcing his head into a very uncomfortable looking height, and a brace adorned his ankle. Leonard wasn't as worse for wear, but sported a good-sized bandage on the side of his head, as well as further bandaging around his hand and wrist.

And Len's heart sank further. No one could save him now.

"Hello," Leonard said. "I see you're in good health, Mrs. Campbell."

"Yes," Jodie said, "thank you. Oh, I'm sorry, is this your colleague as well? I don't believe we've met."

The group turned and saw a balding, brown-skinned man walk up. His mustache was entirely similar to Wallace's, and he bore plenty of hair on his forearms and at least on the patch of chest that showed through the top of his polo. His head was oddly egg-shaped, and his dark, slightly deep-set eyes gave him a hard look that he wore nearly all the time. When he spoke, he spoke fast and rolled every R. This, Len knew, was Claire's father.

"Why do you bother this boy?" Subhail asked her. "Can't you see that he only wants to be left alone?" Claire appeared at his side but said nothing. She and Len met eyes and exchanged tiny nods.

"I'm sorry... but, who are you?" asked Jodie.

"Never mind all that," Subhail said. "My daughter says you are making trouble with Spoiled Goods. Why is it you do not leave him in peace?"

Jodie looked to Wallace and Leonard for answers. "Do you two... do you know this gentleman?"

"I'm afraid I don't," Leonard said with the same perplexed look, and turned to Subhail on the far side of Wallace. "Sir, we're conducting government business, do you need something or can I ask you to step back?"

"I will not step back!" Subhail told him. He pointed to Jodie and his entire arm flailed through the air. Had he been much closer, he may likely have clipped her with it. "I hear this woman is making trouble, and I have every right as an American to stand here in best interest of my family's friends as I need to."

Jodie shook it off. "Okay, whatever. Is there something I can do for you gentlemen?" she asked Leonard.

"Actually," Leonard said with a brief exchange of looks with Len that caught the latter by complete surprise, "it's come up that my partner here and I need to speak with Len."

"Whom?"

"Len," Leonard said, placing a hand on Len's shoulder. Wallace, wincing, turned and hobbled back to their car on the other side of the cruisers.

"Oh..." Jodie said, and renewed what was now a very clearly forced smile. Behind Wallace and Leonard, the three cars' worth of cops weren't leaving. "His name is Leonard, but... why do you need to speak with him?"

"Same thing as ever, Mrs. Campbell," Leonard said. "Tax purposes. You know."

She edged a fraction of an inch closer to Len. "I... thought all that's been sorted out now. Besides, Len doesn't have a job and doesn't have any tax obligations that call need for an audit or anything like that," she said.

"Well, I'd really like to make sure," Leonard said, releasing Len's shoulder to address her head-on. "After all, it *has* been three years since we last saw Len come up in any tax records as a claimed independent or anything like that. Now, since he's alive and obviously hasn't been issued a death certificate –"

'Not yet, but give it twenty-four hours,' Len thought.

"– we need to make sure all those records are in order before we close the case."

Len knew Jodie well enough to see how ready she was to drop her act and scream. Instead, she opened her mouth wide and spoke. "I'm not sure that's very necessary, I –"

"It's just standard procedure, Mrs. Campbell," Leonard said as calmly as ever. "However Len's been feeding and providing for himself all this time, whether it was in fact his doing or a caretaker, the IRS requires that whatever income was required to meet those needs be reported and the gross taxed appropriately."

Jodie threw up her hands. "I don't have time for this," she said, and snatched Len's wrist. "Send me a letter or something or sue me, but we're leaving now."

Subhail stepped forward and uncrossed his arms. "Where is it you think you are going?"

And then, of all things Len could imagine, he could have sworn he saw Leonard grab her arm. It stopped her cold. Dumbfounded, she stared blankly back at him with one foot already mid-step toward the street.

"Mr. Humphrey, I think you're forgetting… you know… our arrangement," she said as low as she could. Len saw then how she didn't want the straggler police to hear.

Leonard stared placidly right back, and even matched her secret volume. "The IRS has first dibs, Mrs. Campbell. Now if you don't release this suspected tax evader I'm afraid I'll have to ask these officers to arrest you for obstruction of justice."

One of the officers, Len saw, got up from the hood of his cruiser. "There a problem, Sir?" he asked.

"It is no business of yours!" Subhail said, but Leonard waved him down.

"No! No, there's no problem," Jodie said over Len's head. He watched as Subhail and Leonard stared her down in tight, and she them, until finally there came a sudden absence of pressure around his wrist. She stepped away from both of them, bowing her consent for Leonard to take over, and just as in his dream, Len could glance back and see the fiery, molten intent in her eyes.

It spread.

"All right," she said. "Go ahead. Take him. But please do update me on when I can take him home."

"Oh, I will," Leonard said, smiling a malevolent smile Len never would have guessed him capable of, as he showed Len into the back seat of the Honda. "You have a good day now, Mrs. Campbell!"

"You too!" she said across the parking lot. She shot Subhail a dirty look and marched off.

Subhail and Claire joined Wallace, Leonard, and Len on the far side of the parking lot. "Are you okay?" Claire asked Len, who was standing in front of the door Leonard had opened for him.

"I'm fine," Len said, "Thank you for calling the cops," he said.

Claire cocked her head. "I didn't call the cops," she said.

Before Len could reply, though, Subhail cut in. "What have I told you about spending time with this one instead of devoting time to your studies?" Subhail asked.

"Dad! Please, I get all A's anyway!" Claire said. "I don't mean to be disrespectful, Sir, but –"

"*But* nothing, my little flower! We are going home now! Say goodbye to your friend, you have school tomorrow and I will not have you wound up and under-slept for it."

"Sir," Len said, "I –"

But Subhail interrupted him again. "No! No comments from you! I see the trouble around you and the mayhem you wreak. My daughter has better things to do than be friends with spoiled goods!"

141

"Gee, how warm of you," Len said more into the open air than directly to Claire's father. "Kinda makes me wonder why you even came today."

Subhail harrumphed, herded Claire into their car, and left. Len watched them go and saw Claire motion, behind his father's back, that she'd see Len soon.

Wallace had started the car, and Leonard was waiting for Len to get in when Officer Clasby walked over with a few cans in hand. He smiled at Len and hopped into the back seat.

Soon thereafter, the Honda was on the road. Len sat behind Leonard. He didn't dare give Buckeye Party & Lotto another look.

They hadn't been driving long. "So you're all right, then?" Leonard asked through the rearview mirror.

Len, who'd been staring out the window and doing serious guesswork about where they were taking him, snapped out of a daydream. "Yeah," he said, "I'm fine… so, where in Columbus did you say your office is?"

"Wha – why do you ask?"

Len shrugged. "I just wonder where we're going, is all," he said. "Isn't that what he's here for? In case I try to make a run for it?" he asked, nodding Clasby's way.

The Honda pulled over. A subtle, car-wide thumping sound marked the unlocking of doors. "We're not taking you anywhere, Len," Leonard said, and thrust the knob between the front seats all the way forward. "Get some sleep."

When he looked out the window, Len saw the treehouse. He looked at Leonard for the literal punch line of some cruel joke, but when none materialized he slipped his hand into the door handle. Still nothing happened. He opened the door. He got out and shut it. Clasby got out as well and stood there on the side of the road with Len, smiling like an idiot, energy drinks in hand. After a moment and the slow lane traffic permitted, the Honda drove away.

"It was Len, right? I got watch tonight. Just in case," Clasby said. "I mean, if you'll have me?"

Len did not at all understand the events of that day, but accepted them. All he knew at that point was that he'd been delivered from evil. Though Claire did not visit before he went to bed, he left the shutters open. For the first time in a while, he spared batteries to whittle by lamplight.

Midnight traffic saw a cozy-looking treehouse that night, with one strange light giving it almost a bayou charm against the starry, leafless backdrop and the still air. Inside, Len paused knife to wood every so often and thought as hard as he could, but he went to sleep that night not knowing whether he still had to make a break for Indiana after all. Subhail had never been particularly warm to him, but at least Claire could lobby her father to Len's advantage, and Len simply could not decide if he wanted to use that in a strategy against Jodie.

He became so distracted by the events of the day that he nearly forgot that woman even existed. Sitting in his bed all night long, Len did finally turn the lamp off, but not before giving his map one last look-over. Clasby slipped out sometime during the night.

In the end, Len reasoned, he could not count on Subhail or Wallace or Leonard any more than he could before. The only one Len knew for sure he could count on, was Len. Len could get Len to Indiana, and in Indiana Len knew for a fact that Len could hide Len from Jodie, because even though she'd been robbed that day, he knew full well she was never going to stop.

There was nothing Claire, Leonard, Subhail, or Wallace could do about that.

So Len kept his plans for Indiana.

Chapter Eighteen

Fog rolled in overnight while a dose of true autumn weather sank in. The treehouse stood proudly in the middle of it all, and although that fog made the day feel dank, it also felt promising. One just had to be bold enough to walk into the gray. Between occasional cars rumbling by, insects chirped and filled the air with a quiet noise that made Len feel safe.

Early in the morning, Claire popped out of the colored air and climbed the rungs. She knocked on the trapdoor. "It's me. Let me up!"

It took a minute, but Len woke up and made to roll off the bed. Half-asleep, he fell off the edge instead, but lay there all the same as he reached awkwardly over – for it could not have been more than twelve inches beyond his side – and unlocked the trapdoor. By the time he sat up, Claire was up there with him, slinging her backpack to the floor.

"Morning," she said.

"Sure," Len said. While he adjusted to the light, one hand stayed on his face. "What's up? Shouldn't you be at school? Your dad seemed pretty intent on that today – doesn't want you hanging out with Mr. Spoiled Goods Len."

Claire started eating an apple from her pack. "No biggie," she said. "I've got a two hour delay today."

"Hunh? Why?"

Claire opened the shutter wing behind her and pointed over her shoulder. "Fog. Too thick for the buses to drive."

"Oh," Len said. He sat there for a moment and looked at it, while his mind thawed. "Anyway!" he said once he remembered himself, "that doesn't answer my question."

"Just checking up on you," Claire said right before a big, crunchy bite. "Last I knew, you were being carted off God-knows-where with the same couple of guys that you were recently fighting to the death with."

"Hm," Len said, and pulled himself up on the bed. "No, I managed to get away from them, and came back here."

"Sounds exciting," said Claire. "Any sign of Jodie?"

"Not since the party store."

Claire faked a game show buzzer sound: "*Eht!*"

"What? Why? What happened?"

Claire reached into her back pocket and tossed Len her phone. Len knew just enough about it to unlock the screen, where he saw a play button and a paused video. "I got a clip on there for you from the news this morning," Claire said.

The green-haired one considered it for a moment, and tapped the screen.

"Hello out there, we're near the bottom of the hour this morning, I'm Loretta Heller. Your top stories so far today: after cornering a suspected green-haired map thief in the same Buckeye Party & Lotto as mere days earlier, authorities are saying no arrest has been made in the case. The suspect has been identified as the same Leonard Campbell of Pennsylvania as had his standoff with police recently, after being surrounded in a treehouse along US-33. Police say it's unclear whether the suspect and these acts are tied to the assault on government officers committed last night, but they assured us that the investigation is ongoing."

"What's she talking about?" Len said. "What assault on government officials?"

"Oh," Claire said, "you don't know? Yeah, after they helped you get away from Jodie yesterday, it just so happens Misters Wallace and Leonard got their own blanket parties overnight."

Len reeled. "What?"

"Yeah," Claire continued, "I see now why you've been freaking out over this lady coming to town. She's bad news, Len. Bad, bad news."

The two of them let it sink in. It was more Claire waiting for Len to catch up. After a moment, though, Len looked up. "You know what that means, though?" he asked.

"What?"

"I was right," Len said. "She really means to take me back, or at least have me to herself – whatever it takes. She must, if she's willing to risk charges like that. Wait, was that story on the news this morning, too?"

"I think so," Claire said. "Here, give me the phone. I'll see if I can find it."

Len handed it over. It took no more than a minute or two for Claire to find it. She sat on the bed and held it before both of them. They watched it, side by side.

Loretta Heller stared them both in the face as the graphics accompanied her report. "Law enforcement is searching for answers tonight after two government officials were found savagely beaten outside their home office in Columbus. Ambulances responded to the scene and found both men lying on the ground, covered with thick blankets from the torso up. Both men suffered a host of injuries including broken bones, large clusters of bruises, and cuts... they're in the local hospital tonight under critical condition. Doctors say that while both men are likely to survive, they can't be sure how full a recovery either will make until the swelling goes down. The officers have been identified as IRS auditors Wallace James and Leonard Humphrey. We'll have more on this story as it develops."

"My God..." Len said. "Should we... should we do something?"

Claire put her hand on Len's forehead. "What? Are you feeling all right? Who are you and what have you done with my friend?"

Len brushed her hand away. "Seriously, now. I kind of feel like this is at least partially my fault."

Claire got up. "What do you care?" she asked. "Aren't these the same two guys that, not long ago, were about to deliver you to Jodie like fresh lamb? Personally, I don't see how you owe them any favors to be even considering it."

As Len chewed on his lip, he looked out over the highway. Morning traffic was slower-going, but he could faintly make out the glow of headlights trying to cut through the fog. He chuckled on accident.

"What's so funny...?" Claire asked.

"Oh," Len said, glancing his way, "I'm just glad it's not tear gas this time."

Claire laughed and said it wasn't funny. "So, back on subject, are you still charting course for Indiana?"

Len sighed and went to the window. He leaned, propped in the windowsill for a moment before his eyes settled on the map hanging in the corner. "I'll have to," he said, "and after yesterday, I'd better hurry it up. It doesn't look like I really have time anymore to be screwing around and gathering supplies.

"And on that note, I believe it's time to see what Bobby has in the way of rides I can permanently borrow." He placed a hand on Claire's shoulder and showed her the trapdoor.

"Hold on," she said. "Why haven't you gone already?"

A small, warm smile adorned Len's face just then. "I wanted to make sure I could tell you goodbye."

Claire looked into Len's eyes, but only gave a series of small nods.

Meaning to really mean it that day, Len started packing. Claire offered her backpack, and they packed what provisions they could from the treehouse. A few armfuls of canned vegetables went in Len's own frayed and worn-out backpack, as well as the only-kind-of-stolen map. Claire fit the collapsed spit in her bag, but there was no way Len's bed was making the trip. It didn't faze him. Len carried his log nightstand over his shoulder, his whittling knife in his pocket, and gave his half-formed carving its own special place in the water bottle pocket on the side of his pack. By the end of it, all of Len's larger belongings remained behind, including his heater, his makeshift grappling hook that he'd made of the hubcap and rope, and the bagged leaves. Fall's winds knicked him as he and Claire began their hike. Along the way, Len thought aloud whether to come back if he could, should they find a car, and at least salvage his heater.

"Not a terrible idea," Claire told him, "and it'll give you one last look around home before you move on."

Len smiled. "I'd like that."

147

And Claire smiled. "I know, Len. I know."

In the fog, they made sure to keep an extra few feet off the shoulder. Len kept a special eye out for Jodie, because he knew that in fog such as this, the advantage could belong to either of them. Although his friend never mentioned it, Len had caught a glimpse of the gun in her backpack, when she'd retrieved the apple. Whether that slip had been on purpose, he didn't know, but Jodie didn't know about it, and for the time being, at least, it meant they could get the drop on her even if she got the drop on them.

"All right, we gotta hurry this up, though," Claire said. "I'll probably be late to school as it is."

"Right there with you," Len said. The map stuck up over his shoulder as they went; they looked looking like a couple of hitchhikers as they made for Bobby's.

Chapter Nineteen

Bobby's Auto Salvage was not the pristine gem of its neighborhood. Had it not been for the general litter and weeds growing out of the sidewalk in that whole stretch of town, people would have remembered the junkyard as an eyesore. Bobby didn't care how people saw his business, as long as he made money. He commemorated that goal with his dollar sign ball cap that he almost never took off – Len shuddered to think how greasy and flea-ridden the black mop underneath it must have been. In one case or another, he and Claire arrived at Bobby's shortly upon mid-morning, with not much time before Claire would have to make for school to risk only mild tardiness.

Their heads rose just into the window to the front shop area, which was markedly more organized and, daresay, slightly cleaner than Willie's office (although, to be fair, it was a pigsty by any standard). In a spring-recline office chair much too small for him, with his feet propped on the counter, third chin on his chest, hands laced on his house-sized belly, slept Bobby. The glass nearly rattled with each snore, though Len and Claire could barely hear it through the wall.

Claire had never seen Bobby before. "*God*," she said, "he's repulsive! I don't even *want* to know what he smells like."

"He's a round bastard, ain't he?" Len said. "Come on – I know how to get over the fence on the side."

A ten-foot chain link fence marked the junkyard perimeter. The links were covered over with a green mesh that thwarted any attempt at a foothold, and the fence wore a crown of thorns. Getting over it, Claire noted, would be no simple task.

Len, however, spoke to the contrary. In the alley running between the junkyard and the abandoned parking lot next door, Len had some wooden planks stuffed away. "If that lazy idiot ever bothered to check this way, he'd see how easy it is to get past his fencing," Len said, "but luckily for us, Karma's holding a few dozen of his IQ points as collateral for as long as he pledges to be an asshole." Claire laughed.

The planks made getting over the fence a touch awkward, but entirely easy. On the other side, a neat stack of crushed-down cars made not only for a convenient landing, but also a platform from which they could see an easy tenth of the yard. Mounds of cars, crushed, picked, and some mostly intact formed aisles and rivers, hills and piles before them. Indeed, other than cars, parts, tires and rims, there was very little else Bobby kept in stock. On Len and Claire's right, on their side of Bobby's office, the fencing had a gate, albeit locked, which Len proposed he could bust open once they found a car he could hotwire. And that would be the end of them knowing each other for some time, until at least Len could perfect his safety.

"Ready to get started?" Len asked from atop their starting platform.

Claire had a look around and released a long breath. "Not entirely," she said, "but I'm right there with you. Let's go."

They split up and looked about for the most intact cars they could find. There were few, which dampened Len's hopes to find one that would run. Once they had a rough inventory of which ones at least had a chassis and wheels, they went one by one, as Claire didn't know how to hotwire, and tried.

The first car – a rusted-over Oldsmobile whose upholstery may have had aliens burst from the seat – had been tried before, Len saw, as the wires were already hanging down and looked burnt. He tried it anyway, and promptly moved to its neighbor. It was a blue minivan, and didn't react at all when Len manipulated the wires. No sooner did Claire lift the hood that they learned why: it had no battery. Just as well, they saw, because it didn't have an alternator, either.

The next three cars showed a touch more cooperation, but failed all the same. A white Neon barely had the gas to start; a black Taurus harbored a dead battery; not quite a dozen cars down the row from them, a beige Crown Victoria – at least Len and Claire guessed it was beige under the rust, dust, and bird poop – had been gutted of its engine entirely.

They tried others, but Claire urged Len to hurry. Len asked for just ten minutes, showed Claire the basics of hotwiring cars, and they split up again. He saw her scurry from the first car he tried as she skipped away.

"What's wrong?" Len said, laughing at his friend's absurd strides.

"Bees!" Claire said. "There's a freaking beehive in the backseat!"

Len laughed harder and sat in a car near the center of the lot. "Glad I'm not using that one, then," he said. After getting the wires he needed for his latest attempt, something caught his eye. There was something shiny in the stack of tires next to this car. He looked. Claire kept trying her luck with cars on the far side of the smashed-down car mountain.

The top of the stack was a tire without a rim, though the one below it did have one. Sitting on that shiny rim, hidden by the free tire, was a revolver. Len checked to make sure nobody was watching him, and no one was.

He reached over and fished around until his hand bumped into the cold metal. His heart skipped, and he breathed to calm himself. Then, carefully, he felt with his fingertips what part of the gun was where, and so lifted it by the handle from the tire stack. Turning it over in his hands, he saw that it was in exceptional shape. Shiny, untarnished, with no smudges or fingerprints, it was as though it had been left by God. He wondered how it got there.

Sitting back in the car in case Claire glanced over, Len checked the barrel. Four of the six chambers had bullets in them. Len stared off into the distance as he considered his options.

He knew Jodie was a threat. After what she'd done to Dianne, Wallace and Leonard, and tried to do to Claire, Len had zero doubts that she was dangerous. But he asked himself, was she worth it? He tapped the barrel against his palm and thought about it. He wasn't sure. He flipped the chambers out again. There were still four bullets.

It would mean four chances to end the nightmare once and for all. Four chances to make things right.

Len shook his head and clicked the chambers back into place. He reached back to stuff the gun at the small of his back, but stopped. Finally, he sighed and, after giving it one last, long, hard look, he placed it on the console. The car didn't start when he tried the wires.

He moved on.

"Hey, Len!"

"Yeah?" Len said, and ran around the mound of car guts until he saw Claire.

"I don't think there's anything here for us," she said. "I can't stay any longer though, I really have to get going to school."

"That's fine," Len said. They scrambled up to the platform of smashed-down cars. Claire went over first.

Len cast a look over his shoulder, where over one of the junk mountain's reaching roots he could see the roof and front end of that last car. "You coming?" Claire suddenly asked from the alley on the far side of the wall, and Len climbed over to join her without another word.

Halfway back to the treehouse, Claire turned to Len. "Well, if you go back and find a car without me, good luck," she said.

Len looked up the gravelly shoulder. "No," he said. "I'll wait until you get back, and then we'll try again."

"Len, you know that's not a good idea."

"I know," Len said, "Jodie's going to be on the prowl again none too soon."

"Exactly!" Claire said. "I say you find a car and get the hell out while you still can. Besides, by the time I'm out of school and get a chance away from my dad, night will have fallen, Bobby'll be up, and we'll have an even harder time finding a car fumbling in the dark. And this is assuming Jodie hasn't caught up with you while I'm away."

"I'm not going," Len said. "Not yet. Get back to me when you can get back to me. I'll be waiting at the treehouse." He saw Claire's concerned look and stopped walking for a moment.

"Trust me on this. I'll lock up the windows and the trapdoor and keep some traps ready in case she tries to take me while you're at school. I have a plan for tonight, though."

"Is there a way maybe I can help?" Claire asked.

"Actually, I think there is," Len said. "When you get back, bring a blowtorch or some bolt cutters, something or the other. Something that can get through metal."

Claire nodded, already thinking how to procure such a provision to get past Bobby's lock, if in case somehow he finally came wise to the planks in the alley. She thought about a blowtorch the hardest. 'Maybe he'll wait for Jodie to come back and burn her face off with it.'

In the meantime, Claire went to school and Len returned to the treehouse. He locked up as tightly as ever and fed his heater. He tried to remember everything he could about how to drive a car, and desperately hoped he wouldn't hit anyone or get pulled over. But these were risks he had to take.

In the afternoon, he withdrew everything from his backpack and, having the time, he organized them. In doing so, he found room for a couple more cans. It even relieved one of the bulging extra outer pockets where he could make use of it; though he wasn't sure what he had to bring that would fit in them.

The fog lifted in late morning, though Len was already hermitted away. When the morning insects settled down, or at least the traffic drowned them out, Len found himself bored, and so he took the batteries from his lamp and put them in a cheap radio he'd found and dropped on several occasions. The clarity was awful, but he spent a couple of hours listening to the news. It wasn't Loretta Heller, but it was just as well to him.

Eventually, the batteries died and Len heard nothing but the traffic roll by for the rest of the day, as normal as before the day Wallace and Leonard first came. Nobody pulled over. Nobody knocked on the trapdoor. Nobody bothered him all day.

He didn't hear any emergency vehicles storm down the highway. The radio didn't mention a thing about police responding to anything major that day. There was no sign of Jodie. Night fell.

Chapter Twenty

A storm was rolling in. Len could hear it a few miles off. He hoped that Claire would return soon, for without the sun to offer him any help, it would be best to try and outpace the rain. He didn't know how much extra he could handle while winging it with his driving. The night would be bad enough; adding rain, Len feared, would make his flight impossible, and he'd already long past outstayed his welcome in Ohio. Jodie was no doubt on the move again, somewhere, and so the less time Len sat there, sitting duck, the better.

In the hopes that it would throw her off, Len opened the windows once the sun was gone, and didn't keep a light on. Not even a candle. He made to look like no one was home.

Sometime after the only light available came from the headlights of highway traffic, Claire reappeared. They could feel Jodie's eyes on the back of their necks, wherever she was. Wasting no time, they stole down the road.

"What's the plan?" Claire asked at the lowest possible volume. "Off to Bobby's?"

"Willie's," Len said. "Did you bring everything we'll need?"

"Right here in my backpack," Claire said. "Let's go."

The storm was very close by the time they reached the railyard. Paranoid from their last visit, Claire had her bow out and nocked before they had to turn any corners. The two of them crept out amongst the tracks unhindered, but tried to stay low anyway. Willie was nowhere to be seen. The same could be said of his crew. There remained no sign of Jodie, and that left just Len and Claire running, crouched over, to where the neat herd of railcars stood much like before at the halfway point. Halide floodlamps were their only witnesses. As they went, the night and the lamps made the shadows deep, and while he and Claire didn't go into those shadows, they reminded Len of Becky for the first time in a long while.

They came to the herd.

"This one looks like it has some," Len said after walking the line. About three cars from them was a railcar full of SUVs. "Claire, over here!"

She, a few cars farther, turned from her search and hurried. Unshouldering her backpack, she placed everything they needed on the ground. Len snatched the tools as he needed them, and the two of them went to work cracking the shell. It was loud, spark-shooting work, and neither of them escaped without burning their hands. They cast looks over their shoulders all the while, and saw thunderheads mounting. In the darkness, the only indication they saw came when lightning flashed among the black puffs of clouds. Len thought it was beautiful, but stayed focused and kept going.

The lock weakened, and Claire used a pipe wrench to break it the rest of the way off. As soon as she did, the yellow-striped metal doors flew wide at the end of the railcar. With much squealing and hollow metal groans, Len and Claire stared into the gut of the beast.

A host of shiny, brand new cars stared them in the face. Len didn't care which one he took, but they agreed immediately there was no use trying for the ones on the top row. After a quick search, they were delighted to find a pull-out ramp on the bottom row. With a touch more finagling, Len and Claire unbound the wheels of the first car – an Enclave, and the only one they could really even access – and squeezed in behind it. Small diamonds of light shone through the sides of the railcar and skittered across their backs when they moved. They shoved the black SUV with all their might, but it didn't budge. Sweating, tired, and without any idea how much time they had or how much attention their blowtorching and lock-smashing had garnered, they pressed their backs to the vehicle, each put a leg on the wall and another on the red Tahoe behind it, and pushed.

"Bastard!" Len said. "Must be in park."

"Can you get inside?" Claire asked.

"Let me see," Len said.

156

Vastly to Len's surprise, the door opened. It banged against the wall and took a scratch and a dent or two, but he didn't care. He sucked in his gut and wriggled inside the car.

He plopped into a seat much more comfortable than he expected and found his nose nearly overwhelmed with new car smell.

"Can you put it in neutral?" Claire asked from the rear bumper. It snapped Len out of a daydream into which he'd only just slipped, and without realizing. He tried the gear.

"Nothing."

"Damn," Claire said. "I wonder where Willie keeps the keys."

"They're right here," Len said, jingling the stupid metal things stuck in the ignition. "What do they have to do with it?" he asked.

It was then that Claire remembered how little Len had been taught about how to function as an adult in society. He'd already missed a lot of schooling and had spent his preparing-to-come-of-age years in the treehouse.

"Grab them!" Claire said. "Grab them and twist them forward!"

"What?" Len asked, and did as he was told. Although it took him a couple of tries to figure out the nuances of the motion, he made it work. He pushed the keys farther than he wanted, however, and the car started.

"Or that," Claire said.

The SUV crept out of the car and down the ramp, where Len put it in park about twenty feet clear of the herd. As Claire hopped down from the car, Len waved her down from putting the ramp back up.

"Don't worry about that," Len said. "Let them see that it's gone, and I am with it."

"But Len –"

"But nothing. The more it looks like I've abandoned town, even without much clue of direction, the more likely Jodie will know she'll have to search elsewhere," Len said. He put a hand on his friend's shoulder. "Once I'm gone, you shouldn't have to worry about her. Between your bow and Subhail showing his colors at the party store, you should be fine."

"All right. Here," Claire said, handing Len a surprise.

"What's this?"

Claire stared into his eyes. They were glazed along the bottom lids. "It's a GPS. I already programmed it to Indianapolis. Stick that on the dashboard and it'll help you if you get lost," she said. She choked back a gasp. "Be careful out there, Len," she said.

"Thank you. You take care of yourself too until I find a way back," Len said. "I appreciate everything you've done for me, Claire."

The two of them hugged goodbye. "So this is really it, then," Claire said, holding on as tight as she could.

Len patted her on the back. "Yeah… for now," he said. "Do you mind if I take the flashlight?"

"Go ahead," Claire said without a hint of hesitation.

"And can I actually borrow a couple of bucks in case I need more gas before I get there?" Len asked. "I mean, the thing's got almost a full tank and all of seven miles on it, but, you know, I want to be sure."

Claire smiled as they broke apart. A hand dove into her pocket and gave something more to Len. "Here's a twenty," she said. "Don't even worry about it."

They stood there. The moment stretched on with several awkward, small nods and the wiping of singlet tears.

Len made a sound somewhere between an uncomfortable groan and a hiss, trying to shake it off and get himself focused for the road. "Okay, I really gotta get going."

"Yeah," Claire said, weakly motioning toward the still-running Enclave. "You take care. I better hear from you soon!"

"You will," Len said. "You take care too."

"Okay."

"All right."

"Good."

"Yeah," Len said. "Good. Good!" He laughed.

"I do have one question before you go," Claire said out of nowhere, and Len jumped at the opportunity to answer. "What happens to the treehouse once you're gone?"

"Hm. I don't know. It's yours now, I guess," Len said. "Speaking of, I need to grab my heater before I go. Never know how cold Indiana's going to be, right? Especially if I have to sleep in the car the first couple of nights!"

"Yeah," Claire said, laughing nervously still. "Good call."

In the end, Len knew he had to get going before Jodie caught whiff and cornered them again. He hugged Claire once more. As he climbed back inside the car and began weaving over the tracks and back out of the yard, he and Claire waved goodbye through the mirrors half a dozen more times.

Claire stood right in front of the yawning railcar for at least another fifteen minutes. By then, a gentle sprinkle began to fall. She kept watching where Len had disappeared around the corner, out of the yard. It didn't feel real. It didn't seem like Len was really gone.

Before he would make for the treehouse and then for Indiana, Len knew somewhere in the black, increasingly rainy void of that night, Jodie lingered. She was somewhere, and to Len that meant she was everywhere. He did mention that he was headed back for the heater, but beforehand he headed to Bobby's, with Claire's flashlight, and leaned the wooden planks against the fencing again. He never spoke a word of it to Claire.

As gently as he could, Len placed each foot on the platform of smashed cars. He didn't dilly-dally; he skulked even lower than before, lest Bobby look out during his cartoons and TV dinner to see someone in his yard. Len saw him in the window, with the pale blue glow of the television screen shining off his fat, gleaming head. The bastard even busted forward laughing at something – probably ridiculous and childlike-asinine – and Len knew his window was as open as Bobby was distracted.

He went immediately for the far side of the central mountain, around the left-hand arm. There he found again the last car he'd tried to hotwire before Claire had school earlier that day, and exactly as he'd left it, Len found the gun on the console.

Stuffing it (and the nearest, rusty license plate he could grab) in his backpack, Len climbed back over the wall. He jogged across the alley quick as a mouse, up the brief hill and sidewalk to the abandoned parking lot of a former supermarket, and hopped back atop his horse. Without a word, he threw the backpack in the passenger seat. The rain was falling in earnest by then, but not so badly that he couldn't see where he was going.

'It doesn't feel real,' he thought at first, and sat there for a few moments to let it sink in. He couldn't help but smile, feeling beside himself in the moment of embarking for Indiana at last. It wasn't long before he was laughing, and giddily. And he had a vehicle, no less! "And now," he said, "if Missus Queen Jodie thinks she's going to stop me now, I'll just run her down, in front of God and everybody."

At last, Len knew and truly felt that he had control of his own life. It felt good. After fumbling with the buttons in front of him, Len figured out the blinkers, and pulled into traffic.

Chapter Twenty-One

As Len rolled down the highway, he wondered what Claire would be up to once he was gone. He figured school would top that list, but what about the time freed up by not hanging out with *him*? Len regripped the steering wheel and focused on staying in his lane, for there was a bend up ahead.

He was being overly cautious about his speed, and tried especially to look far, so he wouldn't jerk around inside his own lane. The smoother he could make his driving, he knew, the better his chances of not getting pulled over and the better his chances of Indiana.

The SUV emerged from an overpass at the end of the bend in the highway, and Len immediately noticed a particularly darker patch of sky over the trees. He looked at it and thought it was incredible. Already, in the storm many of the clouds were bitter with black rain waiting to fall. The sky was angry, and Len saw a patch that was even angrier, finding a way to be blacker than the gray-black already making it impossible to find the moon. The rain didn't help; sheeting rain made Len struggle to see.

There was hardly anybody else on the road, leaving Len at the back of a pack of three cars, which was fine. After another slight curve in the road, he would be rolling down the same long, straight stretch of highway as where he built the treehouse. His pulley system was still there to be put together, and he planned to use that to at least get his heater.

Len wasn't sure how close Claire would be to getting home by that time – his stop at Bobby's had thrown off his estimation of time, and having to concentrate on driving despite the storm certainly didn't help. But, he figured, just before coming to the straight stretch, he would keep an eye out for Claire in case he could get one last wave in before never seeing her again.

The curve ended. Len eyed the darker patch of sky, and a couple of miles off a lightning strike illuminated its part of the sky. By the edge of its light, Len saw that dark patch was a cloud with a really strange shape. He hoped it wasn't a tornado.

Len went underneath another overpass and then, thanks to another lightning bolt, saw it more clearly. He prayed that it wasn't a tornado, because it was already in his neighborhood, already within range of the treehouse on the other side of the next overpass, and Claire's home as well.

Len didn't think twice about flooring it. He had to know what that black cloud was, and defend his home from it. How he would defend his treehouse from a sky-high pillar of unstoppable wind and debris he didn't know, but he also knew he couldn't sit back and let nothing be done about it. His windshield wipers, going as fast as they could, failed him as the wind pelted his car with sheet after cross-cutting sheet of rain. Even when it wasn't, the sound of the falling rain was as though someone had dumped an Earth-sized bucket of water straight from Heaven.

He was able to make out the shape of the overpass as it loomed over him, and was above his head. He didn't track it after that.

The SUV zipped out from beneath that overpass, where Len's godforsaken contemporary had filmed his world-ending video for the news. Len found the ominous black cloud again without delay.

Before he could trace it to its roots on the ground, something on the edge of his vision forced him to glance down. It became more than a glance.

The treehouse was in flames.

As the SUV carried him past it on the road, Len forgot about everything else. He forgot to steer. His foot forgot the gas pedal. All his attention locked on the box shape in the tree as fire danced on its shell. Len could hear the fire laughing at all the water falling from the sky, trying to interrupt its feast. Len could nearly hear the end of each orange tongue licking the air, taunting the clouds, inviting the sky to try harder.

After that, Len was vaguely aware of a few noises, somewhere far off, of a car slowing down and pulling off the road. There was the sound of gravel turning over under its wheels, and a car shifting into park. A car door closed. Shoes

162

walked over loose rocks, and some grass. Rain beat against someone's head. Len wasn't sure. Maybe his.

Len stared up at what was already left of his treehouse. The top third was already falling in on itself. The hatch was lost. A stream of fire ran up the rungs, had devoured the tire's nest. Through a gap in the floor – eaten away into sootiness – he saw his bed would soon be next.

Wherever the heater was, Len didn't know. But he knew the treehouse had never been so warm, and would forevermore be a cold, cold memory.

Behind him, the traffic bastards ran by. Their tires made slick and slap noises as they kicked up water in their treads. Len thought he heard somebody honk at someone else, and then a car speed up. People didn't know how to drive.

The whole time, he watched the treehouse burn.

He fell to his knees, soaked. Water dripped off his head as though from the edge of a roof. For the first time, Len felt truly alone. He took no consolation now knowing what the sky's extra-black cloud was.

Then, suddenly, he peered up for another look – hoping perhaps the fire and the half-eaten treehouse was all a stupid hallucination – he noticed instead something on the tree. He stood again, and walked halfway there. The rain froze him, but any closer and the bonfire-on-a-stick would roast him.

There, facing the road and pinned right at eye level on the trunk for him, waved Len's map. One singed corner flapped in the wind, but it was otherwise untouched by the heat. The rain beat against it as its waving corner seemed to reach out to Len for help. Len stared at it.

Over the entangled lines of roads, highway badges and itty-bitty names of places, someone left some jagged, red letters scrawled on the map. They seared into Len like the very fire that lit them, and read:

Game's done, LEN

WELCOME HOME.

Len sank back to his knees and gazed up at the fire engulfing his home. The sky rained into his eyes, but he refused to close them. For all the good it had done him, Len owed the treehouse to remember it to the last splinter.

At the height of the burning, Len turned his head to the familiar sound of a small car pulling over. Still sitting in defeat, soaked and cold, he bothered to look and saw Wallace and Leonard getting out of the car. Len was on his feet in an instant as the night continued to pour.

The IRS men met him halfway and slowed, their mouths as agape as Len's.

"My God…" Leonard said, and looked at Len. "We saw the smoke from the hospital! Are you all right?"

"Go away," Len said from beneath his soggy bangs.

"I told you not to mess with her," Wallace told Leonard. "See! Nothing good's come of it!" Then, right from that, he turned to Len and sighed. "Kid, I know our involvement hasn't been the best for you and, after all's said and done, we… I, rather, am sorry. For everything. We never meant for anything like this to happen, we just thought…"

And then Len was marching on him, cocking back his balled-up fist and bearing down on the crutch-dependent man. Wallace saw him coming immediately and bleakly raised a hand to shield himself, but Len saw in his posture that he seemed otherwise resigned to the impending blow.

When Wallace dared to crack one eye, he saw Len standing before him, hand raised and ready to hit, but the boy was just staring at him. Wallace lowered his hand.

And then Len lowered his. "No," he said. "You're not worth it." He walked back to what was left of the treehouse. "Just leave me alone."

The fire made something in the treehouse pop. Sparks and fireflies twirled from beneath one portion of it before a few planks of floor fell away. They landed in the drenched grass and had no chance of spreading fire at Len and Wallace and Leonard's level. The rest of that area of floor ensued, leaving a pit in a corner of Len's treehouse that looked like a great popped zit on the underside of someone's jaw. Out fell the rest of his chunks of concrete – first one, then another two rapid-fire, and then a quick burst that was the rest of his stockpile. Most of them rolled into the cattails.

"Len…" Leonard said, daring to come closer. He didn't come all the way, but Wallace stayed back. "Len, we never meant for anything like this to happen. Please, let us help you."

"Haven't you helped enough already?" Len said, and spun back to his feet. He got in Leonard's face. "See what happens when you don't leave well enough alone? Why can't you just call it quits before she finds you again and beats you the rest of the way to death? Wasn't one round enough? Hm? HM?"

Leonard glanced back at Wallace. "I… Len, we only meant –"

"I don't care," Len said with a strange, sudden return to calmness. "Just leave me alone, before I throw both of us out into traffic."

He saw Wallace's lip twitch. After adjusting on his crutch, the man called to his partner. "Come on, Leonard. Let's get out of here." Lightning cracked far away, and it took a couple of seconds before a weakened boom made him pause so as to be heard. "We're wasting our time on this kid. Let's get back to the hospital before the nurses realize we're missing. I don't have the patience or energy to deal with this little brat anymore."

Leonard looked over his shoulder again. When he returned to face a stone-faced Len, the boy saw his face was almost as defeated as he felt. But Len didn't let his own expression falter and betray the question he had pent up. In the end, he let Leonard give up, turn back to Wallace, and leave.

Leonard took his time with it, too, and Len very seriously began to consider retrieving the junkyard revolver from the SUV behind him. "Take ten more seconds," Len murmured. "Ten more seconds, and you'll see how much I like you sitting around like the bastard you are…"

Len only counted to seven before Wallace and Leonard drove away. He watched them go for the last time, surprised that Wallace didn't flip him off again.

Dropping his act, Len returned to the matter of the treehouse. He examined the scene – the map, the collapsing structure, the fire that was beginning to ember in the floor beside the flames mopping up the walls.

A short bit of reason caught him, and it occurred to him that Jodie might be hiding somewhere near him. He stayed where he was and eyed the cattails and the other brush and trees rising from the ditch. He didn't see her, but knew that somewhere, out in that wretched night, she was waiting. He shuddered at the thought of her winning.

"And yet," he said to himself, looking up at the treehouse, "she's so close already."

He cast a look over his shoulder. Traffic kept going despite the rain and night. For the first time, Len considered walking out into the road and letting the bastards decide his fate.

Chapter Twenty-Two

Wallace and Leonard eased themselves back into their hospital beds. It was none too soon, as perhaps five minutes later the nurse poked her head in to check on them.

Wallace, the nearer to the window, stared out it as Leonard wandered channels on the TV. Rain beat against their window, sheeting with each gust of wind. "Ungrateful little shit," Wallace said.

"What?" Leonard asked.

"That kid!" Wallace said. "We go there and try to help him and help him and help him, and how does he repay us? He throws a tantrum like a four-year-old and breaks our ankles and knocks us unconscious and threatens to make us get run over! God! Why the hell did we even bother?"

Leonard threw the remote down on his bed and waited for Wallace to look his way. "Excuse me?" he said. "Have you seen what we did?"

"*I* didn't do anything!"

"Oh, bull*shit*!" Leonard said. "If we hadn't gotten involved in the first place, that kid would be moseying along with his life just as happy as a clam, and it's an honest-to-God shame we ever meddled in his life in the first place!"

"Exactly," Wallace said, throwing himself into his pillows. "I'm going to sleep. Screw him."

"No!" Leonard said. "Screw us! It's our fault that woman found him, it's our fault that he was forced to defend himself, and it's our fault that now he doesn't have a place to go!"

Wallace rolled over to face him. "Leonard, that kid's a delinquent and you know it. It's a good thing we bothered to try to help him."

"Not in the way we did," Leonard said, shaking his head. He leaned over the railing of his bed. "That kid is not a bad egg, and you know it!"

"Please!" Wallace said, and really started to raise his voice. "You know what good kids don't do?" He counted off on his hand. "They don't run away from home, they don't throw weapons and break people's windshields – multiple times, I might add! – they don't build treehouses along the highway and move in to them, they don't come flying out of them gung-ho with a gas mask and start beating up police officers, and they don't go around hunting tax auditors!"

"WE FORCED HIM! Can't you see that? If we had just left him be in the first place and heeded his warnings about everything else, neither of us would be hurt, the kid would be okay! Why can't you see that, Wally? The only reason that any of us are in this mess is because we took *his* side too late!"

"Yeah, because I'm going to take the side of the kid that busted my windshield and nearly broke my ankle," Wallace said.

"You know what," Leonard said, hopping out of bed, "I'm done with this whole stupid thing."

Wallace harrumphed, and rolled over for another go at trying to sleep. "Good, me too," he said.

"No," Leonard said as he stood in the doorway. "I mean I'm done with you. Len I can stand. I feel for that kid. We came along when he had a good thing going and messed it all up for him. And I feel bad for him, but you sit there and you're too stupid or proud to acknowledge that we screwed up and try to honestly do good by him."

"I tried to apologize," Wallace said. "He just turned around and was going to hit me again."

"Wouldn't you?" Leonard asked. "God, Wallace, the kid just became legitimately homeless and you wonder why he's having a hard time being a little compassionate to the guys that essentially made it happen?"

"Screw you, Leonard," Wallace said. He pulled the blankets over his shoulder.

"Screw you too, Mr. James."

"Is there a problem in here?" asked a nurse.

"As a matter of fact, there is," Leonard told her. "I need a different room before things… get unpleasant in here."

"Mmmmm-hm," the nurse said. "I can hear you two 'bout to come to blows all the way down this hallway. Come on, I'll find you another room, as long as the two of you quiet down."

"That would be wonderful, thank you," Leonard said. He didn't bother checking over to Wallace, and followed the nurse down the hallway. That left Wallace alone, who shifted in his bed and watched the rain patter against the window. In the distance, the plume of smoke continued billowing over the trees.

Chapter Twenty-Three

The treehouse was four-fifths gone. One corner of Len's bed hung in the air over the sinkhole in the floor; the trapdoor hung on by a thread; the shutters were all gone except one, and the planks of the walls jutted this way and that like a poorly planned fence. The map at the base of the trunk continued to flap and wave in the wind, but without as much protection from the rain as earlier, it began to get wet and would soon dissolve. Against the blackened tree and the shards of construction left up top, the rungs now looked like the vertebrae of a skeleton's jagged spine.

Meanwhile, the sounds of moving traffic and tires on wet roads continued behind Len. Though the rain had stopped sheeting, the storm had all but run out of things to say. Len was still drenched and would more than likely catch a cold by the end of the night.

Len, however, wasn't sure if he would last till morning. Either by his doing or Jodie's, he simply wasn't sure. He looked at the treehouse, his protection, his shield against the world, and thought a lot about how little a chance he stood. Completely beside himself, he clambered to his feet, bawling, and wandered in the grass to and fro. He formed odd loops and figure eights, dragging his feet and moaning. In particular, he despaired that even his simple carving hadn't been spared. Jodie had of course destroyed that, too. She'd destroyed his entire life.

When none of his stumbling about worked to repair the treehouse or making anything better, and the smoke cloud still presided over the remnants of his home, Len did the only thing he could think of to improve the situation. To end Jodie's chase, to give himself peace, and to avoid ever having to go back to Pennsylvania, Len stumbled further. Tripping over his own feet the entire way, he wandered into traffic.

Nobody was in the first lane, and the nearest car hadn't yet come around the bend. Len didn't keep track of what lane he was in. He just stumbled forward and hoped somebody would hit

170

him. That would be it. It was all he wanted anymore. That was his simple request, his last wish, and the entire world to him. Even as his eyelids flickered open and shut while he drunkenly danced to and fro, he could sense the lights of cars through them. The first car honked and swerved out of the way at the last instant.

Len screamed after him. "You bastard!!" he said, but another car replaced it in the lane. There was one beside that car in the next lane, but Len didn't smile at the relief. He braced himself for it.

The driver laid on the horn and nearly got into a rollover trying to get into the vacant first lane. As that car drove away, Len saw it rock as it desperately tried to correct the teetering chassis.

He tried again, and moved, unable to stand up straight, onto the line between two lanes. A car was coming in either one. Len could just fall into one of them.

When he did, both drivers saw the soaked, sobbing boy at the last second. Both sprayed honks at Len. The one went into the vacant lane; the other scraped the median, and sparks went flying. Neither stopped.

Len went on and on, losing track of time until he was completely absorbed in his quest. At one point, he managed to have a car clip his arm, though it only threw it out of its way. It hurt, but it didn't kill him. And Len kept trying. "Come on, you bastards!" he said. "You hate me and I hate you! Everything you stand for! So come on! DO IT!"

The drivers, of course, didn't hear him say any of that. They saw a young boy with green hair and wet clothes come out of nowhere and tried not to hit him. Len didn't know it, but they didn't need vehicular manslaughter on their records.

A long time passed, and Len began to wonder how Jodie hadn't seen what he was up to, hopped in a vehicle herself and slammed into him. There came a break in traffic, and Len shrieked down the road, into the darkness at the absolute top of his lungs "You BITCH!" he said. He doubled over himself, screaming. "COME ON! HAVE YOUR PRIZE! YOU BEAT YOUR WIFE AND YOU'LL KILL ME, SO COME GET IT OVER WITH!"

At his feet, a light grew across all three lanes. Len took his face from the sky and had a look. Two semis and a pickup were all rolling abreast. Their headlights stared him in the face. The three of them sounded off, and then they bore down on him. Len stood before them, flinging his arms wide, and accepting the brilliant, bright wall of salvation honing in. Their headlights engulfed him. They couldn't have been more than thirty feet away.

Len closed his eyes, and thought a prayer. A force like the hand of God jolted him from place, and Len had no power but to keep from flying. He was struck.

Something heavy landed on top of him. His head bounced off of something wet and soft. Beyond his feet, a huge wind rushed by, carrying dust and rain in its wake that soaked him more. The trucks rushed by. He was okay.

"WHAT THE FUCK'S WRONG WITH YOU, LEN?!" It was Claire. She was beating on Len's chest and shrieking. "WHY WOULD YOU *DO THAT* YOU HAD ME WORRIED SICK WHAT IS THE *MATTER WITH YOU*?"

"What?" Len asked. His mind was too numb to think of anything else. How was he still alive? Was he even? Had he perhaps died and Claire had been killed, and here they were, reunited in the afterlife?

"Len! Len, can you hear me?" Claire shook him. "Damn it Len, TALK TO ME!"

"Claire?" Len said. "Claire, is that you?"

They'd landed on the edge of the shoulder, where the gravel gave way to grass. Claire had barely saved both of their lives, but Len was thankful.

"Oh thank God!" Claire said, and held Len's head. "Len, you scared me to death! What in God's name were you doing out there? My God, what happened? The treehouse! It's gone!"

"I know!" Len said, and immediately fell back into nearly incoherent sobs. "It's no use, Claire! She'll always be there, always right behind me. What can I do except deny her the pleasure? She brought me into this world and she thinks she has the right to take me out, but when do I get the choice for myself? When do I get to have my own life? She won't let me turn 18, Claire, how do I even know that she checked to see if I was in that treehouse before she set it on fire?" He rambled on and on. "Why did you save me?! Why can't you just let me let her win and have the whole stupid thing be over with? You bastard! Why did you have to be such a bastard, Claire! I want to die! Jodie won in Pennsylvania and she's won in Ohio and she'll win in Indiana and Michigan and wherever I go! There's no use! There's no use! There's no use!"

"Len, snap out of it!" Claire said.

"I tried to run away before and it didn't work and I can run and hide but she'll always find me and she'll always be right on my tail no matter where I go and there's nothing I can do about it because she's better than me, Claire! There isn't a thing I know that she hasn't taught me, I mean for God's sake she's the parent, I'm just a kid and what do I know? WHAT DO I KNOW, MAN?"

Claire yelled it right in his face. "SHE IS NOT YOUR MOM!"

Len stopped dead.

"What?"

"She's not your mom, Len!" Claire said, and shook Len for emphasis. "She's not. And your legal name isn't Leonard Campbell. I know."

"What are you talking about?" Len said, wiping the tears from his face. Quite instantly, he'd stopped sobbing. He had no idea what Claire meant, but...

"Len," Claire said, "after Jodie pinned me down in the field, I got to wondering. Once I went home after she chased us through the railyard, I decided to do something about it. So I started snooping around on the Internet for news about

173

something, anything regarding a Jodie Campbell. There aren't any legal records, no court documents, no driver's licenses or marriage records for anybody by the names of Jodie and Dianne Campbell."

"Of course there aren't," Len said. "Pennsylvania doesn't recognize same-sex marriage yet."

Claire shook her head violently. "No. Len, you don't understand. I didn't find records from Pennsylvania, or Rhode Island, or New York, or *any* state for them. Or her in general. Len, that woman is not your mother. I thought you were just disowning her, but you've been right this entire time.

"I was able to find documents about your good mom. Dianne. There was mention of a Dianne Godlewski, and I crossed paths with Wallace and Leonard on my way over here. I asked them about it; they said she exists and gave me a photo that looked exactly how you described. And here's the kicker," she said, "because your mom *was* married."

"Wait," Len said, "you mean Dianne had a husband?"

"Yes!" Claire said. "Your last name is Godlewski, Len. Dianne is your birth mom, but Jodie has no relation to you at all. I don't know everything, but I think it's just about high time you find out."

Len sat up. "How?" He nodded at the treehouse. "She's obviously willing to go to greater lengths to win this game."

"I'm not sure," Claire said, "but I don't think your mom Dianne visited your Uncle Hank for comfort. I think she visited him to pay her respects and pray. Who knows how many others from your family she had to do it for, but there's a record of your Uncle Hank in the system, Len."

"...what did it say?"

"His name is Godlewski, too," Claire said. "I found a newspaper article from about sixteen years ago and his obituary. He died 'under suspicious circumstances,' but no arrest was made. They couldn't or didn't complete the investigation."

"Do you think it had something to do with Jodie?" Len asked.

"It might," Claire said, "and I think you owe it to yourself to find out. The best way, I think, would be to ask her yourself. So we need to find her. I'm going to get Subhail's gun and help you. Tonight."

"No," Len said. "I'm not getting you involved like that. This is my fight. I'll see it to its end."

He and Claire exchanged hard looks. "Are you sure?" Claire asked, but it was much closer to a statement.

"I am," Len said, and stood up.

"That's not all, though," she said. Len gave her his attention. "Len, I know this isn't all easy to take in, but Hank isn't your uncle. I found the marriage records. He's your dad."

Len's eyes went blank as his heart skipped a beat. At some point, the rain had dropped its gusts without him noticing. It wasn't sheeting any more. "My... my dad?"

"Your parents are Henrik and Dianne Godlewski, Len. And your cousin, Sarah, is Henrik's daughter – and by that logic, that would make her –"

"My sister…"

"I don't know where Jodie comes in exactly, or why she wants you back in Pennsylvania so badly, but you've got some heavy questions to ask her. I wonder if she thinks you know."

"She doesn't," Len said. "Otherwise she wouldn't have played Good Mother this entire time."

They stood in the rain, darkness, and quiet for a few moments. Both of them eyed the embering treehouse and shook their heads.

"I'll miss that place," Claire said.

Len placed a hand on her back and they began walking. "Yeah," he said. "Me too."

"So what happens now?"

"I think you're right," Len said. "I need to find Jodie again before she finds me, and I need to find out the truth. And she has more than ever to answer for for what she's done to my mom."

"You know what might not be a bad idea," Claire said, "is if you could get a hold of Wallace and Leonard again. Last I saw, they were willing to help you out. Maybe they could call on the cops again and help you track down Jodie, maybe even help you confront her?"

Len dipped his head. "Maybe. But after all the good they've done me," he said, and motioned to the treehouse, "do you really think it's a good idea to get them involved again?"

Claire had only to glance at the treehouse. "It's up to you, Len. If you don't think any good can come of it, then I wouldn't. I should have listened to you in the first place about all this, and they should've, too. Now they're in the hospital because of her.

"But," she said on the spring of the idea, "that also means they've got beef with her now, too – whether she initially recruited them to find you or not."

"That's not a bad point," Len said. "Okay. I'll try to get a hold of them and see if they'll be willing to help me."

"Willing?" Claire asked.

"We kind of had a falling out," Len said, and said no more. Claire didn't pry. "I think, though," he added, "that before anything I want to visit my Uncle Hank's grave again. I figure if Dianne got some comfort out of it, maybe I can, too."

Claire nodded. She didn't bother correcting the relation; she figured Len had called Hank his uncle for all his life so far, and it would take some getting used to. "Are you going tonight?" Claire asked.

"I had better," Len said. "There's no telling how long I have before Jodie shows up here to inspect the damage and ambush me. You should get back home, though, in case she tries to pull this on your house, too."

Reluctantly, Claire agreed. "Where will you go when you're done, though?" she asked. "You can't come back here."

"I have a car now," Len said. "I'll get to the hospital and find Wallace and Leonard, crash there for the night. Tomorrow I'll brainstorm with them about what comes after."

"Fair enough," Claire said. "Good luck, Len. I'm pulling for you."

"Thank you," Len said. "For everything."

"Can we rendezvous tomorrow?"

"Sure. What time?"

"Whenever," Claire said. "You have my number, and I'm sure Wallace and Leonard have phones."

They bid each other good night. Given a moment to himself, Len suddenly remembered that his carving was in the SUV, not the treehouse. He smiled at it but then his thoughts, completely on their own, turned to his family.

"Uncle Hank is my dad," he said. "And Sarah's my sister... my God." His heart soared at the idea, even if they were dead and he never met them. The idea of knowing where he was from, and having the veil lifted, was more than he ever thought he'd get.

"Leonard Godlewski," he said. He laughed. "Len Godlewski." He shrugged. He'd have to get used to it. His gaze crept over to the Enclave, still running, and once more to the treehouse. It hurt to scrap his pristine last memory of it, but the fact remained: it was still his home.

Rain continued to fall.

Chapter Twenty-Four

Len left the Enclave at the edge of the gravestones. Unlit, the graveyard was difficult to see through the overcast night and rain, but Len had already been there a couple of times and knew his way around well enough to get where we was going. He walked underneath the entrance gate that he could barely make out. It read "In Peace We Lay Thee Here." Falling rain made the dirt paths muddy and the grass soggy. It squished when he stepped and released water like a sponge, leaving his socks long since as soaked as the rest of him.

Greenlawn Cemetery sat on the outskirts of a town called Wapakoneta, across the street from the bowing curve of a river that came from the north before rebounding east. All the oldest gravestones kept guard out front. Toward the newer section, down the slope, Len found a specific row.

He took a deep breath and cut left off of the path. Barely able to make out but maybe ten feet around him, Len found two graves, side by side, with a space on either side. There were two graves on either side as yet unoccupied. Len knew these were reserved for Uncle Hank's family.

Len knelt before the tombstone, glowing with a smile. He set the revolver on the ground in front of him. His hand went up on its own as he felt out the letters – and for the first time, his fingers were able to make sense of the last name.

"HENRIK GODLEWSKI," the grave marker said. "1972-1998. Beloved…" Len could never make out the rest. Did it say father, husband, uncle, friend? He had no idea. One time, about a year and a half earlier, Len brought a flashlight to find out for sure. Someone – with all his money on Jodie – had chiseled out the rest of the message. Now more than ever, it made Len furious. She'd desecrated his father's resting place. She had dared, and she had to pay. Len resolved that she would.

He looked on his left, and saw the next grave in a new light. "SARAH GODLEWSKI," it said. Henrik's daughter, Len knew.

His cousin, he'd been told. He knew better now. He smiled her way. 1993 to 1998 was her marker. Len cried. She was just a child.

"What happened to you?" he asked in the downpour. "I'm sorry that I never knew." He directed this to his father. "I'm sorry that I didn't figure it out, never learned sooner. I'm sorry! Damn it, I've just been an ignorant bastard and you deserved better!"

Len sat there and wept. For how long, he didn't know. Kneeling, with one arm draped across his dad's tombstone, Len wept. "You unfortunate bastard," he said, "I love you…"

Finally, when he got it all out, he steadied his breath. Soon he would catch a cold, but that didn't matter. He squared his shoulders. "I promise I'll do better now," he said. "I swear to you, I'll make whoever did this pay. And then I'll get Dianne out from underneath that bitch that crept into our life after you were gone. She's got no business in it. You knew that, didn't you? You knew she was trouble from the get-go. And yet she remains… but I'll see to that, Dad. I'll make sure Mom can be happy again."

As if agreeing to some dark pact of vengeance, the storm rumbled in the background. It was a deep, proud sound and when it was done, Len nodded. He glanced at his sister's grave. His smile was gone, replaced with a solemn expression of a boy on a mission.

Somewhere, not altogether far from the boundaries of the graveyard, lightning struck behind Len. He looked forward.

"It was you, wasn't it?" he asked, as if begging an answer of God Almighty.

There was silence, occupied only by the hissing of the falling rain.

"How long have you known?" Jodie asked.

Len's head rolled forward on his shoulders. He nodded, but made no attempt to stand or turn around. He used his father as a mediator, facing his epitaph and not the monster standing over his shoulder at the foot of the grave.

"Did you enjoy it?" Len asked. "Did you like ripping my family apart? Were you beside yourself with happiness when you came to Ohio with the opportunity to do it all over again?"

"Len!" she said.

"Oh, don't give me that," Len said over his shoulder. "You live for this, and we both know it."

"That's not how it is!" she said. "That's not how it ever was…"

"But it was you, though, wasn't it?"

"…yes. Yes, Len, it was."

Despite being right, Len felt a pang echo off the walls of his heart. "Why did you do it?" he asked. "What did they ever do to you?"

"Listen, Len… it's complicated, okay?"

Len chuckled in spite of himself. "How is any of this okay?" he asked. "How is chasing me from state to state and beating my mom and killing my dad and sister – how is any of this okay?"

Behind him, Jodie stood, deflated. She gathered the strength, and took a breath, and let it out. "It was never meant to be this way. Nothing was ever supposed to be like this, Len, I –"

"How did it happen?" Len asked.

"I'm sorry?" she asked, as if choking on her surprise.

"How did it happen," he repeated.

There was a long while before he heard her voice again.

At last, Jodie spoke. "After your parents had their first child, Sarah, they had a bit of an issue. Dianne had a lot of complications giving birth to your sister, and one thing led to another and, long story short, it didn't look like they were going to be able to have a son like they'd at least planned to try.

"There were medical advancements available that would have helped them, but none of those were within their reach. After all the bills tallied from Sarah's birth and dealing with the complications, Hank and Dianne weren't sure they'd ever be able to figure it out. The one project they were able to sit down and figure out, would leave Sarah well over ten years old before she got a sibling. Your parents didn't want to wait that long."

"So I'm an adopted little bastard," Len said. He nodded. He could accept that. It gave him a family all the same.

"No," Jodie said. Len's heart reeled again.

Jodie continued. "By the time Sarah was four years old, your parents desperately wanted another child. No hospital, though, would help them with the fertility and prenatal care it would require, though, because they already owed the first one so much money that they weren't paying back with any kind of speed. Around this time, Dianne began her preschool teaching. If she couldn't get a boy of her own, she said she could go to work every day and pretend.

"Without anywhere else to turn, your parents came to my boss."

"Your boss?"

"My boss," Jodie said. "They told him about the situation, and asked for some help. He agreed, on the stipulation that once you were old enough, you would start an apprenticeship and work for him to pay off the debt, since your parents simply wouldn't have the extra money. Your parents accepted those terms, and the mob in that part of Philly financed their way to artificial insemination and a second C-section birth.

"Well, I guess that would be leaving out a few details. So let's start where it started..."

$\mathscr{L}$

A beige overcoat came draped around Dianne's shoulders. She forced her mouth to form a smile (she got about halfway) and leaned into Hank's shoulder as he pulled her in close. He flattened out his tie so it would catch more of her tears. As he cradled his wife, Hank fought off the temptation to chew his mustache. Every now and then, he caught the glance of another patient in the waiting room as they pretended to read a magazine.

He kissed Dianne's forehead. "Shhh, now, everything will be okay. We'll figure this out yet."

The doctor, standing before them, gripped her clipboard with both hands. "But I - I haven't said anything yet. What's wrong?"

"We've been through this enough times to know," Hank said. He squeezed Dianne by the shoulder between sobs. "Let me guess. Outstanding balance."

The 50-something physician searched for words. "I'd love to help, really I would," she said, "but I'd have to pull some wild strings. Maybe there are some extra forms my secretaries could navigate, but..."

She placed a hand on Hank's shoulder, but couldn't think of something to comfort his wife. Swallowing the regret, she offered her apologies before calling the next patient into the back with her.

It had been the same everywhere. The letters had painted such as bleak a picture, but Hank didn't think it would actually be this bad. No doubt when they got home, the neighbor would ask all sorts of questions, ripping open scabs that haven't had an inkling of a chance to fully-form yet. It might as well have been nineteenth-century surgery without an anesthetic. What was worse, this was the last reputable doctor in Philadelphia. Any further out from home and they'd have to pay to fly just to see a doctor. Hank couldn't take that much further time off work.

The appointment concluded. Hank got Dianne to let him check out at the window so they could leave. The secretary passed the documents through the window, including the doctor's business card. Hank held it up, shaking his head and scoffing. "How, wh- why would I need this? I've already come here. I already know about this doctor."

The secretary peered over her glass. "Look at it, honey. And you just go ahead and give 'em a call when you're ready."

Hank turned the card over his knuckles before stuffing it in his shirt pocket. He leaned in and offered the deathliest whisper he could muster. "Is this some sort of joke?"

The secretary leaned over her bosom, getting just as close as the glass would allow. Hank became glad for the glass, for when she spoke, he saw how awful her teeth were - he didn't care to discover whatever breath might have been there too. "No joke, sweetheart. Just a business offer. You take it or leave it, no questions asked," she said.

"But why would you possibly be interested in me? How could you know about me?"

The secretary stood, grabbing a manila folder. "Guess you'll find out when you call." At that, she waddled away.

It took all of six days for Hank to grapple with the idea, let Dianne in on the decision, and for the two of them to make an appointment. Six days after having enough, they met the secretary on her "break" outside the clinic building. She introduced them to a couple of husky, scruffy fellows in toques and jackets, whose names neither of them remembered. It was these two men that escorted the two into a diner not far away, where they sat across the table from a white-suited man patiently stirring his tea and pretending to read the newspaper.

"Mr. and Mrs. Godlewski," the Don said. "So pleasant to meet you. Welcome. Before we begin, I trust you have questions. Please, keep the volume polite and mind the company, yeh?"

Hank and Dianne glanced around. They didn't see any cops, and the diner hardly had anybody in it. Best to keep the conversation, then, where it wouldn't disturb the other few tables.

Hank initiated. "How do you know about us?"

The Don giggled. "That answer should be pretty obvious, Mr. Godlewski. Suffice to say my employees are wide-spread and very observant. Jake here brought your scent to me a few weeks ago after one of my people in the insurance office flagged the file." He didn't indicate who Jake was; Hank guessed one of the men the secretary had introduced them to. "Boring stuff, really. We flag every rejected insurance claim, just in case the client is persistent. Then, y'know, we raise an eyebrow and see if there's business to conduct. So, is there business to conduct?"

"Wait, how long have you been tracking us?"

The Don showed his palm. "Mr. Godlewski, please. We're in polite company here. Your volume."

Hank hadn't realized that he was half-raised out of his booth seat. He sat back down.

Then Dianne spoke. "Tell us what sort of deal you're prepared to make."

The Don nodded at her with a ferociously calm grin. "Of course, Mrs. Godlewski. The terms we've prepared involved no major nor substantial effort on your end for many years, and the child..."

Half an hour later, the Don produced a contract and offered a pen. Hank and Dianne exchanged looks.

"Are you sure this is what you want?" Hank asked.

"We'll do what must be done," Dianne said. "It's our family that's at stake. Our dream!"

"One last thing," the Don said, turning toward the back pages of the document. "As an insurance measure - you seem like reasonable people, I'm sure you understand - the child will receive a bodyguard from among my employees. I spare this personnel for as much the child's protection as for my own. This guardian will have round-the-clock access to the child, no questions asked.

"If you try to cheat me on this deal, they'll find out, and then I will. Not that it's ever been a problem, but it never hurts to... have a bit of insurance, if you will."

As the waitress refilled their coffee, the Godlewskis signed. The Don collected the paper, let them keep the pen, and asked the men in toques to make sure the diner was paid. He and the Godlewskis departed company without another word. One of the Don's men paid at the counter, and the other stopped at the table on his way out. "We'll be in contact. Don't worry about the doctors - we'll get it arranged with your normal physician."

Then the two men went and caught up with their boss. Hank and Dianne weren't sure they'd ever seen those three men again, and sat there at the diner for hours, wondering how good a decision they'd made.

L

"So you see, Len, your birth was a favor to the mob. You are a bartered item and *you* belong to *us*. Of course, it wasn't long before your father started looking for ways to cut us out of the deal, and things turned sour awfully quick. I was assigned to the household during the pregnancy to make sure it all went smoothly, you know, to protect the investment. After you were born, I was told to stick around as an extension of that.

"I had no choice, of course, when your father started acting funny. You were really young when he started sneaking around after work, before he came home, trying to arrange a way for the four of you to flee the state and try to escape your debt to us. When he was stupid enough to actually bring that work home, I caught him red-handed and I didn't have any choice but to make him abandon it.

"My boss, of course, was not at all pleased with those developments. He declared your father a rat, so we shot him."

"Is that how you got Wallace and Leonard, too?" Len asked. "You called some of your crew in from Philadelphia to jump them?"

"As a matter of fact, yes Sir," Jodie said. "They were getting in the way of me doing my job, and I couldn't allow that. Obviously killing government officials on that level isn't the easiest thing to get away with, so we had to offer them a warning, first. Frankly speaking I'm not sure why my boss had me collaborate with them in the first place but, as I'm sure you know, desperate times call for desperate measures."

"So how did it happen?"

"How did what happen?"

"How did my sister and dad die?"

Jodie took a moment on that one. Len could picture her behind him, thumbing at her gun and turning it over in her hand, reveling in drawing out his death. She spoke again, out of nowhere, and it snapped him out of that daydream.

"It was simple," she said. "Or, at least, it would have been had your mother and sister not gotten involved. I knew your

185

father was in the next room fiddling with something he shouldn't have been, so I got up to catch him with it and destroy whatever it was. I threw open the door, this very same gun in hand, and he turned around from his desk. I shoved him aside, and sent his papers and markers flying, and I told him to burn all of it and never speak of it again. In his confusion, he attacked me. I shot him in the side of the abdomen – not hitting anything serious, but enough to stop him momentarily – and within an instant, your sister and mother flooded into the room to stop me.

"I was able to slap Dianne into the corner fairly easily, the lightweight that she is, but then your father lunged at me, blind as ever in his rage and I aimed from the hip. Your sister was in the way. She took the bullet straight in the face and dropped. Your parents wailed over it, but only a moment later your dad pushed the envelope again and came at me with a letter opener. I closed the door in his face and, when I heard a thump as he hit the other side, opened it again and stunned him by slamming it into him. I pressed him between the door and the wall, but he continued to struggle.

"He told me how they would escape, how I would pay for what I'd done to his daughter, how I was the enforcer of the ruination of his family. Henrik told me... with such, *conviction*... that the two of them would escape Philadelphia with you and let their debt become a memory and, thereafter, myth.

"It was at that moment," Jodie said, "that I became the protector of your life, Len."

Len leveled his chin. "What... the hell are you talking about? What do you mean, Bitch?"

She didn't seem at all fazed; she continued as she had been. "I would have to tell the Boss about what happened, why a little girl was dead and all that. If Henrik lived, word would reach my boss of his plans for escape, and then things would become much, much worse. The Boss would have killed you, Len, simply to show your father who's in charge.

"You were just a baby, Len. How could you be at such fault that you should have to die for your father's insistence? To prevent that end, I killed your father right then and there. While he was stuck between the wall and the door, with the knob dug up against his bullet wound, I put the gun against his head as calmly as I could and fired. He fell, and I told Dianne to be silent about it all if she wanted to at least save you.

"She loved you, Len. With all her heart. She wanted dearly to save you, and I used that to stay in the frame for years as you grew up. I was there to save you as well, and now as you approach your eighteenth birthday, the time will soon be upon you to go and serve the Don."

"What makes you think I'll fulfill that promise?" Len asked.

"Personally, I don't," Jodie said. "You're too stubborn and you've screwed yourself on this entire thing!"

"Heard me, did you?"

"What, just now? When you were mumbling to Henrik's rock?"

"Hmph," Len said. "Did you enjoy my little spiel?"

"You were talking too low. I didn't hear it."

'Good,' Len thought. "Then maybe I'll give you the gist of it." He leaned to his left as slowly and subtly as he could, knowing the darkness and curtain of rain would help his cause. He reached out for his revolver.

"Ah-ah-ah!" Jodie said. Her voice shifted into something Len had never heard before. Nearly all femininity dropped from it, replaced with a deep, nearly male quality. "Game's done, Sweetheart." Len heard the click of metal. More than likely pointed at him, no less, Jodie had her gun cocked and ready to go.

He sat back on the soles of his feet. There was nowhere to run. Not even a highway with which to end it on his own terms.

"Good boy," the real Jodie said. "So I'll ask you again, you little pest: how long have you known?"

All the pent-up anger rushed up Len's throat before he could stop it. "What's it even matter?" he asked, and he could feel her expression tighten at the sound of his contempt. "Why even play this part of the game, Jodie? You've got me cornered, you know I'm not going back to Pennsylvania, not to become like you and serve your boss or anyone, and that's the end of it. For me, anyway. You won, so take your victory and let's be done with it."

"Hm," Jodie said. "You got balls, Kid. It was your little friend that told you, wasn't it? That's fine. I'll burn down that little ranch of hers when we're done here. Make sure her daddy-come-to-your-rescue gets a nice little ending, too, before I do it."

'Claire.'

"Wait!" Len said. "Will you… would you spare them if I came home with you?"

Jodie laughed. "What, now you wanna change your tune? It ain't up to me no more, Kid. Never was. I tried to play nice and get all this sorted out, but you and your bitch mom didn't wanna play ball. So now I'm gonna kill your ass, kill your friend's ass and when I get back to Pennsylvania I'm gonna kill your mom's ass, too."

"Tell you what," Len said. "I'll duel you for it."

Jodie laughed really hard at that. "Duel? What, like the back-to-back, ten steps and shoot? Uh-uh, Kid. My game, my rules. You're gonna die, right here tonight, and you're not gonna get anything else done. Kapeesh?"

There was a pause. "Eh?" Jodie asked again, but Len still didn't say anything. She re-punctuated her question. "EH? You deaf, Little Man? I asked you, is that –"

"Do it!" Len said. "Just do it! Unless you're too big and bad and scared?"

Jodie did not reply immediately. She was too busy building up a laugh that turned into something uproarious. "Oh, man, Kid, you're really something. You remind me every bit of Dianne."

Len harrumphed again. "How do you mean? The part where you beat me unmercifully for no good reason?"

"No good reason! Len, I ask you, were you ever in the room when it happened?"

188

"No," Len said, "but that doesn't make you any less the villain. That was domestic violence, nothing less."

"You have no idea," Jodie said, unable to help a whimpered return to the voice Len knew her for. "I saved BOTH of you from being killed! You wanna know how I know that? Because your mother was so insistent on calling the cops time and again, like they were gonna save either of you even *if* I got out of the picture! Every time she would tell me she was reaching for that phone and I had to intercept her, else the cops would carry me away and the Don would call somebody in to abort the whole deal. And that would have meant your death, Len. That would have meant your death."

"So... what? You saved my life by hitting my mom?"

"Time and time again," Jodie said. "Dianne's got no sense, Len. She's got no sense, and frankly she's lucky she didn't get caught comin' over here and promising your dead father all this revenge and whatnot."

"I... I'm sorry," Len said. "I always thought you were this monster, and I..."

"I was just doing my job," Jodie said. "I forgive you, Len. Can you forgive me?"

"...if you let me go."

Jodie sighed very, very loudly. "See, Len, I still gotta do my job."

Len perked up again. He kept an eye out for a window to snag his revolver. "Why do you sound like you're about to say no?"

"Well, mister Len, you had to go and screw that up for yourself," Jodie said.

"What do you mean?" Len managed to ask as the words stumbled through his teeth.

"Well, after you took off, the Don had a couple of men look out on the news for some sign of you. You didn't re-materialize in Philly after a while so we branched out our search. We had a little bit of a bite from Wallace and Leonard, but he really knew to search here in earnest when we got that video of you staving them off. That was all between the two of you, Little Man, and when you refused to come back to Pennsylvania with me and had to make so much trouble, I had to meet with the Don."

"So is that where you've been the last couple of days?"

"Yup. And there's good news, Len. He wants me to finally just forget this whole, stupid thing."

"That's great –"

"After telling me to just kill you and be done with it."

The rest of Len's words died in his throat. He slouched, rain still pouring, gun barely out of reach.

"I'm sorry, Len," Jodie said in her real, unfamiliar voice. "I swear, I'm just doing my job." She leveled the gun at the back of his head, somewhere on the edge of her vision in the dark and weather.

Tears welled up in Len's eyes. He straightened out his back, looking upon his dad's grave in his final moments. "So what's stopping you now?" he asked.

"Nothing," Jodie said. "Goodbye, Len."

Len nodded solemnly. "Goodbye, you heartless bastard. Game's done, right?"

"Game's done," Jodie said. Len's brow curled, for he could not make sense of why she sounded so sad.

Before he could give himself an answer, a bolt of lightning less than a mile off flashed across the graveyard. Len caught the revolver at the edge of his vision. He knew he wouldn't be able to get to it in time.

At his core, though, he knew he had to try. In the flash, his hand darted straight for it.

Jodie fired.

Len's shoulder spewed an eruption of flesh and blood, and he fell forward. Mid-fall, his reaching hand immediately abandoned its mission and clutched the wound. He landed on them both. An all-consuming round of thunder boomed over the graveyard, and as Len lay twisted, bleeding in the saturated grass, he was able to look back and see Jodie on the edge of his vision. She was only there for a moment.

Lightning struck again – cracking a tree somewhere off in the dark – and Len saw the shape of Jodie fall off the edge of his sight as thunder roared with the blinding light. It threatened to shred his very eardrums. The rain kept coming down in torrents, diluting his blood as it pooled, coursing, from his shoulder. His vision fogged out, and Len remembered nothing more.

Chapter Twenty-Five

Len stood before an empty tree. Its leaves were budding, but the spring day was young and just the right amount of warmth. His hand rested on the head of the hammer in his belt. He had a pile of wood between the shoulder and the ditch.

The smallest ones he snapped over his thighs and across the tree's trunk. The small pieces that resulted, he nailed to the tree. A series of them ran up the side, up to where the main boughs went their ways, but Len knew that wouldn't do. Painstakingly, he nailed together a platform in a good position where it compromised with the boughs; he did not cut them, but still was able to use them to support the structure.

He spent the day forming a nice, flat base. At lunch, he sat on the edge of it, appreciating the fruits of his labor. People in the road drove by and gave him queer looks. "What on earth was that boy doing?" they no doubt asked. Len let them wonder. He let them not know. It served them right for being bastards.

He was on his hands and knees, placing nails and starting them, hammering them and moving on. Now he had a good, solid platform. He cut out a square above the rungs. Yes, that was where he would put a trapdoor.

Len smiled the entire time, and sensed that maybe God did, too. It had been mere weeks since he'd last seen Jodie or Dianne, and life was good. It was finally, finally good.

Night came and it was cool and clear, bringing unusually quiet, light traffic. Off in the distance Len could hear crashing waves. He promised himself he would go find them and make that an especially safe place.

The next day brought a golden fog, with traffic coursing by very regularly. Len hammered the day away, forming the walls of his treehouse. He made sure to leave window holes. The planks lined up neatly against one another. He wiped the sweat from his brow. He floated from one area to another, wafting pleasantly from task to task. And it wasn't long before the shell of that treehouse was complete. In another couple of days, he finished the roof. He cut out another trapdoor hole and used some leftover plank scraps to make the hatch. He made sure to leave some extra for the entry trapdoor.

He met a fat man named Bobby and distracted his pea brain long enough to steal his lunch. Bobby was so angry, and Len laughed as he floated away from the lumbering idiot. A week later, Len would return and the man had been so drunk, it was the first time they met. Len knew he would have fun with Bobby.

Night came again. Len was alone in the treehouse. It was an empty, fresh-smelling wooden shell without a speck of adornment to speak of. Len slept on it, and probably should have been uncomfortable, but he was very happy. He had forsaken education, abandoned his family, his home state, good shelter, and the reliability of a meal in his belly, but Len was as happy as ever, because he was no longer where he needed to not be. He wasn't sure if he was where he was supposed to be, but he felt unbelievable solace that he had escaped and was finally free to forge his own life. Len wedged that solace into his heart, and felt full.

He stood on the ground, looking up at his finished treehouse. It was a work of art. The branches stuck out only where convenient; it was otherwise a perfect cube with the rungs crawling up the trunk. Empty window holes were on three sides. Len wasn't sure if he was going to make one on the back yet, facing the field.

A green-haired, fourteen-year-old boy stood in front of a freshly erected tree fort west of Wapakoneta, Ohio. Passersby didn't ask questions, except to the passengers in the car. It became the topic of small talk.

"What's all that about?" they asked each other.

"Is it something for charity?" they wondered.

"I think it looks neat!" the children said, with some adults agreeing.

In one case or another, Len kept his back to the freeway and admired his handiwork. He looked down. At his feet, he noticed some leftovers. He took the wooden knot up into his treehouse, and used his small knife to pare shavings off, little by little.

It was the fuzziest, coziest, and by all accounts best dream that Len ever had. It was nice to feel dry and warm and safe in his head. In the real world, meanwhile, he was cold, sick, and losing blood.

Chapter Twenty-Six

Len opened his eyes. Wherever he was, it was bright and white. He felt a distinct sense of comfort, as though he lay on a bed of clouds straight from God. At first, he didn't hear anything. He stayed still, and let his eyes adjust to the light.

The details of a drop ceiling came into focus. Len became aware of a pulse in his neck and a weird feeling in his right collarbone. It wasn't pain, but there was definitely something extra on it. He tried to wriggle it; it felt sore.

He let his head drop to the side. On his left was a window to a beautiful day outside. Below, a gang of autumn leaves swirled down the road just beyond the parking lot. He was several stories up in a building. Between his bed and the window, Len then noticed, was a chair. It was empty.

He listened. Delicately, the beeping of a heart monitor crept into being. Len sat up.

Claire went to him, and guided him back down. "Whoa, whoa, slow down, Len," she said. "Take it easy. It's okay."

Len looked around. Claire was bedside, and at the foot of the bed stood Leonard, Subhail, and a nurse. They were all watching him.

"What… what happened?" Len asked. "Where am I?" He knew where he was, but he was still coming out of a twilight and couldn't rush back into panic quite as quickly as normal. It hit him that he was in a hospital, and he immediately retracted to sitting up in the bed, ready to leap over everybody and make a break for it.

The heart monitor picked up on it all, but slowed down as Len calmed himself. The second Len had poised himself, his shoulder betrayed him. His arm clicked out from beneath him and, while not contorting into anything uncomfortable, refused to carry weight. The railings of the bed were up as well. He wasn't going anywhere.

"Claire!" he said. "Claire, I can't be here. We need to get out of here, leave, like right now. Come on, let's go! I can't stick

195

around anymore – she's still out there somewhere and last I saw her she shot me and I don't even know how I got here so please, please let's just go before she corners me again and –"

"Len! That's enough," Claire said. Len snapped out of it, and looked at her with an expression that was half dumbfounded and half panic.

Len looked around again at each of them. Their faces made no sense. He opened his mouth to say something, but gave it up as a bad job. He leaned in to Claire. "Where is Jodie?" he asked.

Claire placed a hand on Len's left, far shoulder. "Don't worry about it," she said. "Just sit back, relax." She pushed Len back into the bed. "Do it, before I make you, you hurt and stubborn bastard."

Len couldn't help but smile. "That's my word," he said.

"I know," Claire said as she joined Leonard, Subhail, and the nurse near Len's feet. "So, what's the last thing you remember?"

"I… I remember building my treehouse after just running away from home. Everything was just golden and wonderful. I haven't been that happy in… ever."

"I don't think that was real, Len," Claire said. "You've been in a coma the last eight days."

"Eight days?! How hasn't Jodie come and gotten me? How come I'm not dead?"

"Relax! Relax," Claire said. "All in good time. Are you feeling all right?"

"All in good time, Hell!" Len said, and scrambled into position to leap again. Again, his shoulder refused and he sat back down. "Damn it," he said, clutching his shoulder.

"Len," said a voice, and Len looked up to see Leonard walking up the side of the bed. "You've been through a lot. Don't worry; Jodie is not going to bother you again. Officer Clasby is personally seeing that she's held in custody."

Staring into his sudden ally's eyes, Len found himself wondering what all was going on. He steadied his breaths, amazed and full of questions, and allowed himself to calm down.

"What happened?" he asked.

"We're not entirely sure," Claire said, "but I think you can help us piece it the rest of the way together. So, aside from you building your treehouse again," she asked, "what was the last thing you remember?"

"Ah," Len said. He took a moment. "I went to my dad's grave to see him, you know, for the first time actually knowing that I'm his son. Somehow, Jodie followed me there. Before she shot me, she told me a lot about Pennsylvania. And then... then I had a gun and I tried to grab it, but she shot me before I could get it. All I remember after that was... she was on the edge of my vision and I'm just sitting there, helpless in the grass. Lightning struck really close by, and then that was it. Thank you, whichever one of you it was that saved me."

"We didn't," Leonard said. "When I got there with police, she was unconscious, too."

"What! How?"

Leonard shrugged. "I really don't know. How close did that lightning hit?"

"I don't think it actually hit her," Len said, chewing on his lip. "I'm not sure."

"Hm," Subhail said. To Len's surprise, he wore a witty smile. "Maybe it was God that came to your rescue, Mr. Len."

Len didn't know what to say to that. He turned to Claire. "So she was arrested?"

"Oh yeah," Claire said. "The judge denied her bail, too. Prosecutors are gonna hit her with all kinds of stuff."

"I don't get it. If you weren't there, and you weren't there," Len said, pointing to Leonard and Subhail, "who even called and let you know where I was? How did you know I needed help?"

Claire, Leonard, and Subhail looked at one another. "That's what we were hoping you could help us with," Claire said. "So you don't know?"

"No idea," Len said. The others deflated, but did not slip into sadness. He touched the gauze on his shoulder. "How bad was it?" he asked the nurse.

"Nothing too horrible," she said. Her warm, matter-of-fact voice felt good against his ears. "There was a lot of muscle missing and you'll need some more time taking it easy while the bone heals, but you'll be all right."

"I thought for sure I was going to die," Len said, and nobody had a reply for that. "So," he added, "what happens now?" He turned to Leonard. "Mr. IRS man, I'm sure you have some idea of where all the legality turns at this point, so what happens now?"

Leonard squared himself to Len. "That depends," he said. "Until we track down your mother, you're a ward of the State. A few things can happen, but I should note that your friend's father here has made arrangements with the hospital. He has been so kind as to extend his medical coverage to you, so you won't be footed a bill once you get out of here."

"I don't care about that," Len said. "My treehouse is gone, if you haven't noticed, and I can't go back to Pennsylvania." He shrugged to punctuate his point (and wound up grabbing his shoulder and wincing). "Where do I go now? What happens to me?"

"I... think Mr. Mehta can tell you more about that than I can," Leonard said. He got out of the way as Subhail stepped forward. Len leaned away from the man, who grabbed his wrist in an iron grip and patted his hand.

Subhail struggled to find the words, though Len wasn't sure if he was trying to form the English or fighting past the stigmas he had about Len. At last, though, Subhail looked Len in the eye and began to talk. "I did not know before, how hard life has been for you," he said. "You have been a good friend, a faithful friend, to Claire all these years. I am sorry that I have not gotten to know you, Mr. Len.

"I want to make up for that," he said. "And part of that, I told the hospital I would pay to help heal your injuries." It made Len uncomfortable just sitting there while Claire's dad used his broken sentences. He couldn't help but focus on Subhail's forested forearms. "I do not think that is enough, though."

"Okay..." Len said.

"What I will do," Subhail said, "is I want to help you begin your life for the better. Part of me, you know, will be sad to no longer see that treehouse across the field whenever I go to work. It was fun to look at, and I did not think I would miss it, but I do. In any case, if you wish to go to school, I will help you. Whatever you need. What is the word..." he turned to Leonard. "What is the word you used earlier?"

Leonard stepped forward. "Len," he said, "we know that your eighteenth birthday is coming up in the next month here, and then you're going to head off and try to pick up the pieces of your own thing. We got to talking and we know you're going to do what you will, but if you're up for it, Len, Mr. Mehta has said that he'd like to adopt you."

Len blinked. He looked back and forth between Leonard and Subhail. "I thought... I thought Claire's dad doesn't like me? Why would he want me around like that?"

He'd forgotten that Subhail's hands were around his own, but remembered when, at that moment, Subhail patted the back of his hand some more. "Forgive me, Mr. Len. I did not walk a mile in your shoes. I thought you were just a, how you say, delinquent? I had assumed many bad things about you, and did not understand what you were going through. I cannot undo that or some of the things I said," Subhail said, "but if you will let me, I wish to help."

Len looked to Claire, who nodded. He looked at Leonard, who smiled. He looked at Subhail, who re-punctuated his offer with a soft, friendly look. "Seriously?" he asked, and Subhail nodded. "I need to think about it," he said, and Subhail released him.

"That is okay," he said. "Take as much time as you need." He got up and returned the foot of the bed. Behind them, Claire stood back up and came up on Len's left.

"It's good to see you again," she said.

"It's good to see you again, too," Len told her.

"Please, consider my dad's offer? I know it would take some getting used to, but we'd all feel better about it," Claire said. "I know you don't like people, but, I mean, he's got the extra money set aside in case I ever made it to some crazy-expensive Ivy League school, but I'm not going to. If you want, we'd be more than happy to give you that money to go to college."

Len blinked, then looked at Subhail, who was averting his gaze. "I... had extra," he said. "From..." but a solemn Claire placed a hand on his shoulder, and he left it at that.

Len was at a loss for words. "But…" he said. "I need to…"

For the first time, Len realized that he didn't have an excuse to get out of something, even if he wanted to do it. There was no longer any pressing need to prepare for an attack, a storm, an unwelcome visit. He didn't need to stock up for the winter. He didn't need to think about Indiana. He didn't need to worry about Wallace and Leonard ('I wonder what happened to Wallace?' he thought. 'I'll have to ask'), or live in fear of Jodie, or hope he could find enough fuel to keep warm during the winter. He looked at Claire, shocked and grateful and brought to tears, and he told his friend, before sputtering into sobs, "Okay…" He nodded furiously and his eyes welled up.

"Yes," he said. "It will be good to have a sister. Again."

The two of them hugged, and Subhail placed a hand on Len's shoulder again. They remained like that for a moment as Leonard and the nurse watched from the foot of the bed. They smiled, too.

When Len, Claire, and Subhail broke, Len looked up at Subhail. "On one condition," he said.

Subhail cocked his witty smile again. "Name it."

"Just remember," Len said, "because I never did; I'm a Godlewski."

Subhail smiled, and gave him a single, solid nod.

"That settles it, then," Leonard said when they all settled back down. "I have an in with a judge in the civil courts. I'll talk to her and we'll get the adoption process started. As long as I catch her on the right day, she'll likely make it quick."

"Thank you," Len said, as Leonard had turned and was headed out the door. The remark stopped him dead.

He turned on his heels, slowly. "You're welcome, Len. And on behalf of myself and my former partner, Mr. James, the IRS apologizes that our records indicated you under the surname Campbell. Your government thanks you for your patience and cooperation, Leonard Godlewski."

Giggling, Len waved him to keep going through the door. "Get out of here," he said. Leonard and the nurse disappeared from the room, and Len tried to prop himself up one last time, shouting after the man. "Hey, wait a second!"

"I know, I know!" Leonard shouted from around the corner. "That's not your name, and I'm a bastard!"

Chapter Twenty-Seven

Wapakoneta and the surrounding area tuned in to the local news. They didn't know at the time, but Loretta Heller's broadcast would make her career. She would have Len to thank, and in the coming days, the story strode across all of Ohio and spread across the country within a week. It all started the same as always: the news had its introduction music and graphics, and they flew away in place of Ms. Heller and her co-anchor behind a desk. So it was.

"Good evening, I'm Loretta Heller. Our top story tonight: an update in the Leonard Campbell case."

The cameras on her right flicked on and she turned to them without really even thinking about it. "New details have emerged following the discovery of a teenager last seen three years ago in the metropolitan area of Philadelphia. One Leonard Campbell was reported missing by his mothers Dianne and Jodie Campbell back in May 2011. Just a few short weeks ago, the very same teenager, now age 17, was caught on tape on the side of US-33 right here in Wapakoneta, engaged in an odd, gas-filled firefight with police officers. The Internet video described the scene as an 'attack' on the green-haired runaway, but was headed by IRS auditors Wallace James and Leonard Humphrey of Columbus."

Loretta's face left the screen, replaced by government photos of Wallace and Leonard after a couple of brief clips of their attack on Len, from his contemporary's uploaded phone video.

"Following the attack, a series of odd, unexplained crimes popped up around the Wapakoneta area in connection to Jodie Campbell, Leonard's mother, who arrived from Philadelphia to help take Leonard back home. Not long thereafter, officers James and Humphrey became the victims of savage beatings, though police maintain that the culprits and motive of the attack remains unclear. While the two of them remained in the hospital," Heller said, "a local railyard had a break-in, losing a single vehicle that was sighted at the burned-down remains of the very treehouse Leonard Campbell defended on the famous video, now presumed to have been his home since he left Pennsylvania.

"Later the same night, authorities discovered the Enclave in Greenlawn Cemetary, where they also found Leonard Campbell unconscious at the grave of his late uncle, Henrik Godlewski, and sustaining a serious bullet wound to his right shoulder.

"Not far away, the literal smoking gun lay in his mother, Jodie Campbell's hand as she *also* lay unconscious in the dark and pouring rain. While authorities said that her son had a firearm of his own close by, there was no evidence to indicate that it was a self-inflicted wound.

"Tonight, police have revealed further details of this case, including the charges now being brought against Jodie Campbell. Additionally, the governments of Ohio and Pennsylvania have already finalized, four weeks after the incident, that after she stands trial in Ohio, Mrs. Campbell will face a jury of her peers in Pennsylvania for further crimes.

"In Ohio, it has been determined that Mrs. Campbell is facing charges of arson, destruction of public property, child endangerment, unlawful transportation of a firearm, unlawful possession of a firearm, aggravated assault, attempted murder and, should prosecutors find ties between her and the beatings of officers James and Humphrey, two counts of assault on government officials, two counts of conspiracy to commit murder, and two counts of attempted murder of government officials.

"In Pennsylvania, prosecutors are already readying the cases against Mrs. Campbell, including those brought on by new revelations included in the testimony of her son and his friend – who has chosen to remain anonymous – as confirmed by law enforcement's searches of public records. Regardless of the results of her trial in Ohio, Mrs. Campbell will face charges of child endangerment, domestic battery, and the kidnapping of Leonard Campbell, which brings us to a special part of our segment tonight."

203

Loretta Heller turned back to the first camera, seeming somber. It followed her.

"Law enforcement has also brought to light Mrs. Campbell's involvement in several cover-ups and conspiracies, which will also add to her Pennsylvanian charges the allegations of murdering Henrik Godlewski, kidnapping his son, Leonard, and falsifying the records of his birth certificate, falsifying name documents associated with his wife Dianne, and falsifying the civil union contract between herself and Dianne.

"Furthermore, the Philadelphian Police Department's Gang Unit has confirmed, via Ohio mug shots, of Jodie Campbell's identity. Mrs. Campbell has had run-ins with the law before, in association with the infamous Eagles-Flyer Don of Southern Philadelphia, known by police to run a complicated underground network of hitmen, illegal money lenders, drug traffickers, and other types of city-wide mob-standard crime. Though Mrs. Campbell may be offered a plea bargain in exchange for information leading to the arrest of the Eagles-Flyer Don, whose legal name continues to elude Philly PD, prosecutors say she would still face a lengthy prison sentence.

"In the meantime, her newly freed abductees, Leonard and Dianne Godlewski, face the beginnings of their lives in the aftermath of husband and father Henrik's death. Although our news station has not thus far been able to contact Dianne, we'll keep you updated as the story develops.

"In a related story," Loretta Heller said, "Leonard Godlewski faces a bright future here in Ohio, as one local family has begun court procedures to adopt him. The juvenile has been out of the system for years and, despite missing his birth certificate, contact with his birth mother, and a need to complete high school or a GED, is reported to be in high spirits and good health. The family is reported to be respecting his decision to keep his father's name, but declined further comment.

"Over to you, Bill…"

Two huge, glossy wooden doors opened. Well-dressed people flooded out into the rest of the courthouse, but within a couple of minutes four figures stood, clearly rooted, in the tide.

"I think that went well," Leonard said. Claire and Subhail nodded. "What do you think?"

For the first time since he could remember, Len wore a suit and tie complete with shiny, black dress shoes. He ran a hand through his still-wild hair. Never before had he felt so out of place. He unbuttoned his throat. "Do you know when the judge will make a final decision?"

"Should be within a week," Leonard said. He checked his watch. His suitcase remained at his side. "Sounds to me like she's willing to help you out."

Subhail laughed, stealing their attention. Len thought his gut looked ridiculous in court-appropriate dress. "Could any woman possibly sound more biased in a case?" he said. "So amazing! Isn't it illegal for a judge to be so?"

"Dad," Claire said, "not in India anymore."

"Yes, yes," Subhail said, "I forget that sometimes. Much luck to you, Len!"

"Much luck to us," Len said.

Leonard stood before the three of them and watched Len hug his soon-to-be adoptive father and sister. It warmed his heart. He checked his watch again. "I really have to be off," he said. "Remember, final hearing's in one week."

"You got it," Len said. "Thank you again, for everything."

Leonard threw his smile to one cheek and placed a hand in Len's hair. "No," he said. "Thank you, Len. It's been a pleasure."

"Ain't over yet," Len said. Leonard only patted his shoulder. He watched Len, Claire, and Subhail join the river of people and make their way out the door and down the stone steps. He stood there for a while, just beyond the courtroom floor, with a hand in his pocket and a good, good feeling. He thought deeply about all that had happened, and when he snapped out of his daydream, he was looking across the way, through a glass half-wall and the clerks sitting behind a marble counter.

He walked to one of the windows.

"How can I help you?" the middle-aged clerk said. She seemed annoyed, but nonetheless willing to do her job.

"Yes," Leonard said, withdrawing a pen. The clerk laughed a little inside at that. Didn't he see the pen on the bead chain on his side of the counter? Oh well. "I'd like to inquire about a name change," he said.

She grabbed a paper from beneath her desk and slid it beneath the glass. "Fill out this form, your new desired name and reason will go right here on the Xs, an appointment with the judge to review this will be set within a week and we'll notify you of that hearing date at that time. All right?"

"Excellent," Leonard said. He took the form and walked to the nearest bench. He stared at the form for a moment as it sat limp on his thigh, without filling out anything at all.

Before anything, he clicked his pen and went to the first X. It was the desired name field. He wrote his last name, normal as anything, and added what he wanted to make of his first name. "L-E-N," it read.

He held the mostly uncompleted form aloft in the sunlight for several minutes, looking at his new name. Thinking back months and even years later, he figured a lot of people probably walked by, and gave him funny looks. Maybe they even wondered why he had that stupid smile on his face. None of that mattered, though, because later Leonard filled out the rest of the form, and turned it in to the clerk; and she scheduled his hearing that very week – just like she said she would – and when the time came, that hearing went very, very well.

Chapter Twenty-Eight

On the last warm, lazy afternoon of the year, a little sun squeezed its way past the blinds in Claire's living room. It fell on the crest of their couch in ribbons, with Becky taking advantage. She was fast asleep, curled up on the back of the dark blue leather couch, purring.

The air in the room was still. Nothing had happened for hours. A faint, partial-day's worth of dust accumulated on the mantle above the fireplace which was the central focus of anyone entering and beholding the room. The room itself was separated where its carpet met the tile of the house entrance and the aisle extending from it to the kitchen and the rest of the house. Opposite the couch sat a love seat and some end tables, with moderately heavy Persian décor throughout.

Becky stirred. With a flick of her tail, she came to life and stretched out in ridiculous shapes. It only took a moment, and then she sat upright right where she was, tail flicking side to side, watching the door.

She heard a key enter the lock and turn. The door opened, and in came Claire and Subhail. She wondered why they had their funny dress clothes on, not understanding that they had important things to do. They used their forearms as temporary hangers for their jackets as they took a few steps into the house. They were being very loud. Becky waited on the couch for them to settle back in before asking for food.

Subhail flung his arms wide. "Ah! So good to be out of that courthouse and back home. Would you not agree, Rajkumari?"

"Feels pretty good," Claire said. "Come on, Len, come take a look around."

Becky didn't know Len's name, but when she saw an extra person walk in – also in dress clothes and an un-tucked shirt – she jumped down to weave between his feet. She remembered when they first met and he had hurt his head when she spooked him. If cats could laugh, she would have.

Len's freshly re-dyed hair waved for need of a haircut and lack of product as he looked down. "Hi, Becky," he said. "I haven't seen you in a while! You remember me, maybe? The green-haired bastard underneath the train car?"

Becky had no idea what he said. She purred anyway. Len turned his attention to Claire and Subhail as he set down his bags.

Jodie's trial was well underway, and boded ill for her. The evidence and the State's relentless prosecutors, in addition to Len and Claire's testimony, were all quickly sealing her fate. They could see it on the jurors' faces, and on the judge's. They'd paid little attention to the media and the public reaction, but there was no mistaking that Jodie was going away for a long, long time. Even then, Pennsylvanian authorities were boasting of all the evidence they had ready and waiting for her. A cop visiting from the state had even pulled Len aside one day and told him about it.

Len's adoption case seemed to be going well, too. Retaining his last name didn't seem like a problem to the judge, as long as Subhail was okay with it – which he'd made abundantly clear by standing up so fast and out of turn that the judge had to remind him of court etiquette and bang her gavel. All the while, there was no sign of Dianne; whether she didn't know or was too ashamed to make contact with Len, he didn't know. Either way, he was okay with it. Adopted or not, he would be 18 within the month (Claire had a grand surprise in store for him when it did happen, and Len never saw it coming), and he knew now that Claire and Subhail would be there for him every step of the way for whatever came next. For the first time ever, the future looked bright for Len.

He closed the screen door and stood on the doormat with the main door wide open. He took it all in. "The ranch," he said. "I always wondered if I'd ever see the inside."

Subhail had gone off farther into the house. "Well, it's time to look," Claire said. She and Len exchanged looks, and Len casually wandered onto the carpeted living area.

He looked around at the clocks on the walls, the beads on the lampshade, and the pattern in the glass of the coffee table. He took in the trinkets atop the mantle, the logs in the fireplace, and the blinds on the window.

He pointed to them. "May I?"

"Of course," Claire said. Subhail appeared over her shoulder.

Len leaned over the couch and peered through the blinds. Far off, way on the other side of the field, he could see the blurs of cars passing on the freeway. It felt strange to see such a small road outside, to be so very low to the ground yet still inside safe shelter. He looked for evidence of the highway and the trees, and he picked out exactly where his treehouse had been.

"Yeah," he said, "I can see it."

"We can keep the curtain drawn, until you think you're ready that you can look out there," Claire said.

"No, no... it's fine," Len said, standing back up. "It's just, it'll take some getting used to."

"It is all very well," Subhail said. "What would you children like for dinner?"

Claire passed. "Len?"

Len came out of a half-daydream. "Whatever's fine," he said. "I don't really care." He looked again at the yellow walls and the end of the room. He fixated on the fireplace and planted his feet before it.

Claire and Subhail watched as Len unshouldered his backpack and rifled through it. After a moment, Len found his prize. They began to wonder why he was ignoring them, but then saw a flash of a miniature housecat. They leaned over each other, trying to see.

Len placed his finished carving on the mantle. He smiled, and turned around to his new father and sister. "You know what," he said, glancing back over his shoulder, "let's order a pizza. I'd rather not bother with anything else right now."

$\mathscr{L}$

Hammer met metal over and over again somewhere a stone's throw off in the yard. The sound of it filled Willie's hangout, but Willie wasn't the one doing it. Len came through the choke point of the tracks as though he belonged there as ever. Willie had both arms and a huge wrench in his console, near the front of the yard. He did a double-take when he saw Len walking up, and set his wrench aside for it.

"An' how can I help you today, Young'un?" He leaned on the machine.

"Hi, Willie," Len said. He had street clothes and sneakers on. It had been a couple of days since he'd last been in court, and life really felt like it was going back to normal.

"What you want?" Willie asked. He spat.

Len watched the line of tobacco jet its way to the ground. "You're a disgusting bastard, you know that?"

Willie laughed, craning his head back and balking at the sky. He removed the wrench from the machine and beckoned Len to follow him. Len did. To what end he didn't know, but he did.

They moved up the rise and entered the office, where Willie leaned the wrench against the wall like a sword. The exhausted warrior showed Len through the back door to the grassy, patted-down, makeshift parking lot between the river and the railyard wall. A rust bucket of a pickup truck sat staring at the base of some cement stairs that compensated the rise between the office's door and the bank. It was down this that Willie led Len, and the next thing Len knew, he and the old man watched the clouds waft by from the tailgate.

Willie took a drink from a thermos and offered Len some. When Len declined, the old man sighed. "Yer not gonna leave me alone, are you Son?"

"Maybe," Len said. "I was kind of hoping you could tell me something."

"Oh?" Willie said. "And what was that?"

"Why do you stay here?" Len asked. "At the railyard, I mean. No offense, but you seem barely put together enough anymore to work the computers, let alone the rest of the work. Why do you keep on with it? Why don't you retire?"

"What's it matter to you?" Willie asked.

"I don't know," Len said, "I just want to understand why you do it. I swear I'm not here to take things to cause trouble, I... I just don't get why you do it day after day, year after year."

Willie chuckled, mostly to himself. "Ah, Len," he said, "when I was your age, this country was a lot different. We didn't have all your fancy phones and computers like we do now. A lot of kids from my generation had a work ethic, and didn't go inside from playing each day until the street lights came on."

"What's that got to do with it?"

"Let an ol' man speak, Len," Willie said. "You know, I see you runnin' 'round here all the time, and honestly? You remind me a little of those days. Ya aren't attached to your little gadgets wherever you go. You put things together, and you seem at least mil'ly responsible. That's a good thing. That's why I never shot ya."

"You shot at me!" Len said.

"Ah! But I never actually hit ya," Willie said, raising one finger. "You see, Len, while you've been a complete pain in mah backside for all this time, I can' help but see the good in ya. Maybe that's my fault, an ol' man goin senile, but damn it, that's the way I feel."

Len wasn't sure how to occupy his stare. Looking at the clouds? Staring at the ground, leaning into Willie's words? Making eye contact with Willie? It felt a little awkward no matter what he did, because Willie's eyes wandered too, but Len couldn't help himself from simply listening.

"When I was a little older than y'are now," Willie told him, "I didn't have but a few nickels in my pocket. My parents kicked me out of the house, told me to make my way in the world. They said they'd always love me, and that was true to their dying days. But they wonted some tough love, an' that's what I got. Did me good, too; I didn't know anything else 'cept trains.

"I knew all kinds of trains, all kinds of history on them, where all the major railroads went. I could even tell you up and down all day long 'bout the Underground Railroad. Tha's one of my favorites," he said, leaning in. His shoulder bumped Len's, and the young man smiled. "So I did the only thing ah could think to do: I got myself in with a yardmaster and told him I'd be willing to work. I didn't have a place to stay, so I stayed right there and slept 'neath the bridge nearby till I had some money saved up. Boy, I tell you Len, I went through some overalls during those years."

"You were homeless?" Len asked.

"Naw," Willie said, "my home was right there at that railyard. I built up my strength and my skills, smelled somethin' awful and went some days without eating but you know what? I was happeh. I was real happeh. And everybody knew it. I worked my way up until the yardmaster depended on me. When he retired, I decided it was time to start my own. My heart wouldn' be nowhere else.

"I saved up my money – must've looked awful strange, my bulgin' pockets; I bathed in the river but the bank tellers didn't want nothing to do with me – so I started out with a small railyard. I built it up. And now…" He hopped down from the tailgate and wandered a short distance, where he took a shovel that was leaning against the concrete platform for the stairs. He walked some of the way back to Len and leaned on it. "Now, this is what I done with it."

Len looked back and forth between the old man and the great, rusted walls behind him. "Your name isn't really Willie, is it?"

The old man smiled. "I's a nickname, sure. And I love that, too." He rejoined Len on the tailgate and doodled in the dirt with the tip of the shovel.

Len puffed out his cheeks and watched the river flow. "That's a good story," he said. "I wonder if something like that's still possible."

Willie looked at him more directly then. "You like trains too, little Mister Len?"

"Well, not *trains*," he said. He shrugged, staring beyond the ground between his feet. "I don't know what yet. But something. I guess I still can't help but wonder, though, how I'm even still here. I feel lost. I've felt lost for a long time."

"You shouldn', boy. You got yo whole life ahead of you."

"Almost didn't," Len said as an aside. "And that's part of it, I think. I shouldn't be here right now. Jodie had me cornered and beaten, and yet somehow I walked away and she's on the fast track to prison. It doesn't make sense."

"Wha' happened now?"

"When I visited my father's grave," Len said, "there was a storm. She shot me, lightning struck nearby, and that's all I remember. The best I can come up with is that God smote her right then and there."

"That was the night you busted open my railcar, wasn' it?" Willie asked. Len had forgotten all about it, and tried to make himself small.

"...yes, Sir," he said. He got down. "I'll leave you alone, now."

"Hold it," Willie said, raising the shovel to stop Len. "Sit right on back down."

Len gulped, and did as he was told.

Willie spun the shovel with one hand as he spoke. "Now, I know yer a little trouble-maker sometimes, riflin' through my yard and clangin' against the cars, but I never thought I'd see the day that you actually had the guts to come in *my* railyard and open up one o' *my* cars and steal inventory! Little Mister Len, yer a sly one. But you ain't no spoiled goods."

"Wait, what?"

Willie put up his hand to stop him. "Naw, I heard and saw that bad woman chasin' you and yer friend all 'round the yard that day. I was wonderin' to myself as she walked in, 'Now who in God's glory is this lady, just a-strolling into my railyard like she got some right to be here?' We – that is, my crew and I – saw

213

glimpses of her chasin' the two of you kids down and, well, I know the one you hang out with is a good kid, Len, I really do. And when I saw that woman chasin' you, I realized, maybe you ain't so bad neither."

"So," Len said, "…you *let* me steal that car? You saw us the whole time?"

"I didn't say that," Willie said. "I wasn' here to see y'all." He struck the shovel against the ground. The dirt must have been shallow, because there was an almost metallic clang when he did it. There had to be gravel under there.

"Wait," Len said, and Willie didn't interrupt this time. "Wallace and Leonard and Claire all said it wasn't them that called the cops that day. Was it you? The ones that came to the party store saved me from her. It was you, wasn't it!"

Willie grinned, but stuffed it to the far side of his face in a bad attempt to hide it. "Oh, now I didn't say none of that. You got some wild stories, Mister Len."

"Was it you at the graveyard, too? How did you do it?" Len asked. "Was it you that called the cops, too, so they'd find her there and take me to the hospital?"

"You got some wild stories, Mister Len," Willie repeated. "Every young person has some, I guess. Whatever suits your life fine, there, Mister Len you just go on ahead and believe that." He got back to his feet and spun the shovel in both hands, taking it back to where he'd found it. While the old man's back was turned, Len looked as closely as he could. The back of the shovel had a big, head-sized dent in it, where some great force had clanged it flat.

When Willie returned to the tailgate, Len saw him in a new light. Willie's decrepit elbows let him get up again onto the tailgate yet again, though Len didn't know where the old man borrowed the strength.

"Well, whoever did it," Len said, "I'm thankful."

Willie chuckled. "I'm sure you are. You got every right to be. Now, unless we got some fancy lunch to be havin' out here, I suppose you had better be goin' on home," he said.

Len gazed up at the clouds again. A vast, white, clean one loomed on the farthest horizon. It was gigantic, clean – a mountain in the sky. "I think that's a good idea. You know, with her out of the way, I don't know what I'm going to do. My whole life's just been so consumed by fearing her and trying to stay away from her, but now I'm really just at a loss for what comes next. What do you think, Willie?" He looked right into the old man's eyes, but at that moment Willie gazed off into the distance himself.

Then he hopped to the ground and began to walk away. "If I've gone and learned anything 'bout you or me, Len," he said, "it's that, something like that?" He shook his head. "It ain' up to me."

Acknowledgements

I'd like to extend my gratitude to the people that helped make this story possible. To my family and God, for the support, resources, and guidance, I extend my thanks.

To Roger Ullom, I offer professional gratitude for allowing me the courtesy of showing me a little bit of the world of rail work, as well as clarifying the term "shove." To his crew, especially Perry, I offer thanks as well for the smiles, cooperation, and friendliness you offered me.

To my trial readers, a debt is owed and I thank you very much for your time and help. As an author, I can only do so much to look *Len* over and see where it is flawed, what works and what does not, and your perspectives are infinitely useful in this regard. Thus, thank yous go out to Josh, Kelsey, Cathy, Stephanie, and Hannah.

To Gary Wilson, I extend gratitude. Your class on creativity – a wonderfully non-slack-off surprise of a class – was supremely beneficial to this effort. Without it, discovering how Len's story unfolds would likely have been more difficult. In fact, it may be a reason it took two years for me to get the ball rolling and understand where the story was supposed to go – at all – following the opening scene with Wallace and Mr. Humphrey.

To my talented friend Hassan Zafar, who took the time to design the cover, I say thank you. Your idea for the design turned out to have more promise and sense than I initially had. I am glad you were able not only to suddenly adopt the project as your own and infuse your own ideas to it, but that you did as great a job as you did.

To Bob, Kyle, Melissa, Larry, Aaron, Tim, and Donna: thank you for putting up with me as well. Thank you for helping me, each in your own small ways, to make this whole thing a reality. The conversations I had with each of you were beneficial, both directly and indirectly, to the emergence of *Len* into this book, and it is sincerely appreciated. I know I've annoyed each and every one of you at some point, and for that I apologize. But that's okay, because you'll deal with it. Besides, if I don't give you a hard time, who will? (Probably Larry. But that's another thing altogether.)

To Mom and Dad and Stephanie, there's a lot I could thank you for, and I do. You helped me beyond just allowing me the ability to make this. You helped me take my first steps into the world, that I might make a difference and shape it for the better. This is my first attempt. I hope to make you proud. Thank you for everything.

And lest we forget: thank you, dear Reader. Your interest in this is appreciated more than you might think. Thank you for reading, and take heart that if you liked *Len*, it is not the only story bugging me to be written. You may get more yet.

God willing, of course.

Thanks.

Cheers,
Ryan J. Dareul

P.S. The "J" stands for Lukas.

P.P.S. If you have read this far, you have no doubt realized that Len's "parents," Jodie and Dianne, are engaged in a faux same-sex relationship. It is worth noting that since I initially wrote this story (which is set before 2015), the civil rights movement for the LGBT community made some specific ground in the Supreme Court of the United States. Please observe that the falsification of Jodie and Dianne's relationship in this story is **absolutely not** an indictment against same-sex couples nor the LGBT community. Neither, of course, is any tie perceived between their lesbianism and any negative characteristics they have. These are entirely separate things. As Stephen King would likely affirm, we don't always have control over the story's realest content. The facts of this story are therefore laid true, despite my reservations.